A Lost Tribe

To a teacher and a gentleman
at Scoil Treasa Naofa, *fadó, fadó*.

A Lost Tribe

WILLIAM KING

THE LILLIPUT PRESS
DUBLIN

First published 2017 by
THE LILLIPUT PRESS
62–63 Sitric Road, Arbour Hill
Dublin 7, Ireland
www.lilliputpress.ie

ISBN 978 1 84351 714 6

A CIP record for this title is available from
The British Library.

10 9 8 7 6 5 4 3 2

Set in 11 pt on 15 pt Dante by Marsha Swan
Printed in Spain by GraphyCems

We are not wholly bad or good
Who live our lives under Milk Wood,
And Thou, I know, wilt be the first
To see our best side, not our worst.

Dylan Thomas, *Under Milk Wood*

ONE

THROUGH ONE of the high windows of Coghill House, Tom Galvin scans the lawns fronting the houses of St Paul's seminary. The great copper beeches at the far side, which line the boundary walls, are shimmering in the heat. Now and again a light breeze flicks through the leaves on its way to Griffith Avenue; the trees then settle back into their noonday sleep. Diagonally across the lawn is O'Kelly House, a clean-cut building of Portland stone in neo-Georgian style. Free-standing and partly hidden by larches and fir, it resembles a fine country house in parkland.

The building was opened and blessed sixty years before in the mid 1950s when St Paul's was, like all seminaries in the country, overcrowded; wooden cubicles with a curtain for an opening were set up in the Junior House gym to take the overflow. After blessing the foundation stone, Archbishop Browne addressed the students – boy-priests with army haircuts, Roman collars and black soutanes. On the raised platform in the Academy Hall and flanked by the rector and staff of the seminary, the archbishop was glad to announce that by the end of the century, 'we will be ministering to well over a million souls. The harvest is rich, dear students,' he assured them with forefinger and thumb of one hand on his glittering pectoral cross, the other fidgeting with the folds of his purple silk cloak. 'This auspicious day is a source of great encouragement for me, and a sign that we are responding to the motto of this great seminary: *Omnes ad te Domine.*'

By the end of the century, Archbishop Browne's coffin, covered with a patina of green dust, would be resting among the pile of other archbishops' coffins in the crypt of the Pro-Cathedral. The houses of St Paul's would be cold and empty, with paint flaking from the walls; the few remaining students would be accommodated in one wing of Wansborough House. Priests were saying that the seminary should be sold and the students sent elsewhere for their training, but Browne's successor put his foot down. 'St Paul's was the cradle of my vocation; I will not be the one to close the gates.'

No sooner had the next archbishop been installed than he transferred the remaining seven students to Maynooth and drew up a leasing agreement with Anna Livia School of Business and Marketing. The agreement brought millions to the diocese – much of which was spent in compensating victims of clerical sex abuse. Some of the land – once the back pitches and the farm – was sold off to a developer, who built a housing estate, mostly duplexes, and called it The Friary.

Heavy lorries and diggers trundled in to demolish the old ball alley and to prepare the ground for a student car park and bar. In jeans, design-torn at the knee, young men and women, carrying books and flirting beside the noticeboards, animated the dead corridors. Over the urinals, and the women's toilets, the students' union posted notices giving information on safe sex. One read: *Going out for the weekend? Stay safe: bring your condoms.* Lecturers – in economics, business and marketing – wove their important way in and out of chattering students as they hurried to lecture halls or to interviews on the radio about the Celtic Tiger's latest achievement.

A clause in the transfer of the campus stipulated that the former seminary be made available to the priests of the diocese at a reduced rent, for their annual retreat and other meetings.

NOW, as Galvin scans the lawns, his fellow seminarians of many years before take shape in his mind. In the room where he stands looking out, about eighty of them wearing soutanes and birettas and carrying theology books, gathered each morning. The scraping of chairs and the clatter of books as they took their places at the long rows of desks that faced the lecturer's podium echo in his brain.

Waking from his reverie, he becomes aware of the few diocesan seminarians helping out while on their holidays from Maynooth – the last seminary in Ireland to remain open. They flit around, tidying the room, gathering up hymn sheets that have fallen on the floor and arranging the chairs for the next talk. Since the retreat began, they have been hurrying about the corridors in soutanes. One of them wears a wide sash around his waist. He is checking the PowerPoint and the microphone.

The evening before, as priests were drawing up in cars and others were gathering at the foot of the stairs to chat, Galvin came across a man who had been in St Paul's with him. He was struggling with his bags.

'Here, I'll give you a hand,' Galvin offered.

When they reached the landing, the priest leant on the bannister to catch his breath. 'A bit of company; ah, sure isn't it great ... especially nowadays.' Looking down the stairwell, he said: 'When I was coming out this evening, cars were pulling up across the road; families arriving for supper with the grandparents – you know the scene. Taking their toddlers out of the SUV. Mickey Mouse sunshades.' He smiled and shook his head. 'Wouldn't you feel you're excluded from the party? Life I mean.'

'Indeed.'

He took Galvin's measure. 'You're looking fit, Tom. What are you on?'

'Keeping the best side out. A jorum at night goes a long way. Although my doc keeps telling me to cut back. Sure one or two does no harm.'

'I can't touch it anymore.' He rubbed his stomach. 'Where are the retreat talks?'

'One end of the theology room in Coghill; the one near the library, remember?'

'Hah. What next? And to think we used to fill the chapel. Seems like only yesterday.'

'And the poker sessions till morning.' The heavy look gave way to a twinkle. 'You weren't bad yourself with a hand of cards.'

'You learn a lot on a Kentish Town building site on a rainy day. The summers of my *real* education.'

Down below, other priests were hauling in bags and greeting one another. The priest took a Sunday paper from one of his bags, giving Galvin a view of his dyed comb-over.

'Look.' He sighed and slapped the page with the back of his freckled hand. On the photograph, a priest they both know is hand-cuffed to a guard and being led to the open door of a Black Maria. In the dim light of the corridor the two fell silent. The priest stuffed the newspaper back into his bag and forced a smile.

'Getting ready now for five days of peace. No phones or funerals or someone complaining that the crown of lights over the Blessed Virgin's head is not switched on, or that the vacuum cleaner for the church isn't working. Sheer bliss.' Some of the old sparkle from when he had been the life and soul of clerical golf days was returning.

GALVIN PICKS UP a leaflet containing the retreat director's summary of the previous night's talk. 'Despite the dreadful revelations that have unfolded,' the Benedictine with the clipped English accent had said, 'the Church and you and I have to make atonement for the crimes and sins of our brothers. Do not, on any account, try to deny that dark side of our nature. Learn from it. And remember *the angels of darkness disguise themselves as angels of light.* That said, do not lose hope nor the dream that brought you to this seminary many years ago.'

'My brother priests,' he had continued, 'there is a lack of true spiritual energy among the presbyterate. It is called by different names – low morale, or burnout. I call it the noonday devil. Remember the desert fathers and how they were inclined to despair, having been weakened by this demon. This must not happen to you.' Despite the gravity of his message, he managed to break into a smile from time to time while he took in his audience.

The dream. Galvin scans the grounds again. Yes, the senior students – those close to ordination – and their assured footsteps resounding beneath the vaulted ceiling of the ambulatory on that mild October evening when he had first set foot in St Paul's, come bounding back. 'Incontrovertibly, the Vatican Council will bring about a renaissance. The best time to be coming into the priest-hood,' one student had assured him.

He returned to the Benedictine's summary. 'I cannot give you a key to understanding what has happened to the priesthood in this country in the past thirty or forty years. The Book of Job will be my main source for this retreat: it teaches us that precise lesson, which is, Job would never understand.' He had cited chapter twenty-eight of Job.

In the Bible, Galvin finds the reference: *Where does wisdom come from and, where is the place of understanding? It is hidden from the eyes of all living ... and kept close from the fowls of the air.* Cold comfort. He looks through the open window again. Priests are strolling up and down outside, so close he can hear their conversations.

'Ah God, is that the way it is?' The silence that follows is broken by the scuff and scrape of their shoes on the gravel path.

'Yeah, diagnosed last January. Had a scope. It had gone too far.'

'He won't be back to the parish then?'

'Unlikely.'

'We're all in the waiting room now, lads. How quickly it all ... .' The voices fade.

At each side of the main door of Wansborough House, where the driveway becomes an apron for turning cars, more priests relax on garden seats, or chat, as cheery as schoolboys on the first day of the long summer holidays.

Galvin steps out of the room, down the corridor, and through the dim vestibule. Outside the high double doors, the seminarians, now finished their tidying of the room, are playing with a black cat. One of them, with braces on his teeth, looks up as the cat rubs its head along his soutane. The seminarian is in a jaunty mood.

'The retreat director is excellent, isn't he, father?'

'Excellent.'

'If there's anything you want during the next few days, just let us know.'

'Thanks. I will.'

'It's a beautiful life, father.'

'What's ...?'

'The priesthood. It's a beautiful life, isn't it?'

Galvin keeps sidling away. 'It has its moments.'

'I mean saving souls.'

'Yes, of course. That's what our life is about.'

'Father, the deacons in Maynooth are *so* looking forward to ordination day. Will you remember them in your mass?'

'I will.'

The seminarian is anxious to talk. 'They had a couple of days off after Easter, and guess what? Didn't they go to Rome to buy vestments at Gamarelli's. Isn't that good?'

'Gamarelli's! My goodness. Yes, that's very ... interesting.'

'Celibacy is a great gift from God, father. It's going to be the heart of my priesthood.'

'Good.'

To avoid offending him, Galvin stops for a moment. 'How many of you are there in Maynooth now?'

'Seven. One for ordination this year, and then no one for the next four years.'

'Changed times.' Galvin begins to open his breviary as he moves off. 'Nice cat.'

The seminarian bends down and talks to the cat. 'Yes, you are a nice moggie, aren't you? A lovely moggie.'

By the rose bed a priest tries to light his pipe; he nods in the direction of the seminarians and says to Galvin, 'God help them. Little do they know.' He shakes his head. 'I was at an ordination last week down the country. You won't believe this. The candidate for ordination was wearing a fiddle-back chasuble – you know, pre-Vatican – made out of his mother's wedding dress. Well, the braiding anyway.' He chuckles between puffs. 'Old man Freud would have a lot to say about that!'

'TILL DEATH do us part.' Galvin gives a little laugh and continues walking around by the narrow path that runs along the perimeter of the grounds. In places, overspreading trees form a green roof and dappled sunlight falls on the cedar needles. All the while, fragments from the retreat director's talk run through his mind: 'The Book of Job, fathers, shows us that Job would never understand the misfortunes he had encountered and would have to make peace with that mystery, which is at the centre of life. You have had that darkness in your souls for the past few years.'

Priests walk up and down in front of O'Kelly House, heads downcast, as if looking for something they have lost. Rosary beads sway behind their backs. The papal and national flags lie limp on the poles in front of Wansborough House.

Galvin rests for a while on a garden seat and looks around. He needs these few days to mull over the twists and turns his life has taken for over forty years as a priest, but more especially the horrific revelations of the Hegarty Report, which divulged how priests abused children, and his own guilt that, as the archbishop's secretary, he didn't wake up to the full force of events, even if excluded from the discussions on camera.

He would never have survived the ups and downs of life, he now knows, if it hadn't been for the overnight stay with the monks at Mount St Joseph's. For years he has packed a bag once a month and driven down to the monastery surrounded by the lush Tipperary fields; there he found a space to reflect on the rugged path he had chosen.

The tide is receding for the Church; some vital force is dying within Galvin too: faith in life, in God, his sadness at the naked ambition of those who once had prostrated themselves in humility before the bishop on the day of their ordination. He is striving to recover the dream of his youth but, like an ageing marathon runner, he no longer has the legs. These few days will give him an opportunity to reflect and to try and understand why it all collapsed in the blink of an eye. To stir his memory, he has brought with him diaries going back many years.

Among the ancient trees that dominate the lawn is a giant oak, known to generations of students as Old Pompey. Youthful voices full of confidence return from his seminary days, the clink of cutlery in the refectory: 'Did you know that Beresford, the Lord Lieutenant, had rebels hanged from its branches during the '98 rebellion?' 'No, I didn't know that.' 'Oh, he did. Bad bastard.'

Farther left and at the top of the curved driveway is the centrepiece of St Paul's, Wansborough House, with its plain Doric front and, by contrast, the ornate swags and yellowed alcoves on the side nearest the Pugin chapel. In cut stone over the door is a Latin inscription: *Venite ad me omnes qui laboratis* – 'Come to me all who labour'.

He rummages through the miscellany of thoughts from the retreat director's talk: how St Ignatius of Loyola used keep a death's head on his desk to remind him of the shortness of life. And he gave them a motto: *If you want to live, prepare to die.* It was an echo of the same message from the rector on Galvin's first night in the seminary. 'Faster than a weaver's shuttle, young gentlemen, your time will pass in St Paul's.' Yes, like the fifty years that have gone by since that evening as he and twenty-six others arrived at the seminary.

TWO

THAT AUTUMN EVENING of 1962, crows clamoured in the wide-spreading branches of the same chestnuts and beeches of St Paul's, as if they too sensed something important was about to unfold among the warm terracotta colours of Rome. To mark the opening of the Vatican Council, papal and national flags had been hoisted on the flagpoles. Red, brown and golden leaves formed a collar around the base of the trees, and fell too on the sandy path and on the curve of driveway up from the main gates. From down by Church Road, smoke curled from a mound and mingled with the faint smell of the sea. Cars were pulling up to the front door of Wansborough. Senior students rushed to help take suitcases from car boots. Wearing deep black suits and holding felt hats, the first years – Galvin among them – made a brave effort to look casual.

When all the cases had been hauled upstairs to Coghill House, the rector, slit-eyed when he smiled, nodded and made his way from one family to another.

'Tis a mighty place ye have here, father,' Galvin's father said, as if he were calling across a bog in windy weather.

'Mighty?' The rector looked at him. His eyes narrowed. 'Oh, yes, mighty.'

'Tommy is a great worker, you know, father. We'll miss him at the hay and the pickin' of the spuds.'

'Rest assured, Mr Galvin, that Thomas's youthful energy will be put to good use in the Lord's vineyard.' He stole a glance at his watch. 'We'll speak again before you go.' He thanked Galvin's parents for giving their son to the Church and, raising his voice, announced to all that tea would be served in the Academy Hall.

Later, the parents began to clamber into their cars. Waving at their sons, they cruised down the driveway and disappeared at the curve just before the main gates. Galvin's parents waved awkwardly from the back seat of a hackney car headed for Kingsbridge Railway Station.

All over the grounds, students were chatting. Senior students wore a row of shiny buttons down the front of their soutanes, a sign that they had graduated from university and were studying theology. They exchanged an odd mixture of jokes and fears. The priest to be feared was Murtagh, the junior dean of discipline: known as the Phantom from the way he stole through the early morning darkness to say mass for the Christian Brothers in Marino, he was a dark figure in a slouched hat and long black coat. He appeared out of nowhere, lurked beneath the main stairs to check if every student was in time for Lauds and slunk across to the archbishop's house after nightfall to make regular reports.

One of the Shiny Buttons looked steadily at the papal flag.

'Vatican II will change everything. I can't wait to hear the recommendations,' he declared. The floor made a hollow sound beneath the arched roof as they walked along the ambulatory. A deacon, who would be ordained the following June, stopped to make a point. He had a serious look on his delicate features.

'If it hadn't been for the Council ... I mean prisons like this.' He swept his outstretched hand over the front of Senior House, gaunt and gothic. 'I can assure you, it's the hope of the Council that's keeping me here.'

'Me too,' another said. Nodding, they moved on.

One of the group, a second year called Mac who bore a remarkable resemblance to Michael Collins, leaned over to Galvin as talk of the Vatican Council and Pope John XXIII progressed, and spoke in a low voice: 'Some of these fellows think the sun shines out of their arses. Take no notice. Anyway, getting out every day to the uni makes it easier. Eoin MacCarthy,' he said, and extended his hand.

They passed by other students, some sitting, others standing around a fountain. A senior student was pointing towards the folly like a tour guide. Names were forgotten as soon as they were introduced, but one stood out for Galvin. Damien Irwin, a second year arts student. All afternoon he had been popping up here and there, giving advice: how not to incur the Phantom's anger, how to manage an extra visit from one's family.

'Give us the High Command, Damien,' one of the Shiny Buttons said.

'Yeah, go on, Damo.'

'Who is the High Command?' a first year asked.

'Shh!' one of the senior students said.

'The archbishop,' a student at the back of the group piped up.

Irwin made sure the coast was clear, and then, like a professional actor, he worked himself into the role, dipping one shoulder and holding in place an imaginary pectoral cross. He spoke in a low, measured way, mincing his words: 'I aim to ensure that the seminarians at St Paul's will be well nourished – prunes and porridge every morning; they will have regular bowel movements.' Then he arched one eyebrow and pursed his thin lips as he scrutinized his audience. Those who recognized the accuracy of his impersonation laughed loudly. He picked on one student. 'Always use Astral soap, young man.'

'Why, Your Grace?'

Scrunching up his face, he turned on the student. 'Hygienic reasons, young man. Shouldn't that be clear to you? Wash the private parts of your body.'

'What do you mean, Your Grace?'

The High Command gave him the dreaded stare. 'Your mickey, young man. Wash your mickey with Astral soap.' They guffawed again.

'The holidays haven't changed you, Damo,' someone said.

'Have you met the Phantom?' Irwin asked one of the first years.

'Not yet.'

'Different kettle of fish,'

He moved on to a take-off of the junior dean of discipline. Squinting, and in a voice filled with intensity, he hissed: 'My job is to get rid of half of you before next June.'

Suddenly, Winters, the senior prefect, was standing at the door of Wansborough, frowning and clapping his hands. He barked: 'All freshmen will go to your rooms and dress in soutane and biretta, and then proceed in silence to the refectory for supper where Dr Murtagh will address you. Monsignor Curran, the rector, will then read the rules in the oratory and, because this evening is special, all students are granted the privilege of speaking during supper.'

'Let's go, lads, or your man will have us up before the Phantom,' Irwin muttered under his breath.

THE DARK WOOD of the long refectory tables and stools, set end to end, and the heavy brown wainscoting and pulpit completed a picture that was both cheerless and Spartan.

'Except on feast days or other special occasions, you will eat in silence: a student will read from up there.' Winters pointed towards the pulpit high above the tables with steps leading up to it. Metal chandeliers, like giant spiders' legs, hung from the ceiling. Dull brown oil paintings of sullen bishops and Monsignors clasping prayer books to their chest lined the walls and rested on dado boards. At the head of the room, beneath a painting of Abraham taking his son to the mountain to be sacrificed, was a table perpendicular to the others. 'This table is for the rector and staff,' the prefect told them. 'And occasionally we are privileged to have His Grace, Archbishop Browne, dining with us.'

In their new soutanes, the first years stood in line between two rows of tables. They had been assigned seniority according to the date they had applied to the seminary. Not long out of primary school, two boys with white aprons were wheeling a trolley: its wheels made a grating sound across the red and black tiles.

The Phantom had stolen in without their noticing and, having inspected their soutanes and shoes, began walking up and down the refectory. Suddenly he stopped dead in front of a student.

'Where's your biretta, young man?' He made fussy gestures with his hands. 'You should have your biretta.'

'In my suitcase, father,' he replied in a thick country accent.

'*In my suitcase,*' the Phantom mimicked. 'The right place to have it, I don't think. Don't let me catch you without your biretta again.' He chopped the air with his hand. 'Do you consider yourself above the rules? Is that it?'

'No, father.'

'Doctor. You address me as doctor.'

Muttering about how 'some people manage to get in here,' the Phantom tripped to the top of the refectory and stood beneath the picture of Abraham and his son.

'Be clear about this. It is my aim to see the rules are kept. Any student who thinks that he will pull the wool over my eyes had best leave his bags unpacked. The archdiocese requires men who will be obedient to the Divine Will, which is always', his forefinger shot up towards the spiders' legs, 'expressed through your superiors.

St Paul's was here before you and will be here after you, in case you have lofty notions about changing the way things are done.'

Galvin stole a glance at the student. He had the same lost look he'd had that afternoon at Kingsbridge Station when Galvin had come across him, pushing his bicycle.

'Are you going to St Paul's?'

'I am.'

'Where are you from, *garsoon*?' Galvin's father was standing nearby and heard them talking. He'd only been to Dublin twice: to see Kerry play Armagh in a football final and when his uncle, a priest of the Los Angeles diocese, was dying in the Mater Hospital.

'I'm from outside Abbeyfeale, sir.'

'Don't mind your "sir", young lad. Good, honest people in Abbeyfeale. I sold calves there once. Come on with us and throw your bike in the back of the hackney car.'

AFTER SUPPER they joined the Shiny Buttons in their common room. It was loud and claustrophobic: blue smoke formed a haze around the hanging lampshades. The senior students knew all about plays in the Gaiety and the best films showing that summer in the Dublin picture houses. They recounted the jobs they had got picking strawberries in England's West Country and working in factories around Manchester. A surge of anxiety rose within Galvin: his mouth was dry and he felt trapped, like when he had been a child and the Wren Boys had burst into the house one St Stephen's Day playing melodeons and flutes, and he had hidden under the kitchen table.

One of the Shiny Buttons was doing the rounds of the tables: he was tall and loud and had a cigarette dangling from his lips. 'I'm John Mike Noonan,' he said. 'Don't mind the gobshites that run this place. Just do your own thing. Very soon we'll have a half day every week, and newspapers, and they're also promising a television set. Any of you lads play rugby in school?' Before they could answer, he announced, 'I played second row on the Senior Cup team that beat 'rock a few years back. Back door at three tomorrow. See if one or two of you might make the team this year.' He moved on to another table.

Mac leaned towards Galvin. 'Your man, Noonan,' he whispered, 'thinks he's God's gift to the world. The father came up from Limerick, arse out through his trousers, made his money out of a couple of cash-and-carry places and one or two pubs. Loaded. Big house in Greystones and now racehorses. This place is top heavy with bullshitters like Noonan.'

The din of conversation in the smoke-filled air was getting too much for Galvin, but he kept smiling and picking up fragments of conversations, as if from a badly tuned wireless.

'A television?'

'Yeah, but only to watch the opening of the Council.'

'J. Desmond won a scholarship again this summer.'

'Tell us something new.'

One of the Shiny Buttons gave the first years a heads-up. 'Don't be caught in another student's room after lights out. Jesus, if they find you … .' He made a throat-slitting gesture. 'A fellow was caught two years ago and his parents had to collect him the following day.'

'Why so?' the lad from Abbeyfeale asked.

'*Why so?*' The theology student grinned and looked around slyly at the others. 'You'll find that out in time.'

Mac hissed at the Abbeyfeale lad: 'Let's take a stroll. I'll show you around. Anyway, I need to clear my head. Tommy,' he beckoned to Galvin, 'will you join us?'

'I will.'

THE NIGHT AIR was filled with the smell of smouldering leaves and the promise of good tidings from Rome. Mac raised his head and sniffed.

'Paddy the caretaker was at it again today.'

'At what?'

'Burning leaves,' said Mac, laughing to himself. 'By the way, he has a fantastic-looking daughter, Gill. Lovely Legs, we call her; she won the Lovely Legs of Glasnevin competition a couple of years ago.' He pointed towards a cottage inside the main gate. 'She lives there. The gingerbread house.'

The Westminster chime was tolling in a nearby Protestant church. Swan-necked lamps lit up the sweep of avenue and the walkways along the perimeter of the grounds, setting off the limestone facades, recesses and decorated walls of Wansborough House. They illuminated the students moving in the semi-darkness, their shoes scuffing the gravel path in front of Coghill House. An orange glow hung over the city. Cars passed by on Griffith Avenue and church bells tolled.

'I'm sure you're finding all this a bit strange,' Mac said to both of them. 'Don't. You'll learn a lot in here about life if you keep your eyes open. Many of the fellas come from well-heeled families. Fathers are doctors and lawyers. Jesuit boys. They're the ones given the privileges and sent to Rome for further studies. Lick-arses, if you ask me.' He laughed.

Only half listening to Mac, Galvin was caught up in the beauty of the seminary campus, in the hopes and expectations of the senior students, and how everything would change after Vatican II. And in this flurry of excitement he was aware of Mac telling them that he was from Skibbereen and had got on the Cork minor football team a couple of years before.

'Take no notice of that gobshite the Phantom,' he said. 'After coming here, I wrote to a friend, not knowing that the Phantom opens all letters. He called me up. "Is that your letter, Mr Mac-Carthy?" and he screwed up his ould face as if he were holding a piece of shit. "Yes, Dr Murtagh," I said. "Read it for me." And he made me read the letter. I was giving out about the place and saying that there's a bollix here called the Phantom and that he's the worst of all. I had to plead with him not to expel him. "My parents would be very upset, Dr Murtagh. Please give me another chance. I want so much to be a priest." I was grounded for a month, and when the whole college got a half day on the feast of the diocesan patron, I had to watch from my room on the top floor of Coghill as the students got into their parents' cars and disappeared around the sweep of the driveway.'

A sudden gust of wind threw up a shower of leaves that capered around the lights. Galvin and the others came across students who stopped to pass on the news that the rector was providing a television so that they could watch the opening ceremony of the Vatican Council.

'I'll guarantee you,' one vowed, 'it will shake up the Church in this country. Fasten your seatbelts, lads. Celibacy will be history in ten years.' He drew heavily on a cigarette.

'Not a day too soon.' Mac rubbed his hands together. 'We came at the right time, lads. I heard theologians are saying that mass will be in English, with the priest facing the congregation, and the congregation will be singing and making the responses.'

At the entrance to the ambulatory, they stopped to talk to Irwin. He swept his hand over the grounds. 'The biggest garden party ever held in Ireland – *ever held* – was hosted here at the Eucharistic Congress of 1932. Did you know that? Cardinals from America and Australia. De Valera. The High Command was the brains behind the whole thing. Dev put in a word for him in Rome.'

As they headed back to Coghill House, Galvin remarked to Mac: 'Irwin is great gas. Seems a nice fella.'

'Irwin, oh yeah, great fun all right.' Mac's tone changed. He stopped and lowered his voice. 'There's another side to Irwin. Be careful. He'll sell you down the river if you became a threat to him. I saw him make it hot and heavy for a lad who wanted to get one of the free places with the Lourdes pilgrimage he'd earmarked for himself. He can be a right bastard.'

The sound of the bell ringing out across the lawn caused a quick end to the conversation. 'Come on, lads,' said Mac. 'The Phantom might be hiding under the stairs.'

IN THE ORATORY, which smelt of fresh linoleum, Galvin knelt at the front with the other first years and tried to pray, but the newness of everything had his head in a spin. Stepping off the train with his parents at Kingsbridge, driving in a taxi up O'Connell Street, crowds, double-decker buses, Nelson's Pillar. His mother, who had never wanted him to enter a seminary, had been sullen. His father had stretched his scrawny neck to admire the decorated ceiling of the Academy Hall and rummaged in the inside pocket of his jacket for the safety pin that secured the college fee; his country accent had caused women in tweeds and diamond rings to turn their heads and smile to one another.

The senior prefect announced that they would join in prayer 'so that the Holy Spirit will guide His Holiness and the bishops assembled in Rome for the Council'. He nodded to a student sitting at an organ to the side of the altar. Irwin and others rushed around with armfuls of hymnals. The heavy swell of the organ led them into song and the oratory filled with the sound of 140 spirited voices:

> Veni Creator Spiritus,
> Mentes tuorum visita,
> imple superna gratia
> quae tu creasti, pectora.

During the period of reflection, squelching footsteps approached from the back. The rector genuflected in front of the altar, bowed his grey head and knelt to pray the 'Our Father' in Latin. When he unhooked the gold chain at the neck of his long black cloak with its velvet collar, Winters rushed to take it from him. The rector sat at a baize-covered table and welcomed everyone again, especially the first years. He hoped that the rest of the student body had had 'a refreshing holiday'.

He opened the rule book and put on a pair of dark-rimmed glasses. 'The rules are for your own good, gentlemen,' he said with a lisp. 'To make you into good priests and to join the generations of men who have gone out from this seminary to save souls.'

After reading aloud a page or two, he stopped, removed his glasses and looked around. 'Does anyone here know the most important rule of all? That which is the distinguishing mark of the good priest?' He paused. 'I will give the freshmen the opportunity of answering first.'

'Is it saying his prayers, father?' One of the first years, who was sitting in the front seat next to Galvin, spoke with such innocence that a titter spread through the oratory.

The rector's mandarin eyes looked around for another answer. 'Yes, that is a *sine qua non*. Good man. But even more important ...' the smile was now deserting him, 'I want this implanted in your minds: the most important rule is obedience. What you have to remember is that the voice of God is mediated through the semi-nary authorities, who are subject to His Grace the Archbishop. Another important rule – a corollary of the first – is loyalty to the archdiocese. Loyalty, gentlemen. All the men who have gone out of this seminary have been loyal.'

The rules covered all aspects of their daily lives in the seminary, including raising one's biretta when passing a statue and behaviour at university. 'You shall show politeness at all times to lay students while at university college, but you shall not linger with them or engage in idle gossip. This applies also when you happen upon students with whom you were in school, or even family members.' The rector paused, and flicked one side of the soutane cape over his shoulder so that the satin lining showed. 'Remember custody of the eyes. Before going out to the university, you will assemble in the oratory with your prefect, who will lead the prayer for purity.'

He continued in a solemn tone. 'One rule that is strictly enforced: on no account shall a student ever enter another student's room. I enjoin you gentlemen, never, ever to break *that* rule.'

He knelt again at the foot of the altar. A prefect rushed across with his cloak and held the gold chain for the rector to clasp around his pink neck. Then he recited another Latin prayer before squelching out.

THE COMMON ROOM was so crowded for the viewing of the Vatican Council that some had to stand at the back. Winters switched off the lights as the newsreader announced that they were now going over to St Peter's in Rome.

A hush descended; a communion of expectant faces reflected the flickering movements from the screen as the assembly watched an endless procession of bishops, vested in flowing robes and mitres, walking with great dignity past the Egyptian obelisk of the Bernini piazza and ascending the steps leading to St Peter's Basilica. In a solemn tone, the commentator named some far-off places where the bishops were serving and recalled other Councils of the Church. The Pope, carried high on his throne, appeared and blessed the cheering crowd. The commentator fell silent so all could hear the burst of sound from the organ. The loud applause of the thousands gathered in St Peter's Square was like the crack of a rifle shot in the dry air. Inside the basilica, the Pope dismounted from his throne and made his way between the tiers of bishops stretching the entire length of the nave until he reached his place at the twisted bronze columns supporting the canopy. Here, with clouds of smoke rising from swinging thuribles and filling the sanctuary, he intoned the opening liturgy.

When the broadcast was over, one of the prefects broke the spell by switching on the lights.

'Now you will go in silent procession to the oratory for night prayer.' His tone was flinty. 'And you will pray especially for the Holy Father and the bishops gathered in conclave.'

After praying for the Holy Father and the bishops, everyone went as bidden to their rooms. A succession of doors closing sounded along the corridors before the seminary settled down for the night. Like a child on Christmas Eve, too excited to sleep, Galvin's head was filled with images of the Council: he felt he could reach out and touch the hope inspired by the reassuring face of the elderly Pope. His scattered dreams that night, however, were not about the twisted bronze columns and the Pope with the homely look, but about London and the summer just gone, when he had worked side by side with men hired by his brother: M.J.'s laughing face glistening with sweat as he hopped off the old army jeep he used to rush from site to site. Whipping up bags of cement in his powerful arms and shouting good-humouredly at one of his men: 'Move your arse, lad, we've houses to build!' Galvin himself, pushing loaded wheelbarrows up planks to plasterers and brick-layers. And dancing in the Galtymore Ballroom with Maureen from Claremorris whom he had kissed and fondled down a dimly lit lane across from the dancehall.

GALVIN WAS a good student. He kept the rules and gained some respect from his ability on the football field and as 'a cute hoor from the country who took it all in and said little'. Every morning, along with seventy or so students, he cycled to the university in Earlsfort Terrace.

If he was strolling around the grounds with others or playing snooker, the Abbeyfeale youth hung steadily at his shoulder, content to hover on the edge, and he seemed satisfied with the small change that fell from their conversations. One afternoon when he was watching a rugby game and saw a scrum for the first time, he burst out laughing. 'Lads, aren't they like pigs feeding at a trough? Now aren't they?'

The comment was passed around in the common room and by evening they were snorting like pigs every time they met the lad in the corridor and sniggering at Compline when someone did a pig impression. 'Muck-Muck' they began to call him and, like a group of lions converging on a lone zebra, they began to close in.

One morning the lad from Abbeyfeale sidled up to Galvin and asked him to go for a walk; there was something he wanted to tell him.

'I'd like to be a priest, Tommy,' he said when they were out of hearing distance of those who were leaning against the columns of Beresford's Folly, smoking cigarettes or pipes, 'and one day say mass for my mother's soul. But I'm in the wrong place. I know that now.' He was near to tears. 'Maybe I'll apply to one of the other seminaries down the country where I'd be among people like myself.'

'That's a pity,' Galvin said. 'Sure, if you give it time, you might settle down. I wouldn't mind some of those bastards that were getting at you. That will pass. Take no notice and they'll stop.'

'No.' He shook his head. 'This place is too stand-offish. The other day I met a priest on the corridor and I said: "Hello, father, isn't it a lovely day?" He had a sneer on his oul face, and looked at me as if I were a dog that had strayed into the house.'

Galvin stopped and turned to him. 'Lookit, they don't salute any of us, except the chosen few, but you have to ignore that if you want to be a priest. '

The Abbeyfeale lad left in early November, just before dinner, when the students were in the oratory for Particular Examination of Conscience, a midday review of any sins they might have committed since morning. On the way down the avenue with his suitcase and his bicycle, he pitched his soutane onto one of the laurel trees. The students cycling out to university passed it every morning until the Phantom asked Paddy to remove it.

Dark evenings invaded the grounds. Leaves began to rot, so that the bare branches of the tall trees stood like membranes against the sky. By Christmas, three of the first years had left. One had begun to have agonizing migraine attacks. To each of them, the Phantom issued the standard instructions: 'You will pack your bags, say a brief word of goodbye to your class fellows and leave quietly while everyone is at study. Do not delay.' They left behind empty rooms with rolled-up mattresses and wire coat hangers on the iron bedstead.

Once the excitement of the early days had worn off, Galvin's recurring anxiety returned, a condition that had flared up in adolescence. He had thought that going to St Paul's would cure him, but, instead, when he switched off his bedside lamp at night, he couldn't sleep for a couple of hours. He needed to talk to someone but feared that if he told the spiritual director, he might be asked to leave. Nevertheless, he couldn't go on like this.

One night during study time when rain was lashing against his window he went downstairs along the stone corridor and knocked on the spiritual director's door, half hoping that the priest would be out and he'd be saved the ordeal of facing up to his troubles.

'Yes.' The voice from within sounded peevish. Nevertheless, he turned the door knob and stepped inside. The spiritual director was using a screwdriver to open the back of a transistor radio. A two-bar heater glowed at his side. With the screwdriver, he indicated a seat in front of his desk.

'Yes, young man.' He continued to work on the radio, turning the knobs and putting it up to his ear. 'Talk to me.'

'My nerves, father. I'm having strange dreams.'

The spiritual director stopped and looked at Galvin. 'Ah, sure, don't we all have trouble with our nerves. Sure, that's nothing to be put out about.' He returned to his poking. 'Tell me more, my son.'

Galvin stumbled through a story about his younger brother's death; all the while the spiritual director kept moving the dial and fiddling with the screwdriver until the radio began to croak and splutter, then cleared. Nat King Cole's smoky voice filled the room: *'Pretend you're happy when you're blue, It isn't very hard to do ... .'*

'Ah good,' the spiritual director said and lowered the volume. 'Give me one more minute now. A test run.' He eased the tuner into another position. *'And you'll find happiness without an end, whenever you pretend ... .'*

'Good. Now then, Mr Galvin. Some men who come to St Paul's ... hmm, worry too much about their vocation. Are you eating well and getting on with your class?'

'Yes, father.'

'Do you play football?'

'I love football, father.'

Through milk-bottle lenses that magnified his pale eyes, the spiritual director smiled at him. 'Ah, just worrying too much. You'll make a fine priest. Oh, I'd have no fears about you at all. *None at all.* And, yes ... hmm, it is very sad the way your poor little brother died. Offer it up, Thomas, for the most forgotten soul in purgatory. Good man.'

Galvin's step was lighter when he walked back to his room, but after a week or so the nightmares began again. This time he plucked up courage to climb the stairs to Murtagh's room, where students were waiting for permission to take the bus to the university. His heart was pounding when it came to his turn, but he knocked and was called in.

'What do you want?' the Phantom asked, not taking his eyes off a sheaf of lecture notes. 'To take the bus like the others ... wasting my time?'

'I'd like to see a psychiatrist, Dr Murtagh,' he said, standing in front of the desk.

The Phantom stared at him. 'A psychiatrist! What in heaven's name would you want to see a psychiatrist for? The college physician is an excellent doctor.'

'Something ... I don't know. I feel nervous, Dr Murtagh. And maybe ... well, a psychiatrist is the one to help me.'

'Nervous!' He started to align the edges of his lecture notes against the desk. 'Many feel nervous but they don't give in to themselves, or go traipsing off to psychiatrists!' The overhead light caught the sheen on his black hair.

'But I'd feel happier.' The wind soughed in the roof.

'I'll have to talk to the college physician about this. And to the rector.' He looked towards the rain beating against his window. 'This is a serious matter. It will go down on your file, and be brought up at the Academic Council meeting when your suitability for Minor Orders will be discussed. I'll let you know, Mr Galvin.'

A momentary pang that his worst fears were being confirmed coursed through him.

THREE FLOORS UP in his Fitzwilliam Square consulting room, the white-coated psychiatrist sat behind his desk and took Galvin's measure.

'It's my nerves, professor,' Galvin said. 'I've bad dreams and nightmares and once or twice I've found myself sleepwalking in the corridor.'

'You are able to follow the lectures? Study? Take part in college life?'

'Well, yes, but … .'

Taking his pipe out of his mouth and placing it on an ashtray, the psychiatrist began to write. 'Tell me about yourself – where you grew up, details like that.'

'I'm from the country, professor, from Kerry. I'm the second youngest of eight, all have now scattered.' He blushed. 'They had … very little for them at home. A rundown farm, you see. Two nurses in Coventry and three brothers who went to London. M.J. is the eldest; he started a building company and the others are directors. They began small – refurbishing houses, that sort of thing, but now they're building office blocks.'

'Glad to hear they are doing so well.'

'Another brother is a guard here in Dublin.' He lowered his eyes and started to smooth the nap on the armrest of the chair. 'Then there's my young brother; he got killed off his bike.' Galvin spoke for about half an hour, coming back again and again to his brother's death. 'I can't get him out of my head, professor.'

'Go on, Mr Galvin.'

He told about the incident when he was ten or eleven and his little brother had got a new bike for Christmas. Like the house, the Morris Minor car and the herd of in-calf heifers, the bicycle had been bought by M.J.

'I was teaching Joe to ride the bike and one evening I didn't want to help him and, instead, went off playing football with my friends. He went away on his own, professor. Well, he was knocked down by a turf lorry ... and my mother used to say, "If you had looked after Joe, he'd be alive now." He was her favourite.'

'Most distressing for you and your family. So sorry to hear that.'

'I wake up shouting, that I was ... well, the cause of his death. And the student next door, I think he heard me one night and asked me in the morning if I was all right.'

When he had finished, the professor said: 'It was a tragic accident, Mr Galvin, with painful consequences, but it happened and you were not the cause. Life is like that.' A paternal smile showed around his mouth. 'Now, do you feel better for having told me? Perfectly normal to have a reaction like that. You seem healthy – a bit anxious – but you'll make a good priest.'

'Well, could you give me a prescription for tablets? You know, to calm ... .'

The psychiatrist glanced at him. 'I'm not happy with giving out sedatives, especially to a young man like yourself. However, yes, for a month. Come back to me then, and we'll see.'

'Thanks, professor.'

Clutching the prescription, Galvin rushed down the stairs and got on his bicycle for Hayes, Conyngham & Robinson, dispensing chemists on Lower Baggot Street. While he was locking his bicycle to a railing, he noticed a rakish-looking man growling to himself; he was resting his arms on the parapet of Baggot Street Bridge and gazing into the canal. His brown hat was battered and worn at an angle. Over his shoulder, he glanced at Galvin. 'The world is full of troubles, young fella.'

'It is.'

The man turned away to admire two swans in the canal. 'Full of troubles, and you know, young fella, half the time we don't know what's wrong with us or what it's all about – *through a glass darkly*. Life is a mystery, young fella.' He lowered his head and spat into the canal. 'Great beauty too.'

'Yes, great beauty.'

'Look at them. Wouldn't it do your heart good.' Galvin looked at the swans skimming the water.

'I suppose,' said the rakish man, 'you wouldn't have a bob to spare for the meter. My gas has run out and I'm famished.'

Galvin searched his pockets and gave him an English shilling.

'You're a dacent young boy. You're goin' for the Church, I see,' he added gently.

'I am.'

'I hope you save many souls.'

'I hope so too,' Galvin said, heading for the chemist.

'Say a prayer for me.'

'I will.'

When Galvin returned to St Paul's after the Christmas holidays, the High Command sent for him. After he had genuflected and kissed the archbishop's ring, the prelate indicated a chair beside the glowing fire. 'You're just a bit scrupulous. Of course, some of the great saints were scrupulous.'

Emboldened by mention of the great saints, Galvin told his story while the High Command regarded him with one raised eyebrow, just like Irwin had mimicked. When he had finished,

Galvin said: 'Could I ask you something, Your Grace?'

'Yes, of course. I am a spiritual father to all my priests and seminarians.'

'If I died and I was going for the priesthood … I mean, would God forgive me my sins?'

From his chair, higher than Galvin's, the High Command joined his hands as if in prayer and peered at him. 'Now, my son. I'm going to ask you to do this for me.'

'Yes, Your Grace.'

'I want you now on this eighteenth of January 1963 to put out of your head all notions about being a big sinner. Will you do that for me? You are not responsible for your young brother's death. And as for your suitability, well, we all rely on the grace of God. We are earthenware jars carrying a great treasure, St Paul tells us.'

An impish smile played around the High Command's thin lips. He turned to his desk and took a crucifix from the drawer. 'This reminder of our Divine Master's passion and death for our sins will help you to ward off any thoughts about the opposite sex. Keep this beneath your pillow and Our Blessed Lady will be your consolation.'

'Thank you, Your Grace.'

'And finally, Mr Galvin. We all come into the priesthood motivated by ideas that lack substance – irrational guilt in your case – but never forget: God calls us in our brokenness and with His grace and the guidance of good spiritual directors, we refine our response to His call. You'll be a good priest. I know it.'

On his way back to St Paul's, Galvin decided: *Yes, I'll be fine, there can't be anything wrong with me. These men are very learned. I mustn't go back and be a nuisance.*

He threw away the tablets and followed the High Command's prescription: football, walks in the fresh air and applying himself to Aristotle's and St Thomas's understanding of the world. This advice helped to push aside the demons of the night and that worked, in a way, but he always remained what his friends called a worrywart, blaming himself when something went wrong. (This became especially acute years later in the wake of the Hegarty Report, when he was accused of knowing more than in fact he did about the appalling scandals.)

Like all students were required to do, Galvin went for confession to the spiritual director in the oratory every Saturday evening. Invariably the sin was always the same. 'Bad thoughts, father.'

'When you are going or coming from university, my son, and if a girl passes by on a bicycle, and the breeze ... ah yes ... lifts her summer dress above, hmm, her knee, you look away immediately. To linger on that would be a matter for confession. It could lead to serious sin.' The milk-bottle lenses held him captive. 'You would be placing your vocation in jeopardy if you indulge your base desires. Follow the spiritual exercises, play sport and maintain clerical friendships. Our nature is such that during our youth, we have, hmm, strong urges of the flesh ... these can be controlled by prayer and plenty of exercise. Say a decade of the rosary for your penance.'

'I will, father.'

Despite the reassurance, however, he woke one night after a dream of Sarah Clifford, with whom he had danced only two weeks before entering St Paul's. A wet patch on the sheet was still warm. He didn't want to get back to sleep, but longed instead to wallow in the delicious sequel to the dream and the sheer pleasure of losing himself. Somewhere down the corridor a student, in his sleep, was berating the world for all his worth, but Galvin was back in the dancehall with Sarah.

AFTER SPENDING the summer driving men to his brother's building sites in Reading and High Wycombe, Galvin had returned home with a bulging wallet two weeks before he was due at St Paul's. One evening after football practice, while he and other members of the team were changing into their clothes beside a hedge, they asked him to go to a dance in Ballybunion the following Sunday night. 'I'm getting the Hillman from my ould fella. A last fling for you, Tommy,' one of them said.

As soon as they stood inside the hall door, the clashing of cymbals on the stage, the twirl of skirts and the revolving crystal globe showering the laughing dancers with confetti dispersed from his head all thoughts of St Paul's and 'the body is a temple of the Holy Ghost'. He danced with different girls until he noticed one across the hall. A beauty. Time stopped. He took in her dark hair and shapely figure. In an ashes-of-roses dress, flared out by buckram, she had him transfixed: music, colour and laughter fell away and, when the bandleader announced another set, he plucked up courage and jostled his way across the dance floor.

'Would you like …?' He indicated the dance floor. She nodded and tidied loose strands of hair above her ear.

They danced a second time and, when the set was coming to an end, he looked at her. 'We could go for a walk. The fresh air, you know, good for you.' His heart was pounding in fear of a rejection.

With mock innocence, she smiled up at him. 'Good for my health?' He felt the pressure of her fingers in his back.

'Oh yeah, all the doctors say so.'

'Better obey the doctors then. Let me get my cardigan.'

When she returned from the cloakroom, she had a white cardigan slung over her dress and buttoned at the neck. They gave their pass tickets to those crowding around the door who didn't have enough money to get in. Then, holding hands, they tripped away from the dancehall towards the ocean.

The wholesome smell of the sea carried lightly in the breeze blowing up from the strand and the rush of the waves heightened their excitement. They continued on down the slope, passed the Castle Hotel on their right and the small shop that sold periwinkles, KitKats and ice-cream. In the distance the band was playing the hit song of the summer, 'Sealed With a Kiss'.

'I can't wait for university in October. What about you, what will you be doing?' she asked softly.

'Going to college in Dublin also.'

'Trinity or UCD?'

He raised his head. 'Great song,isn't it?'

'Great. So?' She was smiling. 'Which?'

'UCD'

'We'll be able to meet up then.'

'Oh, let's not talk about schools or colleges.' She was moving near to truths about him that might rob the night of its magic and, to deflect, he tightened his grip around her waist. 'Spoil things between us.'

'Spoil things!' She wriggled away from him. 'You're telling me nothing about yourself. Have you a couple of wives or something?'

'No. No, I've no wives.'

'Relax, I'm only having you on. Although now you're a bit of a puzzle.' She snuggled against him. 'Maybe you've killed someone. C'mon, mystery man, what's the story? How did you do it? ' She poked him in the ribs. 'C'mon, Jack the Ripper. Confess.'

'Yeah, I give myself up. I did kill someone … a young woman who was asking too many questions. Threw her into the sea right down there.' He pointed to the white horses breaking on the strand and while she was looking towards the waves, he put his arm around her, buried his face in her hair and began to ply her with questions. 'What did you do for the summer, Sarah? Why did you pick social science? Have you seen *Come September*? Sandra Dee and Bobby Darin are great in it.'

Light from the street was showing up the white spray that rippled across the pebbles, spent itself close to their feet, and then slipped out to sea again. Steadying herself with one hand on his shoulder, she removed her shoes.

In the distance the bandleader was announcing the next song: 'Maybe Baby', a Buddy Holly hit. A couple hidden in the darkness joined in: *'Maybe baby I'll have you / Maybe baby, you'll be true / Maybe baby ...*' From the direction of the Nuns' Strand came the murmur of other couples. A girl laughed provocatively. 'No, you're not going there again, you cheeky bastard.' The whole strand was alive with the sounds of summer's love. Sarah looked up at him.

'What are they up to at all?'

'I've no idea, but he seems to be a boyo.'

'You wouldn't be like that now, would you?'

'Me? God no.'

Light from one of the lamp posts shone on her smiling face. They had stopped chattering and, as they grew silent, became aware of a pull towards one another, one they no longer wanted to resist. He jettisoned all advice from the priest to whom he had gone to confession the previous week. 'I'll overlook the appalling way you behaved with that young woman in London.' Galvin could see the priest's finger wagging inside the grille. 'But from now on you will steer clear of girls.' When he kissed Sarah's upturned mouth, he caught the same healthy taste of young love he remembered after dances at the Galtymore.

Arms around each other, they climbed the hill. She was quiet for a while before she said: 'We have a couple of weeks before we head for Dublin. Will you be here again before you go up to college?' Her brown eyes were eager.

'Yes ...' he hesitated, '... I might be, but I've to explain, well, something I haven't told you.'

She looked at him while he explained, then turned her head away towards the ocean. 'I hope this doesn't disturb your intention.'

'No, not at all.'

'Good.' She started to put on her shoes and, for balance, rested her hand again on his shoulder. 'You certainly know how to court a girl for a fellow going to become a monk.' They kissed and then climbed the pathway to the main street where the dancers were spilling onto the street and lining up at the fish-and-chip vans.

Despite his confession to the spiritual director every Saturday, the urge to meet a natural desire surfaced in dreams, which left starchy patches in the sheets.

'Ah, yes, a product of our nature; pay no attention and yes, hmm, keep your crucifix under your pillow to ward off any lingering thoughts.' Creaking in the darkness when the spiritual director shifted in the confessional. 'Nocturnal emissions, yes, very natural.' From then on Galvin kept his distance from Sarah, even when she sent him a six-page letter. Lucky for him the Phantom was away when the post arrived that day.

Just before Halloween, they had a chance meeting outside the high doors of the Kevin Barry Lecture Hall at UCD. She had on a black turtleneck jumper beneath a cream mackintosh and her faculty scarf and was carrying a ring binder and books.

'You look the part,' she said, gesturing towards his black suit and tie. He tried to be casual and used a line he'd heard someone say and thought very clever. 'Dead to the world, Sarah.' They chatted about lectures, St Paul's and dances she'd been to in the Four Provinces in Harcourt Street.

'Out of bounds, I suppose, now you've joined the monks.'

'Afraid so, Sarah.'

She was staying with an uncle who had a pharmacy across the road from the Botanic Gardens. 'Not too far from your monastery. By the way, we promised to have coffee together, do you remember?'

'Yes, we did. We could go to Newman House, even though the monastery – as you call it – forbids us to go there. Could be an occasion of sin.' Despite his caution, he was back in the flurry of Ballybunion and the white horses breaking on the strand. 'Yes, let's have coffee some day.'

They met at the sinful place and sat near a sunny window looking out at the Iveagh Gardens where students were strolling along the gravel paths between rows of cypresses. All the while, Galvin kept a peeled eye out for Winters or one of the other prefects. After that, they met occasionally for coffee and, on a free day the following spring, just before they broke up for the Easter holidays, had sausage and chips at the Metropole and then went to the cinema upstairs for the matinee.

'Let me know when you're having another one of these free days.' They were lingering after getting off the bus at the corner of Griffith Avenue and Gracepark Road. Spring had arrived that night. A full moon was shining through the young leaves of the beeches inside the high walls of the seminary. The scent of cut grass carried in the air. They stepped from one foot to the other to keep warm, but were delaying the moment of parting by clutching at fragments of news and, when that was spent, going over the film again.

The next evening Winters rapped on his door during study time; as ever, he didn't wait for an answer and was standing in the doorway before Galvin could rise from his desk chair. 'You are to report to Dr Murtagh in half an hour,' he declared, then walked off down the corridor, leaving the door open as he always did when summoning a student to the Phantom's office.

The Phantom was in a rage. 'It has come to my notice that you were speaking to a young lady last evening, mister.'

'A friend of mine, Dr Murtagh.'

'A friend! Explain yourself.' He tapped his desk while Galvin explained how Sarah was a neighbour from home and they had gone to a film at the Metropole.

When he had finished, the Phantom glowered at him. 'You mean to tell me that you sat beside a young woman in a dark cinema?' His voice was hoarse with vexation. 'Have you any idea – *any idea* – how that could be a source of grave temptation and could compromise your vocation?'

'We didn't mean it like that, Dr Murtagh.'

'Don't you know that company-keeping is forbidden, even for those who are not in training for the priesthood? Asking to see a psychiatrist, and now this!' Colour drained from his sharp features. 'Do you want to be expelled?'

'No, Dr Murtagh. I don't want that at all.'

'Then you are never again to see this … this *friend*. Never again.'
He did a karate chop with his hand. 'You have given a bad example
to a devout woman who saw you on the street in conversation with
this … this *mulier adulescens*.'

'It won't happen again, Dr Murtagh.'

'I should hope so for your sake. I advise you to go to confession.'

The following Saturday evening the spiritual director shifted in
the confessional and turned his Old Spice face towards him. 'You
kissed a young woman! Don't you know you could have endan-
gered her immortal soul? And you a student for the priesthood!' He
was no longer the kindly old man with the screwdriver probing the
back of his transistor.

'I didn't mean any of that, father. I couldn't help it.'

'Are you set on throwing the divine invitation in the face of the
God who chose you?'

'No, father.'

From then on Galvin avoided Sarah, and whenever they did
meet in the main concourse or on the wide stairway, he told her he
was rushing to a lecture and dashed away.

'Any free days, Tommy, we could go the Metropole? Sausage
and chips?'

'Well, yes, but you see, we've house exams and other things
coming up.'

Her eyes dropped to the ring binder. An ache coursed through
him; he wanted to expunge the Phantom and his rules from his
head and draw her to him but, instead, he tightened his grip on his
briefcase and made to move on.

'Oh,' she said, 'ok, I understand. Well, thanks anyway. We'll run
into each other again.'

'Oh we will.'

THREE

ON THE TUESDAY, the second day of the retreat, Galvin wakes with an erection. *Life still in the old dog* crosses his mind and causes him to smile. And as he eases out of sleep, bits and pieces of a dream come back to him. Sarah in her ashes-of-roses dress, the strand at Ballybunion, Brendan Bowyer leaping on the stage of the Central ballroom – but he clamps down on the stray images and makes ready to meet the day.

Washed and shaved, Galvin picks up his breviary and stands for a moment at the main door of Coghill House. A foghorn booming out in Dublin Bay and the sound of a window being raised invade the silence. Solitary priests pace the gravel path beside the tennis courts where grass is growing through the tarmac, reading their breviaries or fingering rosaries held behind their backs.

He scans the grounds as he walks by the statue of Cardinal O'Kelly, founder of the college, on whose head a seagull is surveying the world. Every shade of light, every curve in the walk is saturated with the past: it was here that the Phantom caught them throwing snowballs during the heavy fall of 1963. Over there at the cemetery where cypresses forever block out the sun, fragments of a classmate's goodbye wing back to him. 'I'm off, Tommy. Suffocating here.'

'What will you do?'

'Get my degree for starters.' One of the brightest in the year, he became a principal officer in the civil service and eventually moved to New York to take up a senior post with the United Nations.

By the grotto to the Virgin Mary, he is reminded of the student who couldn't wait until he was out working in a parish. 'I want to be a *good* priest, Tom, but I'm worried that I might not be worthy to change the bread and wine into the body and blood of Christ or give the proper advice in confession.' Two years after ordination, he was able to shed his scruples and head for London with a woman he had met while on the staff of a comprehensive school. 'I have found the love of my life,' he told a startled congregation in the parish church where he was helping out. 'So the honourable thing for me to do is to leave.' Listening in the sacristy, the parish priest's face and neck had been puce.

Passing through the dim corridor that leads to the room where Lauds is recited, Galvin glances at the ordination photographs now relegated to the twilight. Until the seminary was leased out, they had pride of place in the Stone Corridor: the older class pieces in sepia, then cameos in black and white, fresh faces and Pioneer pins on lapels. Fewer every year since the brouhaha after John Paul II's visit had faded. All are now replaced by colour photographs of students throwing their mortar boards in the air, posing with a goat in Tanzania or climbing Kilimanjaro for some charity or other.

The upbeat mood at breakfast is shattered by the arrival of a priest with news about a curate down the country who has hanged himself. 'The PP there is a friend … we were in Maynooth together. Seems the poor guy was accused in the wrong. Awful stuff.' 'Jesus save us' comes from down the table. They lean towards the man with the news as if hearing about a parasite that could attack and kill at any minute.

Harry Sheerin is the first to speak: 'Only a matter of time before one or other of us gets zapped, even if we're innocent! And if you ask me—'

'What are you talking about, Harry?' A man sitting directly across the table rounds on him.

'The Church bosses won't lift a hand to save us. We'll be left swinging in the wind, mate.' Sheerin's curly head, grey now, is bent over his egg and rashers. One end of his plastic Roman collar hangs loose.

They are dumbfounded. The priest with the bad news breaks the silence. 'My friend hadn't a bull's that the poor bastard was in cold storage in his parish – what d'you think of that?' He has their full attention. 'The community guard found him. Used to drop in purely out of sympathy.' He gives a running commentary on the report.

'Well, that's about the measure of it.'

Sheerin is sitting sideways at the table, one arm resting on the back of the empty chair next to him. 'The bishops will always pull the trigger to cover their arses.'

'Oh my God, and we always thought that there was a father-son relationship,' says Cyril, known in his student days as Dominic Savio, the boy-saint. In the early 1970s, when growing beards had become a fashion among young priests, he had tried, but the result had been a thin covering, sparse and patchy, that stood out from his acolyte's face.

'Father-son, me arse,' Sheerin snorts. 'That was never the case, never will be.'

'What's going to … oh, I don't know,' Cyril says. 'I never saw anything like this in my life.' He looks around with panicky eyes, desperately searching for a solution. 'Harry is right … they've no regard for us.' While Sheerin continues to lambaste the bishops,

Cyril leans over to Galvin. 'I've given up, Tommy, I stay in my house, or potter around the garden, and my dogs – I'd be lost without them – they keep me going. Great company.'

'I know, I've a dog too. Sam. He's a Labrador.'

'With their sad eyes, I think they understand what I'm saying.'

Stories about Cyril going on his house-to-house visitation with his Chihuahuas were well-known in the diocese; how he would refuse to cross the threshold if his dogs were not welcome.

'Then I spend a couple of weeks' holidays with the lads – those of us from the ordination year that are still above ground.' He smiles weakly. 'We go to the Canaries in January.'

'Two others in the country did it last year.' Sheerin does a rope-hanging motion and then shrugs. 'You know something? I'm not at all surprised.' He looks around for a reaction. 'I mean, we're expected to live this nonsensical life. Drudgery and isolation. Not surprised at all. And d'you know what, lads? It's killing us.'

'What can you do except get on with it, Harry. Keep the show on the road.' Cyril pours milk onto his cornflakes.

'Cyril,' the man beside him says, 'that's all any of us is doing. I've only two more years to retirement. It's curtains then. I'd gladly have stayed on but ...' he shakes his head. 'Ah no. Not the way things are now. The tank is empty.'

Despite the gloom, their combined presence to one another offers comfort, unlike mornings when they sit alone in their pres-bytery kitchens with the jug propping up the newspaper while they suffer another account on *Morning Ireland* about a priest being sentenced for child abuse.

'Bad work, Tom. And here's something to cap it all,' says the priest who had brought the news. 'The bishop down there has refused to have prayers recited for the priest next Sunday in any of the parishes he served. Canonical directive, he says. Canonical, me arse. Where's the compassionate Jesus, hah? And the lepers.' He speaks close to Galvin's ear. 'We're the fucking lepers.'

After breakfast, Galvin, who knew the PP where the tragic death had happened, phones with his condolences. He is given a blow-by-blow account from the time the patrol car with its flashing lights screeched to a halt outside the PP's door two evenings before. They rushed him over to the dead priest's bungalow.

'This way, father,' the sergeant said. 'Prepare yourself for a shock.'

The smell of death hit the PP as soon as he entered the room, but, except for the slate grey of his face and neck, the dead priest looked as if he had fallen asleep with his head resting on one arm of the couch.

The sergeant broke the silence. 'God rest him. The poor man deserves more than to end his days like this.' He spoke as if he were in a church when mass was about to begin.

The PP fumbled with the anointing oils. 'We'll say a few prayers if that's alright, sergeant,' he said after anointing the ice-cold forehead and hands of the dead priest.

'Oh, do.'

After the siesta that day, life returns to Coghill for the afternoon snack in the coffee dock – a gravelled atrium in Galvin's time, now a dining room with heat-sealed prints in pastel colours decorating the walls: Dali, Monet and vintage posters from Le Moulin Rouge showing young women in a variety of provocative poses, 'Au joyeux Moulin Rouge'. Bright sunlight streaming through the glass panels on the roof falls on the cane chairs and round tables where students flirt and write assignments on their laptops during term time.

The priests are still mulling over any morsel of news about the dead curate. One man had gone out for the evening paper and is passing it around. 'It says here that he had been dead for a day or maybe longer. God help him. The poor fellow had a letter of dismissal from his bishop only yesterday. It was lying beside him when he was found. He is being buried early tomorrow morning. May God rest his soul.'

In accordance with the bishop's directive, a requiem mass is said at seven o'clock in the parish church while cars speed by on the main road, the postman delivers the mail, young women in pencil skirts trip along the pavement and commuters hear on the radio that a Cork syndicate has won the Lotto. The only people present are the priest's mother, an aunt – a frail nun who had spent forty years in Kenya – and a brother and sisters. A few seats behind and across the aisle his classmates from Maynooth kneel closely together.

After mass, while the undertakers are lifting the coffin off the trolley and sliding it along the deck of the hearse, a priest of the diocese, who had been delegated to 'journey' with offending priests, is standing beside the sergeant. 'Sad day, sergeant,' he remarks.

Without taking his eyes off the coffin, the sergeant says in a low voice of suppressed anger. 'Is there any screed of humanity left in your organization?'

The priest's lips tighten and his eyes become defensive. 'Well, as you know, the diocese had to keep the poor … yes, unfortunate under surveillance for his misdemeanour. I was delegated to journey with him.'

'Even after the DPP had thrown it out?' The sergeant makes to move off, but turns on his heel. 'He'd have been left to rot if it hadn't been for the community guard – he was the only one who dropped in to see him. The only one who was *journeying* with him as far as I'm concerned.'

The nun places a red rose on the coffin before the driver closes down the hatch. Slowly the few mourners get into their cars and follow the cortège.

GALVIN'S REMINISCENCES and the retreat director's talks course through his head while he kneels in the chapel or strolls around the grounds. During that evening's conference, the Benedictine had spoken about building a new Church where friendship, not power, would reign. Resting on the garden seat in front of Wansborough, he reviews the jottings he has made. 'Jesus came on earth, fathers,' the monk had said, 'to set an example of service. Have we fallen to pride like Milton's Satan? *Better to reign in Hell than serve in Heaven.* Is that why our churches are becoming old curiosity shops? '

Priests are walking up and down in twos and threes, a return to the habit of their seminary days. The smells of cigarette smoke and freshly cut grass mingle in the breeze. Galvin glances at them and sees, in his mind's eye, their youthful versions: the one who was *victor ludorum* of the college sports every year is now battling prostate cancer; another had starred as outside half on the St Patrick's Day match against the priests. He has shrunk, and hobbles along with the help of a walking stick. 'We're blessed with the weather, Tom,' he smiles bravely when they pass by him.

'Makes all the difference.'

They continue along the sandy path and disappear into a grove of copper beeches, their footsteps fading. Galvin turns over a page of his notes from the director's talk. 'Child abuse is more about the abuse of power: power over the smallest and the weakest.' He rests the notebook on the seat and looks around.

The priest who had ended his life rekindles the recriminations in the wake of the Hegarty Report and casts a pall over Galvin's reflections; the demands for his own resignation as one who knew 'what was going on' drag him back to those dark days when television crews from Britain and America, along with newshounds from all the home papers, scrambled across the lawn. Laden with cameras and boom microphones, they rushed from one press conference to another in Wansborough House. As the rain lashed down, satellite trucks drove over the kerbs and, as wheels sank, the driver revved up the engine and a jet of puddle shot up into the air and smeared the windows of O'Kelly House. After they had long gone, Paddy filled in the furrows with a spade and re-seeded the broken lawn, and for a couple of weeks, the badgers and foxes that came out at night in that part of the grounds went into hiding. In the Academy Hall, broadcasters and journalists thrust microphones in front of terror-stricken bishops whose word is seldom questioned.

In basement kitchens of nineteenth-century presbyteries, where the net curtains were yellowed from cigarette smoke, Galvin drank coffee with accused priests. One man had sat with his elbows on the table, his hands covering his face. Crumbs, an open milk carton and curled heels of bread were strewn on the oilcloth. 'What's happening to me, Tom?' He raised his head towards the sound of passers-by on the footpath outside.

'From what you tell me, you have nothing to fear, and the DPP is saying there's no case to answer. It will be over in a couple of weeks. Then you'll be reinstated.'

'Are you trying to cod me?' He turned a baleful look on Galvin. 'My fate is sealed. I'm finished. My life is ruined. They'll say no smoke without fire. When this thing is over, I'm going to head for Australia, to my brother.'

'That could be a fresh start. And when you get settled there, I'm sure any parish would be glad to have you.'

'Do you take me for a right jackass? I'm finished with this fucking Church. There's no more Christianity in it than in communist China. I'd sweep the roads or bag stones before I'd consider the priesthood ever again. And, by the way, I've made it clear: if I die in Ireland, I don't want to see sight or light of a bishop at my funeral.'

FOUR

TO GET Sarah Clifford off his mind, Galvin plunged into the daily routine of the seminary. He rose at the first sound of the six o'clock bell, did his half-hour meditation in the dim oratory, ten minutes' break in the cold, dark air and then mass. After that he joined the stream of cyclists freewheeling down the avenue and onto Church Road: like tributaries meeting other streams, they merged with those from neighbouring seminaries, crossed Butt Bridge and down City Quay. Football in the afternoon and then study. His examination results at the end of the year elicited a positive comment from the rector: 'A second-class honours, grade one, is very commendable, Mr Galvin. You've been an excellent student. Keep it up.'

The 'bad thoughts' continued, however, and when he went to confession, the spiritual director repeated his stock advice: 'Keep the crucifix beneath your pillow, Mr Galvin. And if you do that, you will be fine.'

One morning during Lent he was in Second Arts. A biting wind blew across from Siberia and the trees stood naked against the March sky. He was checking the tyres of his bicycle in the grey light of the shed when he noticed Damien Irwin standing at the far end.

'We're stuck with each other, Tommy,' Irwin grinned as he lifted his bicycle off the rack and settled the black hat on his head. On the way to the university, Irwin had a succession of jokes and funny voices so that Galvin hardly noticed the journey until they were cycling down Hume Street and turning onto St Stephen's Green. The ease of their relationship surprised him, because he wasn't in Irwin's circle of friends and did not share his interests. Though only a year ahead of Galvin, Irwin was always to the fore of seminary life – making out lists to serve the bishop's mass at the Pro-Cathedral or playing the organ for Benediction.

After lunch the following Sunday, he was waiting for Galvin outside the refectory door. It was the day of the annual inter-house rugby match. Ahead of them, as they walked down the slope where scaffolding was being put up for the new extension, three students were passing around an imaginary rugby ball. Irwin threw them a withering look.

'Would you look at them? Bloody boarding-school boys. Can't understand why they chase a bag of wind around a field. But you'll probably be joining them.'

'Yeah, I managed to get on the team.'

'We've time to do a stretch of the legs. The Long Walk.'

They strode across one of the playing fields and along by the Tolka. Irwin was absorbed in thinking out loud a list for the Holy Week and Easter ceremonies at the Pro-Cathedral. 'Would you like to be on it?'

'No. I'm a bull in a china shop when it comes to anything like that.' The matted grass and the dead weeds of winter swished against their soutanes. 'How is it that you know your way around so well?' asked Galvin.

'I've been coming in here since I was in school. My parish priest asked me to help out during the priests' retreats. Serving mass, helping in the refectory, that sort of thing. I was selected to give a hand with the paraplegics in Lourdes. And the PP is always good for a few bob.'

Two senior students were placing corner flags on the rugby pitch and another was running a lime-roller along the touchline. The tang of YR sauce from the factory across the river carried in the raw wind.

'To be honest, I need it. The dad has eight mouths to feed and working in the yard for Tedcastle's doesn't bring in a whole lot. You won't tell … .'

'No. Not at all.'

'In here, they pour shit on someone from that background, but I think, yeah, I can trust you, you cute hoor.'

'"Live and let live, and never judge anyone because it's a strange old world." That's my father's motto, and he was never inside the door of a secondary school, never mind a university. And, until M.J. became a millionaire in London, the father struggled to make ends meet on the few acres of land.'

When they had completed their walk and were approaching Coghill, Irwin spoke in a low voice: 'Not a word of what I've told you.'

'Not a word.'

Priests who came in to watch the rugby game were parking Volkswagen Beetles and Ford Anglias to the side of O'Kelly House; others talked and smoked in front of the main door. They were wearing Crombie overcoats and had a high shine on their shoes. Some had on galoshes. A few months away from ordination, Noonan, head and shoulders above the rest, and with a cigarette dangling from his mouth, was showing them tickets for the forthcoming international at Lansdowne Road. Irwin glanced at them.

'Jesus, always the schoolboy. Anyway, play well. And kick Noonan in the goolies for me.'

BACK FROM the Easter break the year Galvin was preparing to sit the May examinations, a group of senior students, already changed into their Roman collars and soutanes, were standing around Beresford's Folly, smoking and recalling games of golf at Lahinch. He was lugging a suitcase up the stairs when he met Irwin tripping down. 'Did you dig up all the turf, Tommy boy?'

'Most of it. Did you polish the parish priest's candlesticks and lick his arse?'

'Let's do a round before night prayer.'

Some, still in their black suits and carrying their hats, were dotted all over the grounds; they stopped now and again to chat to others. A student was simulating a golf swing. The hawthorn hedge at one side of the Abbey Walk, bare when they had left for the holidays, now had on a fresh green cover. Irwin was anxious to share his news.

'I was in here over the holidays, helping out with the usual, tidying up after Easter, and guess what? Didn't the Phantom ask me if I would be master of ceremonies at the Pro-Cathedral. Couldn't say no.'

'You couldn't.'

He was upbeat. 'This is the place for me, Tommy. No doubt about that.'

'I wish I could say the same. Not sure even from day to day.'

But Irwin wasn't interested in Galvin's vocational crises. 'Even when I was an altar boy, I caught sight of a world ... .' His expression softened while he described the summer's evening when he had been serving at the men's sodality in the Church of St Joseph, East Wall. In his red soutane and white surplice, he was reclining on the side steps of the altar with the other servers. The sun's rays had overlain the pews in amber. The lighted candles on the altar and the blood-red sanctuary lamp, hanging from a silver urn – all this enchanted him. After placing the blessed sacrament in the monstrance, the parish priest mounted the pulpit. He placed his biretta on his head, crossed himself and then, like a consummate actor whose timing is perfect, rested his hands on the pulpit and paused before quoting scripture.

'I sneaked a glance at the congregation. Their heads were raised towards the priest, now whipping out a handkerchief from the folds of his soutane and wiping his glasses or lacing his sermon with Latin quotations. This was even better than the parish hall during a Lenten play, Tommy, I swear to you, when you could hear trickles of water in the radiators.

'Yeah, that was for me. And then the curates joking in the sacristy about card games or some oul wan annoying them about mass cards. High Mass on Christmas morning. The beauty and mystery of the Latin. A far cry from the drab look of St Brigid's Terrace, I can tell you.'

Two of the Shiny Buttons were sauntering across the pitch. One of them shouted: 'What've you got in the briefcase, Irwin? A mitre?'

Always on the lookout for one of the prefects, Irwin cast a beady eye over the grounds before he replied: 'No, a dangerous reptile I'm going to let loose to deal with gobshites like you.' He returned to his topic. 'Don't know if I ever told you. I used to do a dry run at home.'

'How do you mean?'

'Saying mass. Got one of my brothers to be the altar server. I wasn't going to be just a priest, though. I had a rosary beads around my neck – my pectoral cross and chain.' He opened the briefcase and took out a prayer book. 'See, I'm taking my vocation seriously, not like the rest of you slackers.' It was then that Galvin noticed a window cut into the cover of an old breviary; inside was a small radio. 'A prezzie from my parish priest for helping out. As well as a few crisp notes.' Irwin grinned and rubbed his thumb and fingers together. 'Keep me going for another while. And I'll be able to pick up foreign stations, including Vatican Radio. Learn a bit of the lingo.'

'You'll be in trouble if the Phantom finds out you have a radio.'

'But he's not going to find out, is he? Unless you rat on me, and I don't think that's in your nature. Anyway, you cagey hoor from the country, if you don't take risks you get nowhere. By the way, the same parish priest has a live-in housekeeper.' He threw a sly look at Galvin. 'More than a housekeeper. Say no more.'

The bell for night prayer rang out over the grounds, causing those who were smoking in front of Coghill to stamp out their cigarettes. The chat and bursts of laughter ceased. The Phantom might be on the prowl. The grounds fell silent, except for the rush of footsteps along the gravel walk towards the oratory.

As if unconsciously fitting in with the laws of natural selection, groups formed every year in St Paul's and, as long as the Phantom didn't receive a report of a student caught in another's room, or breaking the rule against 'particular friendships', he was content to turn a blind eye to such formations. The Guns, six or seven students who shared the top places in every exam and were admired because they did so with apparent ease, paraded up and down the ambulatory after breakfast, smoking cigarettes and outdoing one another in discussing world affairs. They affected a detailed knowledge of General de Gaulle's political career and T.K. Whitaker's economic plan.

While others were racing up to the playing pitches each afternoon, another group of four or five strolled the grounds. Their ringleader was Rossiter. Theatrical in his mannerisms, he was always vying with Irwin for the job of heading the archbishop's list for the Christmas and Easter ceremonies and holding up the cappa magna, the archbishop's long trail of washed silk. His soutane was spotless, his surplice well-pleated and he gave off a strong smell of aftershave, which some said was scent. The group could often be found in the library looking up some book on stained-glass, playing bridge while guffawing at some witty remark Rossiter made, or sniggering at a piece of gossip he had gleaned from the diocese.

They shared a common interest in rubrics, and managed to get on the list for the annual diocesan pilgrimage to Lourdes. There they ingratiated themselves with the High Command: it was said that he invited them to afternoon tea in his hotel to winkle out information about priests on the staff who might be stepping out of line in their teaching.

The soccer and rugby players, like Noonan, also banded together. They were loud during recreation time, and Noonan was forever telling the joke about the evening he was trotting out to the back pitch when he had come across an elderly couple out for a walk who were looking up at windows where jockstraps were draped across the sills. The woman pointed and asked: 'What are they, young man?'

'They're scrum caps, missus. Worn on our heads when we're playing rugby, to protect our brains.'

As long as the cache of duty-free cigarettes they had bought in France the previous summer held up, the jockstrap brigade smoked Gauloises and Gitanes in front of Coghill and the strongly flavoured cigarette smoke swept through the vestibule every time someone opened the front door. They were forever selecting teams in the billiards room during the rugby season: teams to play in the inter-house competitions, teams to play against All Hallows or Holy Cross, teams to play in the inter-house rugby game in December or against the priests on St Patrick's Day. Nearly every evening they togged out: their shouts and the thud of wet leather resounded against the walls of the handball alley. And while December mists rolled in from Dollymount, they knocked mud from their football boots by striking them against the concrete steps outside the back door of Senior House.

Irwin avoided the jockstrap brigade and, instead, skirted around the fringe of the other groups. Anyway, he spent most of his time studying in his room, listening in to Vatican Radio on his transistor, or making sure he outsmarted Rossiter to head the High

Command's list for the ceremonies. In winter, as darkness fell over the seminary, he could be heard practising on the organ high above the front door of the chapel.

FIVE

A CONSTANT of the priests' retreat is the annual mass for those who have died during the year. On the Wednesday morning just before the mass, Galvin and the others are vesting in the chapel. The air is filled with the churchy smells of furniture polish and candlewax. The rustle of freshly pressed albs and a purl of whispers worm into the silence. The organist is trying out pitch and chords with the cantor, a young woman with a red rose on her low-cut black dress. The flautist too is warming up. Someone is tuning violin strings. Through the high windows, the sun rests on the long pews and forms slanted columns in the sanctuary.

The seminarians rush to help feeble priests with cinctures and to fix stoles over their shoulders. Others are checking that everything is ready on the altar: one hooks a smoking thurible onto a silver stand. Soft plumes rise and drift through the church.

Eventually, the full swell of the organ causes heads to turn towards the main door where acolytes in soutanes and surplices are leading the concelebrating priests in procession up the central aisle; at each side are the stalls facing each other in choir formation.

Galvin's gaze falls on the cross-bearer and suddenly he sees through his mind's eye another procession when he was in Junior House. Boundaries of time collapse.

He is back in the dark of a November morning, when pairs of students wound their way through the ambulatory to the chapel for the requiem mass. A cold wind from the direction of the college cemetery stole through a gap between Coghill and Wansborough: white surplices ballooned and then were slapped tightly against soutanes. A snigger caused Winters, the prefect, to turn round and rake the long line with a scowl.

Across the rolling lawn, stars twinkled through naked branches of sleeping trees. After a long night's journey, the moon, in its last quarter, rested just above the roof of Wansborough. Another gust and a pile of leaves rose and danced around the statue of Cardinal O'Kelly, where, stolid and indifferent to the weather, he looks eternally out over the grounds towards the city he once ruled.

In the chapel, the music professor raised his baton and the dreadful dirge of Death and the Last Judgment resounded in the incense-perfumed air: *Dies irae, dies illa / Solvet saeclum in favilla / Teste David cum Sibylla.* 'That day of wrath and doom impending.' Black cloths were wound around the tall candlesticks on the main altar. A catafalque draped in a black pall and decorated with gold thread showed the diocesan coat of arms.

The conversations at lunch on that day of the retreat focus on priests who have passed away during the year: the 'characters', like the canon from Seville Place parish who, on the day the archbishop made new appointments, had his housekeeper prepare sandwiches and a flask of tea and then settled himself beneath the plane trees across from the archbishop's house to see which priests would drive up the avenue. As soon as he got back to the presbytery he would phone his cronies and give them a blow-by-blow account of who was summoned to the palace and who was going to get to the Gold Coast – a ribbon of parishes from Sandymount to Greystones – where the Sunday collection was many times that of others.

Harry Sheerin has no truck with nostalgia. 'Pompous old gits. The rector and the staff had little respect for you, unless your mother wore fur.' Propped by one arm on the table, he is ready to preside. 'A prison, pure and simple,' he adds, looking around for a reaction.

'Oh, Harry,' says Sylvester O'Flynn, 'it wasn't that bad.' Sitting stiffly and, as always, fixing his cuffs, O'Flynn had once entertained hopes of becoming Professor of Liturgy at St Paul's, like his uncle. Now, as a parish priest, he writes booklets on how people should behave in church: when they should kneel and when they should stand, and how they should chastise their children. Before every meal, he makes the sign of the cross over his food.

Sheerin turns to him. 'The bastards screwed me. Refused me Minor Orders when the rest of my year were taking another step closer to the big day. The Phantom snookered me. Made me repeat a joke I'd told one evening during the Solemn Silence about the guy who went to the doctor because he couldn't do it with the wife.'

Cyril's anxious eyes are searching for light relief to steer clear of the rising conflict and he chirps up: 'Will you ever forget when the High Command arrived to give us Minor Orders in the chapel? And the little scissors he took out to snip the lock of hair?'

'You were now tonsured,' Sheerin sniggers. 'I'm surprised he didn't cut off our *liathroidí*. He may as well, the way the Church has emasculated us.'

Cyril giggles. 'Harry, now, now. You're very bold.'

Like when they recited the Psalms, they take turns to act out the rituals they performed to receive Minor Orders.

'Open and close a door of the chapel.'

'You're a porter. You could now stand at the door of a church and protect it.'

'Hand on book.'

'Reader.'

'Sprinkle holy water.'

'Exorcist. You could drive out the devil.'

'Ring a bell.'

'Acolyte.'

'And we going out loaded with testosterone and not a word about it,' says Sheerin. Smirking, he looks around for a reaction. 'The pits.' He thumps the table with his fist.

'You're not being entirely fair, Harry.' Sylvester O'Flynn's voice grows even more shrill. Parted down the middle, his silver hair is perfectly groomed and the stud at the back of his high Roman collar seems to be cutting into his pink neck.

'They could at least have given some time to the urge.'

'I beg your pardon. The what, Harry?'

'Do I have to spell it out for you? The snake, Sylvester. What Eve fell for.'

'Well, I don't care what anyone says,' O'Flynn cocks his head and does a waving-away motion with his delicate hands, 'they gave us a good education and prepared us well for parish ministry.'

'Too puffed up,' Sheerin is only getting into his stride, 'with their red soutanes. You know, lads, I've come to the conclusion that when old geezers have little to say about life, they dress up and use titles. And then the gear – the pointy hats. Chief Sitting Bull. And what do you make of those young guys only a wet week out of the seminary?' He leans towards O'Flynn, who jerks away from him. 'Prancing and pirouetting around here in soutanes. And one of them – did you notice the sash?' He rests back again. 'Jesus wept!'

'Oh goodness me, Harry,' O'Flynn splutters. 'I think they're great. So committed. I have one of them in my parish – just ordained. I'm blessed. He does the Stations of the Cross in Latin every Friday night during Lent. The elderly parishioners just love him. And they say, "there's nothing like the old Latin mass".

He plays the concert flute for them after the rosary.'

'Do you know how someone gets promotion in the Church nowadays, Sylvester?' Sheerin relaxes, safe in the knowledge that he has the upper hand.

'I assume it's by having the proper spiritual disposition and high intelligence. How else could it be, Harry?'

Sheerin laughs. 'No, Sylvester. By having the gear: roman clericals and silver cufflinks. And most of all ...' He pauses for effect. 'Loyalty. *Loyalty*, gentlemen. In other words ... no *liathroidí*.'

'Oh, Harry, you're a panic.'

After lunch Galvin makes his way to the old library off the stone corridor, picks up the rule book and leafs through it. The rector's stock reminder after the summer holidays comes winging back to him. 'Your time here, young gentlemen, will pass swiftly; "Swifter than a weaver's shuttle", the Bible tells us.' The cycle, however, of going out every morning to the university, togging out for football and preparing for the St Patrick's Day rugby match and the concert that night were small pleasures they embraced, and they conferred a kind of meaning to the best years of their lives. Time had slipped by and the weeks and months had gathered speed, just as the rector had predicted: 'As a wheel going downhill, gentlemen.' And as they were once shown around the grounds, so too, they helped first years with their bags, and pointed out the special features of Wansborough and how Beresford had hanged rebels from Old Pompey.

Galvin runs his fingers along the parchment cover of the Year Book for 1965. That was the time when the Vatican Council, now in its final few months, was raising expectations in convents and seminaries. The concessions already in place – a half day on Thursday, a television set in both common rooms and newspapers every morning – pointed to greater changes yet to come. Students could now have a radio and a record player in their rooms. On Church feasts, the rector granted a Mix Day: juniors could walk around the grounds with the Shiny Buttons, or visit each other's common room.

Masses in the Pro-Cathedral marked the passage of time, as did the Feast of St Laurence O'Toole, Dublin's patron saint. Holy Week for the Passion ceremonies and Easter Sunday morning for the Resurrection of the Lord. For these ceremonies, the students formed a long procession that wound its way up Fitzgibbon Street, turning onto Mountjoy Square and then down Gardiner Street. In accordance with an edict from the High Command, they were dressed in the style of seminarians in Rome: Roman hats and long black garments with red piping, called sopranas.

Barefoot children scurrying from the open doors of tenements called after them: 'Holy pictures, father.' 'Any holy pictures, father?' Others swung from ropes tied to lamp posts and shouted, 'D'youse want a go, father?' Thick girders supported gables in danger of collapsing. Posters on poles advertised meetings at which a Jesuit priest from Gardiner Street by the name of Scully would speak about the disgraceful way the government was refusing to provide housing for poor people. Another poster showed a smiling Butch Moore and the Capital Showband: they would be playing at the Town and Country on Easter Sunday night.

On one of those days – a Holy Thursday – when the Mass of Chrism had ended, Galvin waited on the steps of the Pro-Cathedral for Irwin, who had been assisting as the archbishop's master of ceremonies in the sanctuary. Canons of the Chapter wearing their ermine were lining up to genuflect and kiss the High Command's ring at the front door. Down at street level, with their hair rollers showing beneath their scarves, women with prams waited to have their babies blessed; others from the Buckingham Street flats were hurrying so that their babies would also slip within the aura of the blessing.

Irwin appeared from inside the lofty doors and made his way through the crowd to where Galvin was waiting. He sniggered and gestured towards the canons. 'Will you look at the woolly backs – all the High Command needs is a sheepdog. Let's go.'

Heading towards Cathal Brugha Street, they heard a man calling in a broad Dublin accent: 'Damien! Damien, son. Damien, I'm over here.' Other students, spilling out of the cathedral, stopped to watch and then headed off towards Parnell Street. 'Here, Damien,' the man kept calling. Galvin looked back. A little man with a broad smile was waving his cap in the air; with him were other men who were idling near where a shawled woman was selling daffodils from a cart.

'He's calling you,' Galvin indicated with a nod. 'Damien, that man – he's calling you. D'you see?' The little man was still waving. Damien glanced down the street and a hunted look showed in his eyes.

'Don't mind him.' He turned away. 'He's just a fellow from our road.' He did a frantic search of his briefcase. 'I think I've forgotten my biretta … left it in the sacristy. Let's go in and get it. Come on, we can go out the other door by the back of the Gresham.'

Galvin stood for a moment looking across at the man, who had now given up and was putting his cap back on. He was talking to his cronies and pointing towards where Irwin had been walking.

'Come on! What are you standing there for?' Hurrying up the steps, Irwin nearly knocked into an old woman at the holy water font.

'Sorry, father,' she said, showing wide gaps in her teeth.

The archbishop's car pulled up in front of the Pro-Cathedral. The driver got out and held open a back door, which, by arrangement, was the High Command's cue to gather his robes about him, hurry down the steps and make his getaway. Both sides of the street were lined with people, mostly women and children, waving and admiring their reflections in the tinted glass of the Daimler.

The ragged children were still calling for holy pictures; a policeman warned them: 'Keep well back, children. Do ye want to get killed? I'm telling ye, keep back.'

He gave a formal salute to the archbishop and, when the car had passed by, threw a smiley wink at someone in the crowd. The women with prams crossed themselves and squinted to catch sight of the slight figure seated in the back of the Daimler, his ringed hand raised in blessing.

In the dim cathedral, wisps of smoke meandered upwards from the candles as the fat sacristan used a metal cone with a long handle to quench them. Rossiter pranced around the sanctuary, removing the missal from its stand and tidying up books. 'I think I left it in the sacristy,' Irwin said. 'Wait here a minute.' Galvin stopped by one of the holy water fonts. A woman with a headscarf was lighting candles at a shrine. The glow from the banked-up candles showed up the deep lines in her weather-beaten face. Her lips were twitching in prayer, her fingers working on a rosary beads.

Galvin and Irwin went out by the narrow lane at the back of the Gresham Hotel and hurried in the direction of Cathal Brugha Street. Not until they reached North Great George's Street did Irwin speak a word, or slow his steps. 'He thinks he'll bloody well work out his problems by drink.' He raised his head and looked in the direction of Belvedere College. 'Some people never learn. Makes me sick.'

'What?'

'You didn't come down in the last shower. You know that was my ould fella. Now I'll be the laughing stock of the college.'

'I wouldn't say so.'

'Don't act the innocent. You know what they're like in there. The fancy schools they've been to. And the great J. Desmond with his airs and graces.'

'He seems ok. Genuine.'

'You can be so fucking thick at times. Oh sure, he has fine manners, but did you ever see him when someone dares to cross him? Goes ballistic. No one questions our J. Desmond. Divine right to pontificate. And you should have heard him the other day outside the back door while they were having a last drag out of a cigarette, going on about the way he holidays in France with the Hennessy family: you know, the brandy crowd.'

Irwin quickened his pace again. 'Keep going,' he said out of the side of his mouth so that the other seminarians wouldn't hear. When they reached the main gates of St Paul's, he suggested they do a round of the grounds. 'Time yet before dinner.' Rows of daffodils dressed the sweep of driveway that led to Wansborough. Those who were already back were walking up and down in front of O'Kelly. Some had attaché cases tucked beneath their arms.

'It's the right background that counts in here, but I'll show them. Most of the fellas are from ordinary … well, teachers, guards, shopkeepers, that sort of … you know, Christian Brothers boys. But the in-crowd calls the shots.' He glanced at Galvin. 'And the right school. Effin' snobs.'

'But you went to the right school. I mean, Belvedere's not exactly a slum.'

Irwin threw him a sheepish glance. 'Please don't tell this to anyone.'

'Have I ever?'

'No.'

'The mother has two sisters who never married. They're getting a good wage in Pim's, the furriers, and were well able to foot the bill when I said I was thinking of being a priest. Thirty-five lids a term.' He grimaced. 'The way one or two of them Jesuits looked at me. Bloody snobs. I knew soon enough I wasn't one of their sort.'

As the bell rang for lunch, students who had gathered to chat fell silent and headed immediately for the door of Coghill, but Irwin was still back there fighting his way towards independence. 'By the time I had done my matriculation, Roisín and Colette, my two older sisters, had got jobs in the civil service, so they were able to chip in for my fees here.

'The dad never wanted me to come here. Threw one of his tantrums. "A priest, looking down their noses at us poor gobshites.

What did priests do when men were half starved and Murphy, a so-called great Catholic, locked them out – decent men like me Dad, your grandfather, who spent his life as a deep-sea docker. If it hadn't been for Jem … God bless you, Jem and give you a b … bed in heaven." And off he goes to get drunk in the boozer. I knew I had to get out of the terrace, Tommy. Most of the kids from my neighbourhood never got a smell of a secondary school unless by winning a scholarship, or the Brothers in Fairview took them in and waived the fee. They were for Holyhead in the *Princess Maud*.'

'Like my three brothers,' Galvin said. 'And the two sisters had to go also to train as nurses.'

That Holy Thursday evening, the seminary had been hushed. Only dim lights burned along the skirting board of the long corridors. Students walked alone. The deacons read their breviaries; some students carried a rosary beads by their side.

As he was going through the vestibule of Wansborough to his room, he came upon Irwin at the noticeboard, pinning a new list to serve at the Pro-Cathedral mass on Easter Sunday morning.

'Tom,' he whispered, 'thanks.' He threw a guarded glance towards the stone stairs.

'For what?'

'Come on. No one likes to see his father shaming him.'

'But he didn't … .'

'Ah, you don't know.' He turned back to the list, and continued to press in the drawing pins. 'No idea what it was like. Trying to stretch the labour when he didn't get work. And then, she – the mother – nagging him to have a bit of ambition and do better for himself than pushing a wheelbarrow around Tedcastle's yard. Driving him demented.' He brightened. 'Anyway, water under the bridge. The mother always held that you make the most of what you have and don't waste time licking your sores, or scratching your arse.'

True to form, Irwin recovered and pushed his way to get what he wanted. He and Galvin congregated with the other students in the vestibule each evening after supper while Winters stood two steps up the stone stairway and read out stern messages from the Phantom about students not tidying their rooms or changing their socks, and about those who were not on time for Lauds – he would not tolerate flagrant breaches of *that* rule.

Afterwards, the students would chat for a while and then move off, some to light up their pipes down by Beresford's Folly or around in the ambulatory. On one such evening, Irwin had news he wanted to share with Galvin and nodded in the direction of the narrow path up behind Senior House. One of his brothers was taking a night course in accountancy after his day's work in Lenehan's of Capel Street.

'No silver spoons in our neighbourhood, Tommy. Graft or you go to the wall.' As they were passing the back gates, Galvin's attention was taken by the sight of young women in buckram-stiffened dresses getting on a bus on Griffith Avenue. One girl was straightening the seams at the back of her nylon stockings. They were giggling at some comment the conductor had made. A voice whispered in Galvin's ear – something about missing out.

Oblivious to nylon seams and flirty bus conductors, Irwin was talking about another brother, a car mechanic in Hewitt's. 'If I know him, he won't be content to be a mechanic for long. The old dear keeps telling him to get a job in sales, and says that in twenty or thirty years many families will own not just one, but two cars.'

SIX

THAT EASTER, Galvin, Mac and a couple of others started going to Newman House for coffee, when the laburnums in the Iveagh Gardens behind the sun-drenched café were covered in yellow blossoms. Since this was strictly forbidden, they had to keep a weather eye out for Winters, who would have them up before the Phantom in jig time.

Mac was already friendly with a few girls studying social science: he had been swapping records with them – Simon & Garfunkel for The Animals, or Procol Harum for The Beatles. He had even stolen out one night to have supper with them in their Leeson Park flat. After tea and cake, they watched *Quicksilver* on a little black-and-white television and talked about the Eurovision Song Contest, and one of the girls wanted to know if it was an occasion of sin to let a boyfriend sleep in the flat even if he was in another room.

As he grew bolder, he introduced them to Galvin and those he could trust. Now that they had a television in the seminary and newspapers for both common rooms, they we able to chat to the girls about the previous Saturday's *Late Late Show*.

Turning to Mac one morning in the café of Newman House, one of the girls said: 'We need a break during the Whit weekend. You fellows know all about *our* lives and we never get a glimpse of that secret life you lead behind those high walls. How about an invitation, Mac?'

Mac cocked his head and, with a roguish grin, replied: 'You're on. Next Saturday afternoon. It's Visitation Day and the Gestapo are usually out on a Saturday.'

'The Gestapo! Sounds like a prison camp.'

'Worse.'

'Settled, Mac. Next Saturday.'

When the girls arrived the following Saturday afternoon, Mac and the others met them down at the front gate and took them around the grounds, and even through the ground floor of Coghill. And as the girls' high heels were clicking along the stone corridor, Mac joked: 'We'd like to be more hospitable and take you to our rooms, but we're not allowed. Sorry.'

'That's alright this time, Mac,' said one of them, giving him a sidelong glance.

They were giggly when they inspected the ordination photos lining the walls. 'What a waste,' said another, pointing out an especially handsome-looking priest.

Galvin and Mac had lemonade, Marietta biscuits and bars of chocolate stashed away, so they had a picnic across the lawn near the O'Kelly statue; the students in their soutanes, the girls in their summer dresses. Their chat rose and fell and, like bees for pollen, they flitted from one subject to another: one was going to serve tables at Martha's Vineyard during the holidays, another was going to do Legion of Mary work at Euston Station and then become a summer redcoat at Butlin's. In an idle moment, the seminarians spotted a football lying on the grass and picked two teams: a mix of

St Paul's and Social Science. Four heaps of soutanes with birettas on top became the goalposts. The girls flung off their high heels and, free from revising lecture notes and memorizing answers, their cries rang out across the grounds. Retrieving the ball, Galvin noticed out of the corner of his eye a dark shadow lurking at the side of Coghill. The shadow moved, then froze. The Phantom crooked his forefinger. Galvin rolled the ball back to his friends and hurried to the dean, who hissed: 'Get back for your soutane, mister, then I shall deal with you.'

'Yes, Dr Murtagh.'

The others had stopped, some shading their eyes to see what was going on. 'Come on, Tommy, what's happened to you?' someone shouted out.

The seminarians saw the dark outline and, as if all life had been drained from their bodies, reached down and picked up their soutanes. But the girls kept on kicking the ball. One of them laughed, and called out: 'We'll lash you in the second half!'

Buttoning up his soutane, Galvin approached the dean, who glowered at him. 'Escort those young females off the seminary grounds immediately. Immediately I said.' He dismissed him with a wave of his hand. 'And report to me at six along with those other buffoons.'

'Yes, Dr Murtagh.'

That evening they stood in front of the dean's desk. 'Who are these females and who invited them inside the gates?' he rasped.

Mac spoke up. 'They're our friends from university, Dr Murtagh.'

'Friends from university! Are you aware of the rule that forbids social intercourse with lay students? Hasn't Monsignor Curran made that abundantly clear?'

'We didn't think it was very wrong, doctor,' Mac replied defiantly.

The Phantom squinted at him. 'Playing football with the opposite sex is tantamount to inviting them to your bedroom. Never, ever again.' He scythed the air with his hand. 'Never repeat what you've just done. Am I making myself clear?'

'Oh yes, Dr Murtagh,' said Mac.

The others chorused: 'Yes, Dr Murtagh.'

'Now, out of my sight.'

Like sheep streaming out of a pen after being raddled, they were herded out of the Phantom's office as he added: 'This episode will be inserted into your file and looked at when you are approaching Minor Orders. I don't know how some of you got in here. Get out of my sight.'

'Thanks, Dr Murtagh,' they chorused before closing the door behind them.

As soon as they were a safe distance from Murtagh's room, Mac turned towards the others. 'Football to the bed. Sure if I knew that, I'd have played much more football with them.' They were too fearful to laugh in case Murtagh overheard and instead continued their chastened walk up the corridor to their rooms.

IN THE LATE SPRING, the rector, despite opposition from some of his staff and a strong reaction from diocesan priests, decided to open up the seminary. He invited in professionals in different fields: marriage counselling, education, psychiatry, the prison service and so on, and called a special assembly in the Academy Hall to explain what he had in mind.

'The purpose of this meeting, gentlemen, is to apprise you of changes that I and the staff are making to equip you for your ministry. This is all to fulfil the recommendation made by the Vatican Council.' He tossed a lapel of his soutane cape over his shoulder. 'And to let you know I am granting you permission to leave the college one evening next week to listen to the best of our preachers. They form a hand-picked team that will carry the torch of faith in the years to come. I advise you to pay them close attention.'

Four of them went out to the parish of St Maria Goretti and sat at the back while the hand-picked team conducted a mission in a packed church. On the first night the parish priest introduced the team to the congregation. Like members of a showband (which were sweeping dancehalls up and down the country), the priests stepped up to the microphone and, in turn, waved to the congregation. Noonan, the leader of the team, would deliver the homily that evening. Ordained the previous June, he was already popular as a singer and entertainer at the bingo sessions he ran in Baldoyle and nearby parishes.

For an opener, he joked with the congregation. 'Your parish priest and I are the best of buddies. There's nothing he wouldn't do for me; there's nothing I wouldn't do for him. So we end up doing nothing for each other.' The congregation tittered at first, shy about laughing in a church, but before long they were in stitches.

'Prayer is very simple, my dear people. I pray to God in me own way. I give out to Him. Yes, God can take it.' A tall figure with a shock of red wavy hair, he lifted the microphone from its stand and strode back and forth in the sanctuary. 'And if you're too tired to kneel down on the floor, get into your warm bed and bring God in with you.'

A ripple of surprise spread through the church. Women looked at each other and stifled a laugh, then, like a skilful comedian, he followed up with, 'Hey missus,' to a woman in the front pew, 'you'll bring in worse.' The church erupted.

'Strange old world,' he said, and laughed. 'I'm a priest of the diocese, singing and enjoying meself, calling the bingo numbers in the parish hall of a Friday night, and The Beatles are off in a monastery doing their meditation.' After each of his quips, he primed the congregation by chuckling into the microphone.

He moved on from prayer. 'Don't be worried about whatever changes the Vatican Council brings, my dear people,' he said striding across the sanctuary again. 'The Lord tells us not to be afraid. We have strengths within us that we never dreamt of. We can cope with anything, even death. Not joking you.' He paused and resumed: 'Two women in the bus the other day were chatting.

As sure as God is me judge, I was sitting behind them.' He pulled a face and said in a squeaky Dublin accent: '"Me husband dropped dead the other day."

'"He didn't!"

'"Oh he did. I asked him to go out to the garden an cut a head of cabbage an not to be always under me feet. An he dropped dead."

'"Oh Mary, I'm sorry for your trouble. And what did you do?"

'"I opened a tin of peas."'

When the laughter died, he continued with his sermon on the changes in the Church. 'Sure, God wants us to be happy. Nothing wrong with laughing in God's house.' When he had finished, the congregation, for the first time in that church's history, applauded. And when Benediction was over, Galvin overheard two women as they left the church: 'That Father Noonan is better than a concert out in The Embankment; we could do with him here.'

'You never said a truer word. It would be great to have him instead of the old sourpusses we're landed with.'

SEVEN

DURING THAT MONTH of May, the students formed a procession from the refectory to the chapel for the Miraculous Medal novena prayers and the May devotions. Seated on both sides of the centre aisle, they endured the same tedious monotone of the spiritual director. From high up in the pulpit, he banged on about St Catherine Labouré and the Rue du Bac and, when the prefects weren't looking, the junior students tried to make each other snigger by pulling faces. A few of the regulars from the houses near to the college – those who attended Sunday mass – slipped into the seats at the bottom of the chapel; the dim part near the heavy double doors. When the novena prayers were over, they said a special prayer that the Holy Spirit would guide the nineteen young men who would be ordained priests for the archdiocese in June.

On one of those evenings, while the spiritual director was droning on about the merits of wearing the Miraculous Medal, Galvin felt a sharp poke in his ribs. He stole a sidelong glance at

Mac, who was indicating with a discreet nod towards the back of the chapel where Gill, the caretaker's daughter, was kneeling. Her hands were joined in prayer but she had the same mischievous grin on her pretty face as she had had every evening of the previous June when she had been doing a novena for success in her Leaving Certificate, dressed then in the wine-coloured skirt and black blazer of her school. She now attended the Holy Faith secretarial school in St Mary's Road.

Mac's excitement of a few days before came back to Galvin as he lowered his head and tried to concentrate on St Catherine Labouré and the Rue du Bac.

'Have a deco, Tommy,' Mac had said as they were walking towards the main gates and Gill was turning the key in the ginger-bread house. 'Not a schoolgirl anymore. Didn't she win the Lovely Legs of Marino contest during the summer. How about that?' He was giddy. 'Have to see more of those legs, Tommy.'

Galvin looked at him. 'Are you out of your mind? If you're caught ... .'

'Keep this under your hat. Whenever I can manage it, I hang around here to meet her when she's leaving. And you know that look she gives under them dark eyelashes?'

'She hasn't given me any looks under them dark eyelashes.'

'Well, Lovely Legs will get more than she bargained for.'

'If the Phantom or ... you're dead.'

'You should see her in a summer dress and those open high heels. One of these nights, Tommy, one of these nights I'm going to have a conversation with Lovely Legs of Marino. Deep theological discussions, you might say.'

'How're you going to manage ... I mean ... the life we're preparing for? No girls.'

'Plenty time for getting holy, doubting Thomas. Four more years, that should be long enough for any fella to get holy. Anyway, we should be enjoying ourselves. We're in our prime.'

'You'll be out on your arse before you know it.'

The following week, when a group of them were removing their football boots outside the back door of Coghill, Mac gave Galvin a blow-by-blow account of how he had succeeded in meeting Lovely Legs. 'I found out what time she goes out in the morning, and asked the Phantom for permission to go to the uni by bus. Said I had a blister on me arse.'

Galvin looked at him.

'Ah no. Blister on me foot, you thicko. No flies on Mac.'

When he suggested to Lovely Legs that they should meet some time, she had teased him: 'Now what would we be meeting for?'

'Oh just to talk about the weather, the price of hay and the price of heifers.'

'You and your heifers. Now what would a city girl like me know about the price of heifers? And sure, you're going on to be a priest. I'm shocked.'

'That's ok. Pretend you're going to confession. I need to practise.'

'Will there be a penance?'

'Depends on how you've been since your last confession.'

'Or maybe how much I know about heifers.'

Later that evening in the Common Room, while some seminarians were browsing through newspapers and Rossiter and his pals were colloguing in a far corner, Mac made a beeline for Galvin.

'Tommy,' he said, 'Lovely Legs will go to bed tonight a satisfied woman.'

'You'll be fecked out, Mac, I'm telling you. For the life of me, I can't … why are you taking the risk?'

'Not to worry, Tommy boy, Mac knows how to look after himself.'

All that May and into June, Mac managed to meet Gill once or twice a week in the grove of trees up near the cemetery. After a while, he grew careless and shared his good fortune with one of his year. Before long others got to know about it and decided, while they walked around the ambulatory, that they should do something. They were concerned.

'Bad example.'

'Absolutely, and if it were found out, we'd all be tarred with the one brush.'

'Yeah, he's not serious about his vocation.'

'Lowers the tone of the place, if you ask me.'

When the corridors were deserted two evenings later, and every student was in his room or in the library, 'baking' for exams, Winters sidled up to the Phantom's office to report what he had been told. Upright and stolid as Cardinal O'Kelly's statue, and staring at the books that lined the opposite wall, the Phantom listened.

'Thank you' was all he said when the prefect had finished. 'I'll attend to that.'

For half an hour, the Phantom stood gazing out at the ambulatory. His mind was racing. This was the inevitable outcome of a growing slackness in the college, and the rector's naive notions about freedom and the Vatican Council. MacCarthy had to be made an example of, or students would lose all regard for authority. That incident when he and Galvin had invited females from the university into the seminary and kicked around a football was another sign of the rot that had set in.

At supper in the priests' parlour that evening, one of the professors, just back from Rome, had the other priests in stitches describing how Cardinal Suenens had put the wind up the High Command at the Vatican Council. The Phantom affected a smile but his mind was on his mission and, as soon as he had rushed through his meal, he excused himself and hurried up to where he had been told MacCarthy was meeting Lovely Legs. He climbed into the thicket of the undergrowth and merged with the trees, a huntsman lying in wait for his quarry.

In the chapel, the students were singing the Lourdes hymn; Mac was among them, belting out at the top of his voice, '... *virgin most pure, star of the sea.'* He whispered to Galvin: 'Lovely Legs, here I come. *Pray-aye for the sinner, pray for me.'*

Hidden among the trees, the Phantom spotted the door of the gingerbread house opening and light from the hallway shining on Gill's blonde hair. 'I'll be home later,' she called back into the house. 'Just going over to Church Road to Maureen. We're looking at dress patterns in *Woman's Own.'*

A woman's tinny voice from deep inside rasped: 'Don't be late. You're spending too much time with that one for the past few weeks. Make sure you're back in time for the rosary.'

The Phantom watched. Wearing a trench coat and patent high heels, Gill tripped smartly along the path that ran by the boundary wall and beneath the green roof of overhanging branches. At breaks in the row of trees, her dangling earrings caught the light from the swan-necked lamp posts. She walked directly towards the Phantom and, for a moment, he feared she might decide to step right into the same part of the thicket – instead, she stopped so close he could catch the rich scent of her perfume. Her shining eyes were fixed on the chapel where the lights within showed the beautiful stained-glass images of the Virgin Mary ascending to heaven on a white cloud. The Phantom knew by heart the inscription at the base of that window: *purissima virgo, ora pro nobis.* Lovely Legs took out a little mirror and applied lipstick with the help of whatever light was filtering through the trees.

Soon after the singing stopped in the chapel, and the lights went out one by one, footsteps hurrying up the path caused the Phantom to stand stock still. Against the clear night sky, he made out MacCarthy's tall silhouette searching the grove. And then he heard him.

'Now then,' Mac pronounced like an actor, 'my nymph of the dark woods. Ye gods, how ye have favoured me that I behold yon winsome creature this blessed night! What dark pleasures does this grove offer to me when summer solstice is almost upon us. Lady of the Woods, come thou to rest in my arms?' He grabbed and kissed her and then began to sing: 'My Venus in blue jeans, Mona Lisa with the ponytail ... .'

'Shh,' she whispered, 'you'll have the priests down on top of us.'

'Ah, snuggle into me, you great-looking piece of goods. Most of them gobshites don't know what God put them into this world for.'

She was giggling. 'Hey! Not so fast. Did you say all your prayers, holy boy?'

'Holy boy! I'll show you who's the holy boy.' He backed her up against the nearest tree, their feet causing a rustle in the undergrowth. 'You've been on my mind all day, Gill.' His voice was hushed and tender now.

'Have I? You've been on mine too.'

The silence that followed was broken only by the sound of their kissing and by Gill's pretence at resistance. 'What are you doing with your hands, you randy devil? You're starting early tonight. What did you have for your supper?'

'Curry. It warms the blood.'

'Hey,' she raised her voice in protest, 'that's below the belt, Eoin. Oh Janey, no. Do you know the effect you're having on me?'

'They're not my hands, Gill, I swear. That's a badger – or maybe a fox. Badgers and foxes come out at night and shove their snouts in all sorts of places ... .'

'If you run a ladder in my nylons, I'll give you badgers and foxes. And you'll have to get me a new pair.'

'First thing in the morning, I'll be into Clerys, and I'll ask the woman at the counter.' He put on a thick country accent. 'Give me here a pair of them nylon shtockings for Lovely Legs, Miss.' Both of them laughed. 'She who has the besht legs in all of Dublin. Didn't she win a big prize in the Glen Abbey contesht out there in Marino? And I wouldn't tell you word of a lie. Amn't I in training to be an ould priesht?'

They were silent again until he heard her shout, 'Hey, holy boy, now now!' Another brief silence was followed by a stern 'No.' In his growing excitement, the Phantom shifted his weight, then froze in case they might hear the twigs cracking beneath his feet, but they were lost in each other. Gaping at MacCarthy and the caretaker's daughter, the Phantom was no longer the dean of discipline, but a voyeur spying on two young people satisfying their natural desire for each other; and, despite his resolve, the force of their passion was drawing him in.

Eventually, after much kissing, groaning and whispering, they stopped. Gill smoothed down her dress and fixed her hair; they kissed again and MacCarthy said something about meeting at the end of the week. MacCarthy waited until the sound of her high heels on the path had faded, then hurried across the playing pitch, climbed the steps of Coghill and disappeared inside.

The Phantom couldn't sleep. Despite his best intentions, the rustle of the dress and the glimpse of a shapely thigh and suspenders in the moonlight had woken a hunger that he thought had been satisfied by keeping to the bishop's prescription on the day he was ordained seventeen years before. 'Say your Office and rosary, play golf with your fellow priests and go to bed on time. God will look after the rest.' Now, what he had seen teased him with a mocking voice: 'Despite your status as a priest, dean and your academic distinctions, the pleasures you've just spied on will never be yours.'

He hated them – especially MacCarthy – for awakening such disturbing thoughts in his head and was on the verge of getting out of bed, opening his drinks cabinet and knocking back a few whiskeys, but he knew to his cost where that would end. He set his mind to the day ahead and stared at the roller blind. Thoughts he had managed to suppress now began to escape his control. The college nurse, a young woman whom he met every week to discuss the students' health, came into focus. In his fantasy he replicated what he'd seen earlier and more – and was left with a throbbing sensation that filled him with guilt. He hadn't given in to himself in years.

After resting for a moment, he got out of bed, showered and then knelt at his prie-dieu to say an Act of Contrition. He wanted to switch on the light but another professor might see it and think he was sick. Of one thing he was certain: he would insist to the rector and the seminary council that MacCarthy be expelled.

Rising from his prie-dieu, he realized to his horror that he was on the early mass for the Christian Brothers and, although he had said an Act of Contrition, was no longer in a state of grace, and would commit another mortal sin if he said mass without receiving absolution. For the remainder of the morning he sat fully dressed on a chair beside his bed, staring at the window and, when the edges of the blind began to show light, he stood, recited the Office for Readings and Lauds, then put on his gabardine and set off for Gardiner Street Church.

A couple of afternoons later Mac opened the window of his room and sat down on the wide sill. With the examinations over, the ambulatory below him was in a holiday mood. After Prize-Giving Day at the weekend, they would go home for almost three months. Students strolled around in the hazy sunshine, some wearing their birettas, others carrying them. Rossiter's pals were capering about the fountain, dousing each other with water from the spray and shrieking when someone got drenched. Gill flitted into his reverie. 'I'll never forget you, Eoin; you know that,' she had said the night they agreed to give each other a wide berth when the seminary would reopen in September. 'Yourself and your cows and the price of heifers.'

'Nor will I forget you, Gill, and your Helen Shapiro beehive.'

'Nor my lovely legs, I hope.' Her face had lit up with devilment.

His lazy daydream was shattered by a rap on his door. 'Come right in,' he called airily.

Winters stood at the open door. 'You are to report to Dr Murtagh.' Severe eyes took his measure.

'Me?' Mac grinned.

'Yes, you.'

Affirmed by the love that would be his that evening, Mac was free and easy. 'Probably wants to make me Student of the Year?'

'Get yourself off that windowsill and put on your soutane. Dr Murtagh is a busy man.' Catching a sultry picture of Angie Dickinson on the wall, Winters threw a withering look at Mac. 'Remove that.' He turned on his heel and walked off, leaving the door open.

Mac climbed the two flights of stairs. The call to the dean's office wasn't troubling him: very likely one of the prefects had reported him for breaking the solemn silence after Compline. He planned his defence and rang the bell.

Without asking him to sit down, the Phantom kept his eyes fixed on the green leather inlay of his desk. 'Mr MacCarthy,' he said, 'you are the cause of great concern to the rector and the priests of this college. Repeatedly you have shown scant respect for the traditions of St Paul's. And, now, I am aware that you have been consorting with a young woman in a way that makes you completely unsuited to the priestly state. Therefore, it is the considered opinion of the seminary council that you lack the necessary disposition to become a priest of the archdiocese.'

MacCarthy stared at the head of glossy black hair. This was not about breaking the solemn silence. He listened like one might to a consultant who says, 'I'm sorry, but, yes … we will do everything we can to make you comfortable.'

But there was no hint of comfort in the Phantom's hiss. 'You have to leave St Paul's right away. You may be suited to the priesthood elsewhere, such as England, the United States or Australia, but not the archdiocese.'

MacCarthy's broad shoulders began to slump. Suddenly he was drained of his carefree manner and wanted to bawl his eyes out, but he refused to give the Phantom the satisfaction of seeing his humiliation.

'Will you give me another chance, Dr Murtagh?' His open palms, offered as an earnest of intent, made no impression on the Phantom. 'Please give me another chance. I want to be a priest in this diocese. I can be a good priest, I know I can. I will never again do what I did with Lov … Miss O'Carroll. If I'm expelled, it will upset my mother an awful lot; my father died only a couple of years ago.'

The Phantom continued looking at his desk. He rubbed his chin and it seemed for a moment as if he might relent, but his lips tightened again. MacCarthy had forced him to face uncomfortable truths about himself; he hadn't slept for the previous two nights.

'It is out of my hands, Mr MacCarthy. The rector has made the final decision. I will grant you a day to notify your family. Does your family have a phone?'

'Yes, Dr Murtagh, but … .'

'That will be all.'

As Mac was about to turn away, he pleaded. 'One more chance, Dr Murtagh. I won't let you down.'

'The decision is out of my hands, Mr MacCarthy. And by the way, you are not to reveal your situation to any student. You will stay in your room except for meals.'

For some time after Mac had left his office, the Phantom fixed his gaze on the apple trees outside his window, but his mind was on the way he had influenced the rector to expel MacCarthy. Then, with heavy steps, he went to his sitting room, took a bottle of Jameson from his cabinet and poured a large measure, making sure he had mints to take before he went down to dinner.

After prayers in the oratory that night, and once all lights had been switched off, Galvin heard a tap on his door. Raising himself up on the bed, he could make out the figure of Mac with his finger to his lips.

'I have to talk to you,' he whispered.

Galvin tiptoed to the door and glanced up and down the corridor. The window over Winters' door was a dark rectangle. 'If we're caught, both of us are up shit creek.'

'I am anyway.' He sat down at Galvin's desk and told him what had happened. 'When I recovered, I went back up to the Phantom and asked him who had informed on me. I'd nothing to lose now. I told him I've a right to know. He wouldn't budge. Some fucker squealed on me.'

'Keep your voice down, Eoin.'

Mac lowered his head and nestled it in his arms like a child giving in to sleep. After a while he raised himself and when he spoke, his voice was filled with sadness.

'I'm going to get my degree first, so we'll meet at the uni. I went to see a Carmelite in Whitefriar Street. He's my spiritual director. He knows Cardinal McIntyre in Los Angeles. All is not lost, Tommy. If the Carmelite is able to swing it, I'll go to the seminary in Thurles. The rector said he'd give me a reference and that I may be suited to another diocese.' He made a brave effort to smile. 'So, looks like I'm off to California with my banjo on my knee.'

Just before he left, he added: 'A strange thing happened when I went back up to the Phantom's room to plead with him. I'd swear he had been drinking. His eyes were red. I don't know. Strange, Tommy, I had some sympathy for the poor bastard. I mean, what is he except a fucking toady for the High Command. Waste of a life. And a man with his ability. Knocked the socks off everyone.'

The next evening when the bell rang for supper, each student, as ever, stood at his door wearing a soutane and biretta until everyone was ready to go in double file to the refectory. The stamp of their footsteps was loud on the wooden corridor, army recruits on the march. They passed the open door of Mac's room where the bookshelves were bare, the stripped mattress was on the iron bedstead rolled up and tied with a cord, and wire clothes hangers were piled on the desk. They passed on, down the wide stairway and, as every evening, raised their birettas to the statues in the alcoves.

During supper, fragments of the story filtered through despite the watchful eye of Winters and the other prefects.

'Mac has been expelled.'

'Think it had to do with laughing during evening devotions?'

'No. It was contempt for the staff. Someone said so.'

'The Phantom had warned him.'

'The Phantom is a prick.'

The following day the truth seeped out.

'Caught with Lovely Legs.'

'Jesus, lucky bastard.'

'Someone snitched.'

'The Phantom was seen at the door of the gingerbread house giving out yards to Paddy. Paddy looked shit-scared.'

Lovely Legs was never again seen around St Paul's. The word in the college was that the Phantom had delivered an ultimatum to her family: either she went to live in another part of Dublin or the family would have to vacate the cottage. Good jobs were scarce so Lovely Legs had no option but to take the *Princess Maud* to Holyhead and catch a train to her aunt in Leeds where she eventually trained to be a nurse.

A few days after Mac had been expelled, Galvin trudged down to the riverbank. He needed to get away from the build-up to the summer holiday cheer. The cruelty of the decision to expel Mac was causing him to think through his brother M.J.'s offer to join him in London. 'You'd have a place at the table if you want it and you'd be rolling in dough in no time.' He'd run his hand through his wavy hair. 'And the pick of fine-looking women. I'd be delighted to have one of the family here – the only one with a college education. You could even go to college over in London and become an engineer. Then we'd be made.' M.J. now employed over 200 men. They laid pipes and cables up around Northampton and Bedfordshire and built houses out in Bury St Edmunds as well as an office block in Milton Keynes. 'The directors' table, Tommy,' had been his last words the previous Christmas. 'If ever you feel that priest college is too much.'

Listening to the vexed dialogue in his head, Galvin hiked up his soutane, squatted by the riverbank and was suddenly convulsed with an uncontrollable fit of crying. All the sadness, anxiety about his own future and frustration at Mac's expulsion burst through his defences. A few yards up the river, children were using jam jars to catch tadpoles. They stopped and stared at him. One of them called out, 'Are youse alright, father?'

He dried his eyes with the back of his hand. 'Ah, just something that happened. I'm OK now, boys. Thanks.'

One boy cupped the side of his mouth with his hand while he whispered to the others. They returned to their tadpole search but kept stealing glances at him through the brambles. Farther up, others boys were bickering about the right way to launch their raft, which kept getting stuck on the riverbed. 'And another thing,' one of them shrieked. 'I'm Huck Finn today. You were Huck the last time!' They stopped and waved to the sky as a plane passed over.

'Alright then. I bags Tom Sawyer.' The lush scent of cow parsley and sweet cicely rose from the riverbank. Every now and then Galvin had to swat away flies.

Memories of Mac came flooding back to him. Like the evening they were assembled in the oratory for the customary talk from the rector. 'The rules make you good priests ... for your spiritual ... *mens sana in corpore sano* ...' Mac, suntanned and spare from digging trenches in Luton and playing football with the local club there, was sitting beside him.

Just as the rector was getting into the hygiene part. 'Polish your shoes, change your socks, brush your soutanes ... cleanliness next to godliness ...', Mac nudged him.

'See what I found in a Lucky Bag,' he whispered out of the side of his mouth. Galvin threw a guarded glance at the other man's hands, which opened slowly as if to let a bird escape. He found himself staring at a condom.

'Eoin, Jesus! Put that thing away.'

The rector raised his head and looked in Galvin's direction.

'Is that young man ... Mr Galvin, have you the temerity to talk while I'm reading the rules?'

'No, Monsignor Curran, of course not,' Galvin stammered.

The rector removed his glasses, and Galvin braced himself for one of his explosions. But after a pause he replaced them and went back to the rule book, reminding them that the most important virtue they would need to cultivate during their time in St Paul's was obedience to the college authorities. Even at that dreaded moment, Mac did a whispered imitation of the rector's lisp. 'And loyalty, gentlemen. Loyalty, me arse.'

The soft swish of footsteps through the cow parsley caused Galvin to raise his head. J. Desmond, only a year away from ordination, was approaching, reading his breviary; when he drew near, he marked the page with a silk ribbon and closed the book. 'If I were a Rodin, Tommy, I'd have a ready-made subject for my "Thinking Man".' He gathered his soutane and hunkered down.

'Not one of my best days, Des,' Galvin said.

'A problem shared, they say, is a problem halved. Is there any way I can help?'

While gazing at the children trying to launch their raft, Galvin spoke about how dejected he was at his friend's sacking and how he was going to give it all up. He had to hold back another crying fit.

'Eoin is a fine bloke,' Desmond said, 'a bit impulsive, but so was Simon Peter, and the Lord gave him the keys. The first Pope, you might say. Sometimes, I think they show poor judgment up there, but don't quote me.' He studied Galvin for a moment. 'So what will you do?'

'Might go to the uni in October to study engineering.'

'And from what you say, you could then, eventually, join your brother in England.'

'That would be my aim.'

'If that is what you think the Lord has in store for you, then maybe that's what you should do. But you yourself will decide that.'

With much cheering, the boys managed to get their raft afloat.

'I'll just say one thing – it may or may not help. One has to put up with a lot of crass ignorance in any organization and the Church is no different. I've had my doubts about the whole thing over the years – in truth, the doubts never leave you. And that's healthy. Who would want to give a blank cheque of their life to the Church or to any other institution? Actually, I find it rather worrying that many of the fellows up here', he indicated the seminary houses, 'never question anything. They spend seven years sleepwalking and are never challenged so long as they are seen to keep the rules.'

'And show loyalty,' Galvin said. They both laughed.

J. Desmond stood. 'Anyway, Tommy, I hope you'll come to a right decision.' As he began to walk away, he added: 'At least you have the long hot summer to make up your mind.'

'Thanks, Des.' Galvin turned back to the river. The boys, delighted that their raft was afloat, waved to him. 'Want a go, father?' one of them called out.

'Another time, boys.'

He watched J. Desmond using the silk ribbon to find his page as he walked away. And he remembered the many inter-house debates and open forums when he had stood and challenged the authority system in the seminary, despite the presence of the rector or the dean of discipline. 'Only J. Desmond would get away with that,' someone whispered afterwards, as students were making their way to the common room for a cup of tea. 'You or I would be kicked out.'

AS EVERY YEAR on Prize-Giving Day, a team of caterers arrived to serve lunch before the High Command presented the prizes and delivered the keynote speech. The day before, Paddy and the students had been run off their feet. They had shed their soutanes and were dressed in working trousers and football shirts. They hoed weeds in the rose garden, used push mowers to cut the grass in the quadrangles and cleaned Beresford's Folly of cigarette ends and spent matches.

Inside the college they rearranged tables in the refectory and lugged in extra chairs to the Academy Hall for the priests, who would arrive wearing tonsure suits and holding trilby hats that showed clean silk linings. Designated spaces had been marked off for the priests' cars – Monsignors, members of the metropolitan chapter and parish priests parked in the wide apron in front of Wansborough, while curates who could afford a car parked up in the senior football pitch. Pride of place, near the main door, was reserved for the High Command's Daimler.

Before the meal, the priests strolled up and down by the rose beds. Some smoked pipes and cigars; all were in a jaunty mood. First Communions and Confirmations were now over and, except for funerals and weddings, they would be free for much of the summer.

In a black soutane with crimson piping and buttons, and a flowing cape of washed silk, the High Command stood out. Accompanied by the rector, Murtagh and some of the staff, he paced in front of Wansborough House, fingering his pectoral cross and keeping a peeled eye on the priests. It was said that he would think nothing of summoning a man to the palace the following day if he noticed him without his hat. The priests who hadn't had a chance to meet him already, came up, genuflected and kissed his ring: they spoke for a minute and then genuflected again before backing away as they had been taught to do many years before in St Paul's.

'Look', said J. Desmond, walking the grounds with a few others. He pointed discreetly to a silver-haired priest in a frock coat and shiny black shoes who was studying the rose bed. 'The last of the Raj.' They chuckled. *Après nous le déluge,'* he added.

In the refectory, the High Command presided at the centre of the top table, which faced the long rows of tables stretching to the far wall. Flanking him were the rector and the auxiliary bishop, then members of the staff of St Paul's. All sat at one side, facing out towards the priests and, beyond them, the students. Bottles of wine and small bouquets of flowers decorated the priests' tables. Caterers served the meal, wine waiters stood behind the tables ready to recharge glasses. The excitement about the new extension was shared by the whole refectory; it would accommodate the large number of candidates the college would take in the following September.

Prize-giving took place in the Academy Hall. All stood when the High Command, followed by the staff members, entered and, when all were seated, the rector moved to the podium and opened a folder containing the list of prize-winners.

As in other years, J. Desmond practically swept the boards. The rector read out the results in Latin. It sounded like a litany: *'Primum praemium tulit in Sacra Scriptura: Ioannes Desmondus Byrne.'* The same for the other major subjects, dogmatic and moral theology, and canon law. He was highly placed in the subjects of less importance and, when he won the overall award for academic excellence – the *discipulus optimus* – the priests, many of whom had already known about his exceptional ability, gave him a spirited applause. Above the clapping, one of them turned to the man beside him. 'Next stop Rome, wouldn't you say?'

'Comes from the right stables too.' The other man's jowls shook with laughter.

'Mark him down. Future Keeper of the Seal.'

'Wicked temper though. Could be his undoing.'

Irwin applauded also, nodding in approval to those beside him and managing a smile. He too was named among the prize-winners: first place in *caeremoniae sacrae* and *pastoralis theologia*. To the bright students – the Guns especially – sacred ceremonies were nothing more than rubrics; very much the poor relation. Pastoral theology was also on the margins.

Irwin had earned his *primum praemium*, having spent long hours baking. Tom Galvin won the junior prize in French, which meant a scholarship for two weeks in the Irish College in Paris. Again, J. Desmond took the senior prize.

When the final applause had died, the archbishop padded to the microphone. He congratulated the winners, and encouraged those who didn't do as well to work harder in the coming year. 'To you who will be ordained this month, I say place your trust in our Divine Saviour and seek the protection of His Blessed Mother, and your ministry will be a fruitful one.'

Like everyone else, the archbishop was in a sunny mood and delighted to announce that the new building would commence in the autumn. 'The diocese is expanding. We have a glorious future ahead of us. By the turn of the century we will be meeting the spiritual needs of a Catholic population in excess of one million souls. And while I am heartened to learn from your revered rector, Monsignor Curran, that twenty-eight young men will present themselves for training here at St Paul's next September, we must remain ever vigilant and committed to our task of nurturing vocations in our parishes.'

He addressed the deacons who would be ordained later in the month: 'You have responded with great generosity to the call of our Divine Master. Very soon, by virtue of your ordination, you will have the power to transform the elements of bread and wine into the body and blood of Our Lord and Saviour. You will raise your hand in absolution and forgive sin in the sacrament of penance. Not the greatest potentate on earth, the most able leader – the President of the United States even – has the power to forgive sin. Reverend gentlemen, if the Lord were, in His wisdom, to call you to Himself, just after saying your first mass, your decision to follow in His footsteps would have been worth more than anything you could achieve in worldly terms.

'Some of you here had the opportunity to become doctors, lawyers or to distinguish yourselves in the world of banking; some of your families come from such noble professions. You might have accumulated riches in the marketplace, but all that would be as mere flotsam and jetsam in the rich ocean of sanctifying grace, which will be yours when you exercise your ministry as an *alter Christus*. The reward that is stored up for you is beyond description after a life of service in the Lord's vineyard.

'Bear this in mind, gentlemen, and you who are to be this year's *ordinandi*: as soon as you are ordained for the priesthood, you will, from then on, be set aside from all men. Ordination will have conferred on you that ontological change that Divine Grace has effected in your souls.'

He took his seat and a cricket applause followed. With a mandarin smile, the rector thanked the archbishop for his inspirational words. He wished all the students a blessed holiday and reminded them to be faithful to the *ratio mensis*, telling them that it would be a most useful record of how they had been true to the spiritual practices of a seminarian on his holidays.

'This evening,' he then announced, 'I will call to my office those who have been found worthy by the Academic Council to study in Rome, Maynooth or at the École Biblique in Jerusalem.'

The college had caught the holiday spirit. Room doors were flung open and light shone in the corridors. Students packed. The sound of vacuum cleaners resonated through Wansborough, Coghill and O'Kelly. Sweeping brushes glanced off skirting boards.

The Phantom, accompanied by Winters, patrolled the college issuing instructions. 'Make sure you clean out your room; the priests will be here next week for the annual retreats. And if you haven't paid the balance of your fees, you need to see the bursar. This college doesn't run on fresh air.' His tone was less harsh on this day.

A game of doubles was taking place on one of the tennis courts: the pock of the ball and shouts of 'out' or 'forty-love' carried in the sultry air. Bursts of unrestrained laughter could be heard coming from the rooms overhead.

That evening Irwin and his cronies had little interest in tennis. Instead, they were keeping a lookout for anyone on his way to the rector's office. They hid beneath the wide staircase or loitered around the dim vestibule, tidying up or posting last-minute reminders from the Phantom about leaving keys at the office and polishing the corridors.

Galvin had packed earlier and had rallied a few others to kick a ball around in an effort to lift his cloud of depression. Before going to the playing pitch, he lay on his bed and tried to rationalize Mac's sacking and lessen his own frustration. Mac, after all, had been taking risks and should have heeded warnings about keeping the solemn silence. Galvin's effort, however, to argue himself out of his anger and sadness was futile. Just as he was pulling on his football socks, he heard footsteps approaching his room and raised his head to see Irwin standing at the open door. 'Oh,' said Irwin, 'I wanted to … well, thrash out something.'

'It will have to wait.'

'After supper?'

'After supper.'

That evening they sat on garden chairs near Old Pompey. Paddy the caretaker was lowering the papal and national flags at the front of Wansborough. A fog that presaged more fine weather was settling over the trees along by Church Road. Sitting or standing around a garden seat chatting with students, including Rossiter, were priests who had lingered after the presentation of prizes – occasionally, they took students out to lunch in the Grosvenor, or to the Savoy in O'Connell Street, where they fed them steak and chips and diocesan gossip. Through one of the open windows of Junior House, the Beatles could be heard going at full tilt with 'I Want to Hold Your Hand'.

Against all this, Irwin was brooding. Since he had learnt that the three places for Rome had been filled, he had been moping around on his own all afternoon. Galvin knew the signs by now: the forlorn look, the pout and the eyes ready to fill up, the weighty silence.

'Let's go for a stroll,' he said to Irwin. They took the Abbey Walk and continued under the time-formed arch of the beeches and then emerged to climb the grassy embankment that led to the senior pitches. 'Well done in winning the French prize,' Irwin said at last and added: 'Ioannes Desmondus will be excellent company in Paris. Getting the train for home in the morning?'

'Can't get away fast enough.'

'It's the seal of approval.' As always, when his thoughts were racing, Irwin quickened his pace, so Galvin had to get a move on to keep up with him.

'What?'

'Rome. One of the Monsignors hinted that I had it in the bag. Always the same story – those with pull always get ahead. Why should they, Tommy, why should they be the ones? Fuck it. In the Church you would think things would be different. Well, I'll show them. And I'll get to Rome too. That's where you can bring about change. Give the poor devils of this world a chance. In here, the elite are earmarked for future glory.'

'I don't know if it's that bad.'

'No? When was the last time the High Command visited your house with a case of wine on Christmas Eve?'

'What are you on about?'

'Is your head up your hole, Galvin? The dogs in the street know that every Christmas Eve on his way home, the High Command gets his driver to stop the Daimler at the Byrne mansion. All very cosy. Let me tell you, despite all the fine thoughts about Vatican II, J. Desmond Byrne feels he has the divine right to be top of the pile.'

They continued on their walk around by the handball alley, where a few students were playing cricket: all had on whites, the batsmen and wicket-keeper were wearing leg pads. The bowler made his run up and sent the ball flying in a looping trajectory towards the wicket. The batsman crouched and connected, causing the pock to echo against the gable of Senior House. A cheer went up from the cricket players. Shading his eyes, Galvin turned to look. Figures in brilliant white were leaping and prancing against the setting sun, but Irwin was oblivious of it all.

'Tommy, this isn't going to stop me from getting to Rome. If not this time, then there will be other chances. Let's go this way,' he said, indicating the Long Walk. 'I worked hard. I'm gutted.'

'I know.'

Farther on, other seminarians were lounging on a garden seat. From a transistor radio on the grass, Lyndon Johnson was defending the war in Vietnam.

'Oh, sure, I'm good enough to hold the *cappa magna* for the High Command, but not for Rome.'

'Maybe they need you here for the ceremonies.'

Irwin turned a look of contempt on Galvin. 'D'you think you're talking to a moron?' A heavy silence set in again until they were about to cross the stile. 'I'll get to Rome, make no mistake about that. And why not? Why does it have to be privileged shaggers who get to the top even in the Church? A divine right to rule. They're taught that in their poncy schools with their cricket and their model aeroplanes and their debating societies.' He adopted a posh accent: '"Don't *ever* sell yourselves short, gentlemen" one of the toffee-nosed Jesuits used to say in his Saturday evening talks in Belvedere. "Remember you have been privileged with a high place in society. You've an obligation to maintain that position."'

EIGHT

IN MID JULY J. Desmond and Galvin, along with students from Maynooth, Kimmage Manor and Milltown Park, stayed in the Irish College on the Rue des Irlandais and attended the Institut Catholique de Paris. And while Galvin and the others struggled to hold a conversation in French, the words tripped off J. Desmond's tongue, so he was put in the advanced class.

After dinner each evening they lazed in the atrium. With the heat of the day still radiating from the limestone walls, they drank from pitchers of wine and got high on Rahner and *novella theologia*. Night fell over Paris without their noticing, and a starry sky became a navy pincushion above their heads. They were certain that those great young theologians – Hans Kung, de Lubac and Ratzinger would bring about a reform of the Catholic Church. Promises of a bright future mingled with the whiff of Gauloises drifting up towards the sky.

'I mean, now that we're in the EEC, we will benefit from greater contact with Europe. It will enrich our thinking on all matters,' a Dominican student declared. He stopped as if to enjoy to the full the echo of his own wisdom. 'Yes, give us a global perspective.'

'The hope of the Council is one of the chief reasons I'm staying,' J. Desmond said.

'My situation too.'

One night when the others had gone to bed and only Byrne and Galvin were left in the atrium, J. Desmond looked up at the spires and domes of Paris. 'Did you never find it strange, Tommy, that a hundred and forty of us fellows in St Paul's who are training for a way of life that is most unusual, never get an opportunity to air any reservations about the life we're going to lead?'

'In what sense?'

'Well, our sexuality for starters; something better than the crucifix under the pillow. That's quite daft. And then being wrapped in cotton wool in case we give in to temptation. How can we know ourselves, for God's sake, test ourselves even? Did you know I was refused permission to take up a scholarship to Cambridge, which I'd won in UCD? The rector told me I might be endangering my faith, especially since the scholarship was to do scientific research. He cited a priest of the archdiocese who had gone to Cambridge and had "absconded with another scholar".' His laugh was brittle. 'He didn't specify of which sex.'

'I wanted to be a priest, Des, when I entered St Paul's, so I kept my head down. Now,' Galvin gestured with his hands, 'I don't know … I may not be back in September. I told you all about it that day down at the riverbank.'

'Quite so.'

'As soon as we finish here, I'm off to England for the rest of the holidays. I'll see what happens after that.'

In an impulse, J. Desmond stood and put out his cigar. 'Let's get out of here and do a stroll around the city. Are you on for that?'

'Sure,' Galvin said, but he didn't feel entirely comfortable with a man whose background was very different from his own, and whose learning was beyond his.

They walked for about an hour and then stopped at a café bar on the Boulevard Saint-Michel, where they sat out in front and drank cognac. Young couples were having a great time, laughing, kissing and whispering in one another's ears. To Galvin's surprise, J. Desmond began to open up on his family – their tendency to 'give in to dark thoughts'.

He held up the cognac glass and looked at it. 'My dad used say to my brother and me, "Never imagine that taking refuge in the bottle will brighten your day, boys." His own father had lost his consultancy through the demon drink.'

He went on to the cold war between his parents. 'No fights, just not talking. Then Dad's sudden death when I was in First Theology. Mother was an Aer Lingus hostess, one of the glamour girls of those years. She revelled in throwing parties for our Merrion Road neighbours. Used to drive Dad scatty.' While he spoke, his face took on a vulnerable look: no longer was he J. Desmond, cold, polite and laden with prizes. 'It's hard to fathom. The death of … well, it can change your whole outlook.'

'I know,' Galvin said. 'I know well what you're talking about.'

'You don't.' His tone was prickly. 'I'm not referring to my father's death.' He kept shifting his glass on the round table. 'Hugo. We grew up together – Willow Park, Glenstal and then medical school.' He looked straight at Galvin. 'I've never spoken about this to anyone in St Paul's, so … .'

'It's safe with me.'

'Thank you. He picked up a rare virus that seemed to resist treatment – well, at that time. Two weeks in the ICU of Vincent's and he was dead.' His voice faltered. 'Every summer we went on holidays. We sailed to the Hebrides. And one year as far as the Bay of Biscay, crewing with both our fathers.'

The white-aproned waiter approached and recharged their glasses. J. Desmond continued. 'It's possible to love another ... of your own kind. You know what I mean?'

'Well ... yes. Yes, of course.'

'Look at David and Jonathan in the Book of Samuel, *he loved David as much as he loved himself.* Tennyson's *In Memoriam* shows how close the poet was to Hallam, his dear departed friend – just like someone else would love a woman.'

Galvin cleared his throat. 'To be honest, Des, I'm a bit out of my depth here, but, yes. That's possible, I'm sure.'

'Nothing to be ashamed of. My eldest brother, Mal, he's a qualified psychiatrist now. I borrowed a book from him. Our sexuality is ... well, one thing's sure, it's not black and white. We're not all we appear to be, Tommy.' He shifted in the chair. 'Can you see why I would like some guidance on the strange path sexuality can take?' He paused. 'Not sure if I didn't enter St Paul's too soon after Hugo ... it goes without saying, this is *entre nous.*'

'Most certainly.'

They finished off their drinks and returned to the Irish College. Despite the wine and the cognac, Galvin took some time to get to sleep that night. He woke, as the sun was rising over Paris, opened the tall shutters and sat on the deep window ledge mulling over J. Desmond's revelation until he saw Père René hobbling out to unlock the front gates and limping back with the morning papers.

HAVING GOT a good honours degree, Galvin returned to St Paul's after the summer holidays. Even though he was now among the Shiny Buttons, he still had nagging doubts about accepting Minor Orders, which would be conferred at the end of that academic year. The hopes and expectations generated by reports from Rome, however, drove him on.

'The Church is being reborn, and to be a priest, from now on, will be a life filled with challenge.' The Guns were excited by the document on the nature of the Church. *'Lumen gentium* is ground-breaking,' they asserted as they paced the ambulatory each morning. 'What a great time to be joining the priesthood!' *Aggiornamento* – used by the Council to capture the spirit of change – became their buzzword.

Nevertheless, the trickle of students packing their bags and leaving behind the rolled-up mattress continued. Galvin, however, dismissed his doubts as a product of his own insecurities. Yes, he would make the sacrifice – thousands of priests going back over centuries had done it. So could he. He would be a priest like the curate from his home parish who gave ten pounds each Christmas to the widow whose husband had been killed on a Coventry building site.

Once a month on a Saturday night, the rector gave a status report on the sessions at the Vatican Council, then coming to an end. One evening he announced: 'The mission of the Church, young gentlemen, from now on will embrace human as well as spiritual needs. And so His Grace wishes that you devote some of your formation to pastoral care. To achieve that goal, I am appointing a priest on the staff to supervise your work with various charities that care for the poor of our archdiocese.'

Galvin, along with three others, including Irwin, was assigned work with the St Vincent de Paul Society. On nights when a wintry fog clung to the street lights and children along Mountjoy Square were calling after them for holy pictures, the seminarians in warm overcoats and black hats visited the tenements, which reeked of urine and stale sweat. Some of the hall doors had been hacked down for firewood, so the one-room tenements were freezing. Children scurried in and out; their playful screams and calls and their feet thumping on the stairs caused women to throw open the flat doors, whip a Woodbine out of their mouths and swear at them.

One night a woman wearing a wraparound overall and a jaded look told them through her tears that when her husband came home from the pub he always demanded ... She looked at Galvin, then at Irwin. 'Now d'you get me? I know you are Christian Brothers an ... an anyway, we've six already. And the priest down in Gardiner Street – don't get me wrong, a very holy man, brothers. He says that I'm carrying me cross. An to do me best.'

Walking up Richmond Road with Irwin after their visitations, Galvin kept going back to the woman with the jaded look and ragged children. 'How can any country call itself Christian ... .'

'Yeah. I'm sure you're right.'

'If I go on for ordination – *if* I do – I hope to work in a parish like that. Jesus, make a difference to their lives. Do something. I mean, isn't this really a priest's work? What's the point of giving up so much, like the love of a woman, unless we make some difference? Aren't I right?'

Irwin made sounds of agreement as they turned in to Church Road. At the corner a man was lurching through the side door of The Cat and Cage pub.

'One of the reasons I came here,' Galvin indicated the gates of St Paul's, 'was to try to make a better world for people. Maybe that's unrealistic ... .'

Irwin stopped him. 'You mean to have to put up with all that shite, like tonight? Screaming children and women knackered from having babies, and some waster off at the boozer drinking the welfare. Not for me, Tommy. I'll never work in a parish, not if I can help it. Anyway, all this poverty would remind me too much of ... you know.

'And what's more,' he said as they were walking up the driveway, 'I'm not going to be a sticking plaster for anyone. Higher up is where you can influence things. Rome. That's where the power is. Making contact with those who have influence – civil servants, politicians, ambassadors.'

While Galvin's head was filled with the acrid smell of smoke, Irwin was off on a solo run on the beauties of Rome. 'My parish priest brought me along as a decoy while he canoodled with his housekeeper.

'St Peter's Square, Tommy – nowhere like it on earth. Cardinals and bishops in their robes going to their offices in Vatican City. The parish priest had a contact in the Vatican, so we got into one of those magnificent rooms at the side of the basilica: you know the type – ceilings decorated with scenes from the Bible. And the Swiss Guard saluting us.'

They walked up and down in front of the oratory before going in for Compline along with the other students. Irwin lowered his voice. 'One evening, I slipped away from the hotel – the parish priest wanted me out of the way. I hurried across the city until I was at St Peter's Square.

'I stood beside the Egyptian obelisk and stared at the basilica – maybe for half an hour. The grandeur of Bernini and Michelangelo against a pink sky. The men who sold souvenirs were gathering up their statues and pictures. A few beggars. The heat of the day still rising from the flagstones. Twenty centuries of tradition, Tommy. St Peter buried somewhere near. Few other organizations have lasted that long. D'you see what I'm getting at?'

He stopped and looked at Galvin. 'That night I decided that here was where I wanted to spend my life. And you're welcome to your screaming babies and some shagger's long johns hanging from a fireguard.'

Students were gathering in front of Senior House, their breath and cigarette smoke showing in the frosty air. 'Work in a parish!' Irwin said out of the corner of his mouth. 'For what? To be complimenting old ladies on their crochet, like my parish priest? Jesus, I'd be up in Brendan's, in the high security wing.'

They passed through the dim vestibule and joined a stream of students rushing down the stone corridor towards the oratory, always on the lookout for the Phantom hiding in the shadow of a statue. Irwin threw a furtive glance over his shoulder.

'And here's something else. When I returned to the hotel that night, the parish priest's room door was open but he wasn't in his bed. His sister, a night matron in one of the hospitals, tries to chaperone him on holidays.' He sniggered. 'Wasting her time. A severe case of mickey trouble.'

After Compline, Irwin knocked lightly on Galvin's door. He had a mischievous grin as he put a finger to his lips and checked that the coast was clear.

'For fuck's sake,' Galvin whispered. 'If you're caught, we'll both be—'

'Had to show you this,' he whispered and took a purple vestment out of tissue paper. 'Found it in a press beside the priests' parlour; been there for yonks.' He unfolded a bishop's cloak and put it on.

'How do I look, young student?'

'Every inch a cardinal.'

'Please address me as Your Eminence. Don't you think I'd cut a dash in St Peter's?' He paraded around the room, the hem of the cloak trailing on the floor. Then he took it off and folded it neatly in the tissue paper.

'Keep that safe. Could be useful when you're working with the Curia,' Galvin said.

All traces of a smile vanished from Irwin's face. 'I'd do a much better job than many of them. Put that in your pipe and smoke it, student.'

He eased open the door and peered up and down the corridor before he was swallowed up in the darkness.

NINE

ON THE THURSDAY morning of the retreat, a few priests, including Galvin, are up early. Some read their breviaries while walking with measured steps on the clay path down by the grove of eucalyptus trees. On the lawn, the London plane trees cast dappled patterns on the dewy grass. Galvin opens his breviary and recites the Office of Readings.

Later, in the room where the retreat director delivers his talks, the high windows increase the heat from the morning sun, causing grey heads to sink. Somewhere in the rich foliage of the chestnuts, pigeons make soft murmuring sounds. The priests recite Matins, and Winters, now a canon, announces that they will sing the *Veni Creator* for the only candidate for the priesthood – the first in seven years – who will be ordained in Maynooth the following Sunday.

They grow quiet again for a period of reflection before break-fast. The yawns are infectious and Galvin has to make a determined effort to stay awake. Idly scanning the rows of silver and grey and the shiny bald crowns, he is about to let his head drop to his chest when he is jolted into wakefulness by the dreadful cut of a priest across the aisle. His sullen jowls and the set of his shoulders bespeak the shame and fatigue he had talked about the evening before: 'No let up, Tom, one case of abuse after another. I couldn't take any more. My GP has put me on calmers. Was it all for nothing?' He is hoarse when he releases a scornful laugh that breaks into a cough. 'Never thought I'd be seeing out my remaining years on Xanax and sleeping tablets. And to think it was so good once.'

The priest's nose is a branched pattern of angry veins; his disappointed mouth a tell-tale of his soul's torment. 'Predators, Tom, that's the way we're seen nowadays,' he had said as darkness closed in on St Paul's.

An image comes to Galvin's mind of a 74-year-old boy who wants to bawl and keep on bawling until every vestige of his grief and fear and frustration has drained from his body. His fantasy expands: he sees the old man's puckered face, tears leaping from his eyes like the little boy who has tried his best, but whose schoolmaster has covered his copybook with red pencil marks and called him a fool. And when the priest had dried his eyes, his Church would still lie in ruins but he, at least, would have given vent to his misery.

Like most of the others, the priest's eyes are closed, so Galvin is free to look closely at the man's tortured face. Only a few years ago he was in full flight, a bulky figure on a bicycle powering his way around the parish, overseeing the building of a new school, checking every day with the architect or shooing children away from playing football around the church. God's policeman. He had a reputation in the diocese for striking a hard bargain and 'no builder would pull the wool over Jimmy Joe's eyes'.

In the dining room they settle down to breakfast and to a testy exchange about the fall-off in mass attendance, and wonder if there's any way they could bring young people back to the Church.

Jimmy Joe joins them and sits quietly at one end of the table. He hooks his walking stick on the back of his chair.

'No respect for authority, and I lay the blame at the feet of the parents,' Sylvester O'Flynn says in his high-pitched voice. He brushes notional specks off his deep black suit. 'Not a sign of a religious emblem in the homes.' He settles his cuffs. 'And as for the schools, well, you'd have to wonder. Those young teachers ... sure, none of them is going to mass.'

He blesses his porridge and relates how one Sunday evening he approached a group of young fellows drinking cider in the church grounds. 'You'd better go elsewhere,' he said, but they only laughed at him.

'I'll call the guards,' he threatened.

'Yeah, do, an we'll burn down your fuckin gaff tonight.'

'Watch your language, young man,' he said.

Sylvester stops. 'I won't sully your ears, fathers, but you can imagine ... go an eff yourself ... effin perverts the lot of you. You should be put up against a wall an shot ... ' Then, as he was walking away, one of them threw an empty beer can after him, saying: 'Would you look at the way he walks, must be an effin shirt-lifter.'

'You were wasting your time, Sylvester,' Cyril says. 'I close my door now at nine o'clock – six in the winter – put on the alarm and no one, *but no one*, gets in after that.' He looks around for approval.

'Father Teds,' says Harry Sheerin, who, having arrived late, picks up the thread of their conversation. 'That's what we are nowadays, lads, better face it. Subjects for television comedy.'

'Worse than that, Harry,' says Cyril. 'Whenever I go home and say mass in the town, I've to sign in, can you beat that? And sign out again! I was going into the school one day – in my own parish – and the secretary comes out and stands in front of me. "Where are you going, father?" "I'm going to the classes," I said to her, "like I always do." "You'll have to sign this book. No exceptions."'

The conversation reminds one of the priests of a searing encounter. Rather than moping around his house or the church, he had tried to get out and visit the parishioners in their homes. 'Have a bit of supper with them like I used to do in Canberra; shorten the night, you know what I mean.' The first evening a man answered the door and glared at him. 'Well,' he said, 'what do you want? Money?'

'I'm one of the priests up here in the parish church.'

'So?'

'I'm visiting the parishioners.'

'Well, you won't find any here. Me and me family have put all that stuff behind us.'

'Why is that, might I ask?'

'You might.' He peered over the priest's head at some point across the street. 'It's because of pervs who can't keep their hands off children. Now get out of me sight before I set me dogs on you.'

Jimmy Joe, whose blood was beginning to boil, jumps in. 'Ah for goodness' sake, what's all this complaining about? This is only a phase the Church is going through. We'll be as strong as ever in ten years. I never buy a paper now, except for the Catholic papers, of course.' He raises his fist. 'The media will never win out against us. You mark my words. We were there before them and we'll be there after them. And another thing. When we were young priests, we had real men to look up to. Men afraid of no one. Men who let school principals know where they stood. Men who could polish off a bottle of whiskey while playing cards.' He turns to Sheerin. 'And, I can tell you, they were men who could go out the following morning and preach great sermons at five or six masses.'

He recalls the famous Ned Gilmore, who packed the nine o'clock mass every Sunday night in Westland Row. 'No one could touch him as a preacher.' He smiles at the memory. One night when another priest was on and Ned was patrolling the church, he came upon two louts talking in a corner behind the holy water font. 'Stop talking while the priest is preaching the word of God,' he growled at the youths.

One of them gave him lip. 'He's not saying anything I'd be interested in.'

'Right then,' said Ned, 'this isn't a place for blackguards like you two.' Making a sweep for the youth, he grabbed him by the two lapels of his shirt. Pop went the buttons, showing the young fellow's bare chest. 'Ah,' said Ned, casting him back on the seat. 'You're not even a man. Not a rib of hair on your chest.'

The priests chuckle. One of them lifts the big stainless-steel teapot and holds it at the ready. 'Oh, Ned was the boy for them. Six foot three and a neck on him like one of his father's bulls out in Moynalty. And,' he pauses with the teapot poised over the table, 'as I say, no better man to finish off a bottle of brandy after a day's golf at Woodbrook. I've seen him do it.'

A priest, quiet until then, says: 'No wonder Ireland gave the Church an almighty kick up the arse.' He winks at Galvin.

With a scowl, Jimmy Joe rounds on him. 'There's no need for that foul language, father.'

The priest stands his ground. 'His like are partly responsible for the way things are right now. People have long memories, and now it's their turn – the child abuse thing is only the tip of the iceberg. Ireland has been waiting a long time for this chance.'

Cyril makes a feeble attempt to steer the conversation away from the tension that is now brewing. His small eyes dart from Sheerin to Jimmy Joe and then to others, and he seems to be shrinking inside his jacket. He has the same frightened look he had as a child, when his parents were fighting at the breakfast table before his father whipped up his briefcase, banged shut the door and stormed downstairs to his office in the Munster & Leinster Bank. And when his mother in her dressing gown disappeared to the kitchen, he could hear the cupboard being opened and the dreaded chink of the whiskey tumbler. Now he spends his life insisting on the bright side of every topic and seeing the positive in everyone. And he rarely makes a comment on any issue without coaxing agreement. 'What's Padraig Harrington's chances in the Open, lads?' he says, putting on a brave smile. 'His dad played football for Cork. Did you know that?'

But the priests have gone on to reminisce about other great preachers of the past. Sheerin is grinning. 'John Mike Noonan too was a great man to give a homily. He was God's gift to the human race when we were in the quare place.'

'Whatever became of him? A talented man,' Cyril says, smiling in the hope of an upturn in the conversation.

'He has a few pubs around Manchester. The lads came across him in Cheltenham a couple of years ago. Long leather coat and wide-brimmed hat. The real Ally Daly. He had horses running that day; does well with the nags,' a priest says.

'Did your wan go off with him – the housekeeper?' someone asks.

'She did, and became the mother of his six children, three of each. Blue and pink on an even keel.' Sheerin sniggers and looks for a reaction. 'How about that now? Some housekeeper. I wonder, lads, did Noonan preach before or after doing the thing – you know – the thing that Rome doesn't want us to do? '

'At the same time.' Hoping for agreement, Cyril is trying to put out another fire. 'Few were able to give a homily like Noonan.'

Jimmy Joe pushes back his plate and, glowering at Sheerin, stands and reaches for his stick. 'Such disrespect. Never in all my life … .'

The catering staff, with buckets on a trolley, approach their table to collect the delph.

'Well,' Galvin says. 'We'd better leave these people to do their work; they have a hard day ahead of them.'

TEN

IT DIDN'T TAKE LONG for Irwin to recover from his disappointment at not being chosen for Rome. Very soon he was back to his old self, beetling around the corridors, whispering the latest saucy joke and, in the refectory, keeping a weather eye out for any distinguished visitors, such as cardinals or bishops, who might be guests of honour at the top table.

Since it meant a free holiday for him in Milan or, most of all, Rome, he fitted into the role of the parish priest's decoy and, after these visits, gave Galvin the lowdown while on their way to the Pro-Cathedral for Sunday mass. His face lit up when describing the day he was having a meal with his parish priest in Trastevere and casually mentioned visits to the Nunciature in Dublin.

'How in God's name do you know the Nuncio?' Wide-eyed, the parish priest stopped eating and looked at him.

'Very simple, really. I was helping in the Pro-Cathedral and when he was leaving, he asked me who I was. We fell into conversation.'

That day in the Pro-Cathedral the Nuncio had been impressed by the way the seminarian had helped to put away the vestments in the cupboards, and had joked to the sacristan: 'There's hope for the Church when young men, like this gentleman here, are showing such interest.' The next time Irwin was helping around the sacristy, the Nuncio greeted him. 'Ah,' he'd said, 'Mr Irwin, the hope of the Church.' Very soon, the word in St Paul's was that Irwin was paying his respects after the Christmas and Easter holidays.

Although he was cautious from then on in front of Irwin, the parish priest subsequently told his friends at the golf club: 'He is better to me than the two buckos I have as curates. One of them is only interested in winkling paintings from the old dears he brings communion to. When he goes on holiday, he deposits his *objets d'art* and his late mother's jewellery in a bank vault. And when he was in Rathmines, he got a designer who had worked in Carton House to come and have his apartment done in heritage style. How about that, lads?'

They'd laughed. '*And the son of man has nowhere to lay his head. Oh, Mother of Jesus!*' one of them said as he prepared to tee off.

While Irwin and Galvin and the others were getting their heads around abstractions in theology, going on holidays, putting on the stage play before Christmas, playing rugby and soccer against the priests and moving closer to ordination day, the Irish Church was changing. Priests were dropping out, mostly because they had fallen in love, although a few – the more intellectual – were no longer willing to accept Rome's ruling on birth control. Independent-minded women refused to settle for the halfpenny place and severed their links with the Church.

Jesuits were returning from Fordham and Paris wearing jeans and pullovers and hosting weekends for priests and congregations of nuns on 'how to get in touch with your feelings'. The younger nuns and brothers were booking in to guesthouses as far away from Dublin as they could manage and the nuns, with coy whispers, were confiding to their closest friends, while strolling around the convent grounds, that they had found a soul mate. 'And we exchanged friendship rings in Clarendon Street Church on the Feast of the Sacred Heart,' one nun revealed. 'A private thing – I cried with joy. Never thought I'd find real love.'

Parishioners were delighted with the changes and sang the praises of their curates. 'Not at all stuffy: so natural, and off on weekends with the kids, and don't bother about wearing the garb. The kids call them by their first name, you know.' Ireland was throwing off the shackles of the past. New laws were being put on the statute book. And bishops were trying, like King Canute, to turn back the tide; and when they were pushed aside by a fast-moving society, they phoned up TV studios. 'Disgraceful to be discussing the intimate details of the marriage bed on a television programme. And in a Catholic country!' Rubbing its hands, the nation was glued to *The Late Late Show*. Gay Byrne was laughing. Fewer people than ever were paying any heed to the bishops, except the old, who had been conditioned to whisper their sins of 'bad thoughts and actions, father' in the dark confessional. 'In me past life, d'you follow, father?'

IRWIN WAS ordained with fourteen others in the Pugin chapel on a glorious Sunday in June when the lancet window behind the sanctuary filtered a polychrome on the prostrate figures of the ordinandi. In snow-white albs they promised obedience to the High Command. Galvin was the deacon at the mass; also present in the sanctuary were a couple of Monsignors from the Vatican, Irwin's guests. In the Academy Hall where each newly ordained priest spoke a few words of thanks to family and friends, Irwin, in his speech, was able to speak in Italian when thanking the Vatican Monsignors.

Having been passed over before, he set his hopes on making it to Rome for postgraduate studies. Again he was let down. A few days after his ordination, the High Command informed him that he was to study catechetics. He phoned Galvin, who was staying in Dublin for a few days with one of his brothers, a garda inspector. 'Let's go to the Hibernian, I've got a few bob from my ordination. Tomorrow at one, if you can. I'll treat you.'

'Tomorrow's fine.'

'Washington. They're sending me to bloody Washington! Catholic University. Tell you all about it when we meet. Tomorrow, one o'clock then.'

'The Catholic University. Many would feel honoured,' Galvin said as soon as they were settled in the hotel foyer.

'No, Tommy, you're out of the loop unless you're in Rome. That's where those with clout – you know, the Curia – get to see if you have leadership ability.'

'You'd be assured of a teaching job in St Paul's.'

'I don't want to end up there. Doing what? Teaching catechetics for forty years to weedy young blokes, talking bullshit to the Phantom in the priests' parlour? A fecking cul-de-sac.'

'Well … .'

'And I'm not going to work in a parish, maybe down in Wicklow, praising brown bread with the Irish Countrywomen's Association and off on the annual Lourdes pilgrimage. Fiddlesticks. As I keep telling you: the power is in Rome. The diplomatic corps – Vatican envoy, maybe. I won't be satisfied until I get there. Look, let's have a drink.' He was already hurrying towards the bar and, before the waiter had arrived to show them to their table, had drained his glass of gin and tonic and was ordering another round.

'I won't give in, Tommy,' he repeated when they were seated at the table and the waiter was handing them two stiff-backed menu charts. The light through the tall windows sparkled on the glasses and gave the room the lively aspect of high summer. One of the windows had been opened, causing the edges of a linen cloth to rise and fall. At the other tables were banker types, one of whom had nodded to the young priest and his companion.

After the meal they walked out into the warm sunshine and headed towards Grafton Street.

'When are you off?' Galvin asked.

'September, but before that, I'll make sure I take the Nuncio out to dinner. The Holy Spirit has a strange way of making an appearance after good food and wine.' As they made their way through shoppers elbowing for a bargain in the sales or waiting at a bus stop, he told Galvin about a narrow escape he had had the night before while driving home in his brother's car. 'A farewell party for a priest … well, ex now. He's headed for Chicago with the love of his life. Only two years in the job. Always a stupid gobshite. She's a dragon. I could see she has taken over his life already.

'Anyway, I was in deep shit, when I saw the line of cars and a garda checkpoint ahead. I was well over the limit.' He explained how he had whipped out his purple stole, draped it around his neck and rushed out of the car and up to the sergeant. The guards were busy checking the two lines of traffic. Making sure to keep at a distance, he called out: 'Sergeant, I'm out on a sick call. Can you arrange to let me through, please?'

Without hesitation the sergeant called out: 'Make way, make way. There's a young priest on a sick call. Thank you. Make way.' The sergeant raised his hand in a salute. 'Now, Father. Go ahead.'

Irwin chuckled. 'You've got to use your nut, Galvin. The whole line of cars pulled aside.'

'The waters parting for Moses on the Red Sea. You're a bastard.'

They passed by the Grafton Cinema, which was showing *Room at the Top*. Irwin turned to Galvin. 'I've no choice except to go to Washington.' And, as if imparting a secret, he added in a cold, measured way: 'D'you remember the night we came back from the V de P work in Buckingham Street, and I was high on Rome? Well, they're not going to stop me from getting there. There are ways and means. As the mother used say: never give up on your dream, and remember, you've only one life to live.'

ELEVEN

WITH ONLY two days left before the retreat ended at midday on Saturday, the priests, like children devouring the last scraps at a party, drain every precious moment from their days. They linger at the table after the midday meal, savour dessert, a glass of red and memories of the good times, and pool any snippets of information about the diocesan appointments that emanate from the archbishop's house: what parishes are being amalgamated, and who is 'handing in his gun and his badge'.

'And no one coming after us, lads,' one man says.

'After a hip replacement, I'm now expected to look after two parishes,' says another. More often than not, the conversation gets round to their ailments and their pills. Pills for diabetes, pills for heart conditions, for arthritis and enlarged prostates. Scopes they have had, and colonoscopies.

Like an emigrant returned to his native land and trying to anchor his own identity, Galvin listens closely and takes only a small part in the conversations. Eventually, he makes his excuses and when he stands to leave, they hardly notice. On his way down the wooden corridor to the chapel, he comes across a priest about to climb the stairs to his room. 'Giving in to the noonday devil, Tom,' he jokes, placing his joined hands at one side of his head in a dumb show of sleeping.

'Why not? While you've the chance.' They speak for a while about how the Benedictine retreat director is so refreshing. 'Give you new heart, wouldn't he?' says the priest. 'Although his notion of us priests sharing purpose-built houses to be a support to each other is a bit daft. If I wanted to live in that sort of community, wouldn't I have joined the Vincentians after finishing my schooling in Castleknock? No, I'm grand with my own hall-door key.'

'You have a point there. Anyway, *coladh samh*.' Galvin continues on his way to the chapel.

Inside is cool and has the churchy smell of furniture polish and incense. He kneels at one side of the stalls. The sanctuary, the crenellated altar, every shade of light floods his mind with memories: the Phantom vesting for mass, carrying the chalice and wearing his biretta, and sweeping out of the sacristy. He would genuflect at the foot of the altar and, if the student who was serving that morning wasn't ready to take his biretta, he would let it drop; then in the sacristy, he would lambaste him: 'You're on for another week, student.'

As his eyes follow the grain of the armrest, his thoughts are freewheeling. The Phantom's efforts to implement the Council come winging back; how he had invited theologians and sociologists to talk about ministry in a changing world. It was too late. The poison had spread and, to add insult to injury, when he organized an open forum to promote free expression in accordance with the spirit of Vatican II, he was met with an angry silence.

He had sat alone on the dais, his hair still perfectly groomed but now turning grey at the temples, his eyes fixed on the folder in front of him. When he spoke, his voice was no longer in the hectoring tone that he had used on the first day they had arrived: 'If you are so foolish as to try and change anything in this seminary, you will fail. St Paul's was here before you and it will be here after you.' He had invited suggestions as to how life in the seminary might prepare students for the priesthood. No one spoke and, for about twenty minutes, he'd endured a crucifying silence. He grew pale and beads of perspiration showed on his upper lip; eventually, he slapped shut the folder and walked out. They had defeated him at last.

The memory of what he had done to Mac and others had left no room for sympathy. Their formation had now included object lessons in humiliation, cunning and revenge: lessons some of them would implement years later when they had been put in charge of parishes.

The Phantom's breaking point came soon after. When he repeatedly failed to appear for the students' mass in the chapel, another priest would announce that Dr Murtagh had a cold and he was filling in for him. Word filtered through the oratory one night that he wouldn't be back in September and, despite the strict rule of solemn silence and the cold glare of the prefects, the students raised a loud cheer. Later, as they were passing his door to their rooms, they each viciously kicked at it and walked on.

When Galvin picked up his breviary in the chapel, it fell open at a marker – his own ordination card. At the top was a quotation: *But we have this treasure in earthenware vessels that the surpassing greatness of the power may be from God and not from ourselves.* He took out the card and was transported back to a blustery day in early June, when he and twenty-two others lay prostrate on the cold marble and promised loyalty to the High Command.

ON THE WEEK coming up to ordination, they had made their retreat in total silence, walking the grounds on their own: a portent of the journey they were about to begin. Some read their breviaries; others, with meditative steps, took the narrow path where ground elder and wild angelica flourished by the river's bank. Blackbirds and thrushes, taking a break from feeding their young, eyed them from high up in the poplars.

The rest of the students had kept their distance. As ever, a screen of expectancy fell over the seminary, like during Holy Week. All outdoor games were suspended until after the ordinations; music was to be kept at a low volume. The rector had delivered a special talk on the Tuesday evening: 'All the years of prayer and study, of rising early on dark winter mornings, of observing the rules of the seminary will come to fruition next Sunday when these young men who were called by God will each become an *alter Christus*. One day, with God's grace, your turn will come also.'

To prepare for Ordination Sunday, the students helped to tidy up the grounds of the seminary. In a shirt and trousers, Paddy rattled along on a tractor, sending up a shower of grass behind the mower. His two sons, promising footballers with Homefarm United, painted the garden seats and nailed up a WET PAINT sign on the green slats.

The retreat director, a Jesuit priest with tails hanging from the shoulders of his soutane, spoke in a clipped monotone: 'Next Sunday, young reverends, when the Church calls you to serve the Lord, you will gain a unique status that will mark you off from others. After that and, for the rest of your life, you will stretch out your anointed hands over the host and again over the chalice. At that moment you will change the basic elements of bread and wine into the body and blood of Jesus Christ. And when you raise your consecrated hand in absolution, you will bring divine forgiveness to a repentant soul.

'No one else has been privileged with that supreme power, which will come to you because you said Yes to the Almighty. You will be a priest of God for ever, according to the order of Melchizedek.' His Roman collar hung loose about his sinewy neck. 'Remember that you are embarking on a journey that will be one of great sacrifice. Your courage will be like that of the men I had the honour to serve as chaplain at El Alamein. You too will find yourselves alone, many times, in the Garden of Gethsemane; you will be reviled and rejected. Yours will be a white martyrdom, called *banmhártra* in Gaelic.

'In the words of the great French spiritual writer, Lacordaire: *You will have a heart of fire for charity, and a heart of bronze for chastity … O priest of Jesus Christ.'*

Each evening, while the setting sun was casting an orange glow over the chapel, the ordinandi joined the rest of the students for vespers; together they sang the *Veni Creator Spiritus.* The following Sunday they would lie prostrate on the sanctuary floor to show their unworthiness for the office they were about to assume and their need for God's grace. The High Command would anoint their hands with chrism and then bind them in a linen cloth. When it was over, the photos taken and the prie-dieu returned to the side chapel for another year, the seminary would bask in the afterglow.

Galvin woke sometime after five on the morning of his ordination. The rain that had disturbed his sleep a couple of times during the night had cleared off. He looked out through the window of his room: filmy clouds were passing high above the glazed roof of the chapel. Down on the square, it appeared as if some lavish deity had cast diamonds on the fresh grass.

The twenty-three for ordination were served a cooked breakfast an hour after the other students had had their porridge and brown bread. The college was hushed. The only sound in the refectory was the quiet clink of cutlery or when the serving boys from the kitchen wheeled the trolley over the black and red tiles.

According to a time-honoured ritual, the ordinandi made their way in double file to one of the side rooms off the reception hall in Wansborough. Each of them had his alb, cincture and stole over his forearm: warriors ready for battle. Each had been assigned a deacon, who stood behind like a waiter; his function was to have the vestments in order and to give moral support to the candidate and accompany him to the chapel. They vested in a silence broken only by the rustle of new albs being placed over nervous shoulders, or when one of them uttered a little laugh while having difficulty making a knot in his cincture.

Hands joined, they waited until they could see the archbishop's black Daimler approaching at the pace of a funeral car. Then they stood at the main door of Wansborough: no going back now. The fresh surplices of the vicar-general, the rector and staff were ruffling in the breeze. Monsignors from the diocese stood among them.

When the archbishop's car pulled up, his driver got out and opened the back door. The slight figure emerged and cast a sharp look at the assembly. A smile played about his thin lips. When he raised his hand in blessing, the folds of his washed-silk robes caught the morning sunlight. 'Benedictio Domini super vos praecipue ordinandos,' he said above a whisper and blessed them with index and middle fingers. The rector led the response: 'Et super vos, Archiepiscope,' and rushed to genuflect and kiss his ring; he was followed by the new dean of discipline, now called the vicar for formation, then the other priests on the staff.

The archbishop's master of ceremonies, wearing a pleated surplice, shining shoes and a tetchy look on his handsome face, grimaced at the inattentive student who should be holding up the cappa magna behind the archbishop. Red-faced, the student rushed to lift the purple trail.

The chapel was already full. Family members and guests stood when the full swell of the organ burst into 'Ecce Sacerdos Magnus' – the salute to His Grace, the archbishop. One of the deacons incensed the archbishop and then the congregation; slanted pillars of smoke from the high windows stood in the sanctuary.

The support of his fellow ordinandi, his family and the power of the ceremony now dispelled any doubts that had been surfacing in Galvin's mind during the previous week and which he put down to his nervous disposition. The archbishop's sermon also was encouraging. 'From now on, my dear brothers in Jesus Christ, you will make the ultimate sacrifice: you will give and not count the cost, labour and seek for no reward except that of knowing you are doing the will of our Divine Saviour.'

When the ceremony was over, the tension broke and all strolled out into the sunshine. Parents and guests knelt at the prie-dieu to receive the first blessing and to kiss the freshly anointed hands. Beaming in his long cloak fastened at the neck by a gold chain, the archbishop was in no hurry to move off; he congratulated parents, mingled with families and knelt at each prie-dieu for a blessing.

The boyish faces of the ordained, their satin capes cast over their shoulders, adoring mothers' looks and wide-brimmed hats, children capering and skipping on the grass – all come back to Galvin as he stares at his card. And fathers who might have done root canal treatment the day before or prepared a legal defence, now stand back and adjust the viewfinder to get the best shot of a son imparting his first blessing to his mother: a son whom they had secretly hoped might follow in their footsteps.

Galvin's father looked awkward in his navy serge suit, but he nodded and accepted compliments and good wishes. Vigorous efforts with a serviceable brush and carbolic soap had failed to remove the clay of the hillside farm from beneath his fingernails.

One of the newly ordained returned to St Paul's that evening to take Benediction. Vested in braid with a golden humeral veil over his shoulders, he raised the thurible and, with a pendulum motion, incensed the glittering monstrance containing the Real Presence. Banks of lighted candles in tiered formation shone on the white marble and on the bouquets of flowers. More candles lit up the high altar. And when he genuflected after deposing the sacred host in the tabernacle, the fresh sole of his leather shoe showed. The world was clean and pure. That golden evening the congregation, including Paddy the caretaker and his family, kneeling where Lovely Legs had once knelt, ranked the young priest higher than the angels. Thirty-six years later he would appear in the newspapers handcuffed to a guard and on his way to serve seven years in prison for an illicit relationship with a boy. The students' singing filled the chapel: 'Pange, lingua, gloriosi / Corporis mysterium / Sanguinisque pretiosi ... .' Through the open windows, the Gregorian chant could be heard all over the grounds where nature too blessed the evening: the whitethorns lining the fence along Griffith Avenue, laden with frothy blossoms, gave off a rich perfume.

On the following day, Father Thomas Galvin said his first mass at Eccles Street Convent Chapel where his sisters had attended the boarding school. His private intention at the mass was for the repose of the soul of his two brothers: one who had died when a trench caved in at a High Wycombe building site and the other, Joe, who, at nine, had been killed when his bicycle had been hit by a turf lorry. In the sun-drenched garden after mass, where nuns were fussing about and a photographer was getting the family to stand in front of a statue of the Virgin Mary, a priest who was a curate in Galvin's home parish in Kerry and who had served the mass, sidled up to him and whispered: 'You're looking mighty serious, Tommy. Don't worry about a thing. Priests will have the option of getting married within ten years. The Vatican Council will change everything.' He laughed. 'The bishops won't know what hit them, you'll see.' Within ten years, the priest himself had disappeared to England and married in a London register office.

LATER THAT DAY, Galvin's brother M.J. spared no expense for a dinner and a dance band at the Gresham Hotel. Among the many cards and telegrams read out after the meal, including one or two from men with whom he had worked behind the mixer in Milton Keynes, was a card from Irwin: *Ad multos annos to my best friend. Deep regrets I couldn't make it. You know yourself, Tommy, coming up to exam time.* Later Galvin was to learn that Monsignor Giordano, of the Congregation for Bishops at the Vatican, had been visiting the Papal Nuncio in Washington and Irwin had made sure to get an invitation to a reception for him.

TWELVE

IRWIN RETURNED later that summer from Washington. As ever, he was all ears for news from the diocese, even though he already knew everything that was going on. He and Galvin did Howth again: a walk around the Head and then dinner at a harbour restaurant. He was upbeat.

'Off to Lourdes in September, Tommy.'

'Didn't you tell me one day, you had no intention of hanging around, commending old ladies for their brown bread and going off to Lourdes with them?'

'Ah yes,' he laughed, 'that was then. The Nuncio is going and you don't refuse an invitation from that important bod. Remember the age-old motto of the diocese: *Major appointments are made in Rosary Square*. The Nuncio is a man of influence, and you don't look a gift horse in the mouth: that's if you want to get anywhere in the', he did inverted commas with his forefingers, 'Holy Roman Church.'

FOR THREE YEARS after ordination, Galvin made a brave effort to teach religion to pupils in a technical school. Despite his use of pictures, stories and film, the pupils didn't hide their lack of interest. They sniggered at the back of the classroom and passed around notes, and told him that religion had had its day. A teacher next door often had to knock on his door to complain about the noise. He appealed to them for quiet, but they ignored him. And to distract him they asked questions like: 'Why don't priests get married? Don't they like girls, Father Tommy?' 'We don't believe in any of this. There's no Santa Claus.' 'God is only for them in the posh houses.' 'What do you think of that, Father Tommy?' They were telling him what he already knew: he was not a teacher.

One evening, just before he was to return to school after the summer holidays, he was glad to slit open an envelope and read that the archbishop was appointing him to the Parish of the Immaculate Conception, close to Skerries. That Friday, in his Volkswagen Beetle, he drove past the airport and then through a couple of dusty villages until he reached St Mochta's, where he was expected by the parish priest. The bright harvest day afforded a wide-angled view of the ripe fields of corn that stretched away to the Cooley mountains. A couple of times he had to pull into a gateway on the narrow roads to let tractors towing high loads of bales pass by. In their wake, they left wisps of straw clinging to the hedges.

He stopped at a lay-by to get his bearings. In a farmyard inside the hedge, men were feeding sheaves into the open mouth of a threshing mill. Others were sinking hay forks into the rising mound of straw and making their way to one of the ricks; laughing figures who waded with purpose through the rising chaff in a golden haze. 'Move your arse there,' one man shouted at a youth who was struggling with a bag of grain. Resting on his pitchfork, the man guffawed and called to the others: 'Look at him. Out all night chasin' women. Now he's draggin his arse after him. Look lively, young lad.' He had to shout to be heard above the steady hum of the thresher and the blue Fordson Major powering it by means of a wide revolving belt. Fond memories of Reading and cement mixers and driving M.J.'s men to work down the Kilburn Road came back to him.

The parochial house was grey and threatening and loomed up inside high walls; the surrounding rise made it look more stolid and forbidding. To one side of the presbytery was a small orchard of glistening red and green apples. A clothesline hung from two of the trees; on the line were white collarless shirts and a woman's pink blouse and nylon stockings. At each side of the footpath, chrysanthemums, clusters of hydrangeas and lupins flourished in a mass of colour.

Galvin parked and walked up to the front door. The brass knocker made a heavy thud when it fell against the wooden receiver. Footsteps shuffled inside. A stout woman with a flowered overall and grey hair tied back in a bun opened the door and stood guard in front of a mahogany hallstand on which hung canes and a straw hat.

'I'm Father Tom Galvin,' he said.

She eyed him from head to toe and, chuckling to herself, turned on her heel. 'Ah yes, the new man. Come on.' She waddled ahead of him, down a wainscotted corridor, and rapped on a door at the end. Putting her ear close to the wood, she shouted: 'He's here. Can you hear me? He's here.' After a gruff 'Yes. Bring him in,' she turned the knob, gave the door a hefty push with her shoulder and led Galvin into the room.

Reading his breviary and smoking a cigarette, the parish priest was wedged in a nook between a glass cabinet and a radiogram. A round table was piled with money bags tied at the mouth. Gay Byrne, on the radio, was taking a call from a giggly housewife.

The parish priest looked stouter and more bald than when the Phantom had invited him to come to St Paul's to talk about fundraising, for which he was well known in the diocese. The word then was that he had bundles of tickets for raffles ready in the sacristy and when parishioners came in to have a mass said or to arrange a baptism or a wedding, or even a funeral, he'd push a book of tickets in front of them.

'Wait now,' he said, turning over a page of his breviary and taking another drag on the cigarette. He continued to read, his lips moving as his eyes scanned the pages, the buttons of his waistcoat straining as his wide girth rose and fell.

Over the mantelpiece was a black-and-white photograph of de Valera, tall and austere and towering over the High Command and other clerics; in the background were swags of bunting hanging from the front of Coghill House. Another sepia photo of a couple on their wedding day stood on a deep window ledge, the man seated, the droll-looking woman standing with her hand resting lightly on his shoulder.

Eventually the parish priest inserted a ribbon marker in the breviary, crossed himself and looked at Galvin over his glasses. 'You're a fine strong fellow. You'll be able to use that here.' Without moving from his throne, he stretched out a beefy hand mottled with liver spots, making Galvin cross the room for the handshake. 'So you're the man whose brother made a killing in the building trade across the pond.'

'He's been successful, yes, thank God.'

'I hope he made it honestly. We hear stories about them Irish contractors and how hard they were on the poor workers.'

'My brother earned every penny he got through hard work.'

'I'll take your word for it.' The parish priest's belly shook when he chortled. The housekeeper chuckled in sympathy.

'Lizzie,' he turned to her. 'Give this young gentleman the books for the visitation of his area.'

'Right.'

'And bring the bag of sweets.'

'Faith, *you* had them last,' she said roundly.

'No. You took them with you last night.'

The housekeeper left the room and returned with the visitation books and the bag of sweets.

'A sweet?' the parish priest said. The housekeeper shook the bag in front of his face and got another fit of the giggles. Galvin rested his hat on a sugan chair and took a Yorkshire Toffee. 'Thanks, Lizzie.'

She shook the bag again. 'Take another one, we're not that poor.'

'All right. Thank you.'

Devouring one toffee after another, Lizzie sat in a chair, rocking and throwing sidelong glances at Galvin, who was trying to make conversation.

'Great weather for the harvest,' he said.

'Tis,' she replied, 'if you had a harvest. I don't.' She laughed at her own quip. 'All I have is me garden out there.'

'A fine garden it is.'

The parish priest began to explain what he wanted from his curate, but Gay Byrne kept interrupting him, causing Lizzie to bolt from the rocking chair and stamp across the room to shut him off. 'Now, Mr Gay Byrne, you'll have to stay quiet for a while.'

'You'll be on the bingo every second Friday night; you and Father Stephen Dolan, your companion curate,' the parish priest said, and rolled his eyes. 'That's if the bold Father Stephen is in the parish.'

'If he's in the parish,' Lizzie echoed, her mouth full of sweets.

'You'll have to bring back the money and the stubs and put them all in the safe,' the parish priest declared.

'Right.' Galvin nodded.

'And you'll have to take me for the big shop once every two weeks. I'm not able to be dragging bags now.' Lizzie got up and left the room.

The parish priest threw a dead eye in Galvin's direction. 'I hope you'll be obedient, because the last bucko was anything but. And by the way, if you have any false notion about introducing newfangled ideas from the Vatican Council into this parish, I'd put all those out of my mind right now if I were you. The brave Stephen tried and failed. We've a lot of overheads. We have to pay our debts. We don't have time for fancy ideas from them boyos in Rome.'

He opened his breviary and fingered a Sweet Afton from the packet at his side. 'You're on the early mass tomorrow morning. God bless now and I hope you're happy here.'

'Thanks.'

'And by the way, I do all the weddings and funerals.'

'Fine.'

'Oh, and a last thing: you will come here at the end of each month and Lizzie will give you your wages.'

He flicked a cigarette lighter, switched on the radio again to a laughing Gay Byrne, and went back to his breviary.

GALVIN AND STEPHEN had a house each: Stephen's was in the church grounds, Galvin's was out the country. They didn't meet much apart from in the sacristy on Sundays and counting the collections on a Monday morning. On those occasions Stephen was usually in a jokey mood until the parish priest arrived.

While keeping an eye on the door one Monday, he said: 'Our boss used to get the garage to yank out the passenger seat when he bought a new car. The back for Lizzie; can't have a woman that near you. You know, the Maynooth Statutes. Imagine the pair of them; he behind the steering wheel and Lizzie perched in the back.'

Listening to the banter, Galvin remembered a chance meeting with a priest in Wynn's Hotel who had told him: 'Here's some friendly advice to a young man. Stephen is bright, but there's something going on in that man's head. He was asked to do postgrad in Rome, but said he'd prefer to work in a parish. The uncle was a bigwig in the diocese of Miami. Kidnapped poor Stephen.'

BEFORE CHRISTMAS that year, the parish priest was made a canon of the metropolitan chapter. From then on, he wore the purple canon's cape over his soutane every Sunday when chatting with parishioners at the front door of the church. 'My people expect it of me; it's an honour for them too, you know, to have a canon in the parish,' he said defensively to Galvin. He was also appointed vicar forane, a post that included caring for the spiritual welfare of priests in the deanery.

Every Sunday, he sat at a desk in the sacristy, reading his breviary and listening to his curate's sermons. 'As the parish priest, I've a responsibility to see that my curates' preaching is in line with Church teaching,' he rounded on Stephen when he accused him of treating them like schoolboys.

On Monday mornings while counting the Sunday collection, the canon presided at the top of the table, a notebook at the ready and, when the count was complete, he would refer to his notes and take the two priests to task.

'By the way, father,' he said, turning to Galvin one morning. 'You said a ferial mass last Thursday, when it was the feast of St Joachim and St Anne.' He studied his notes again. 'Just because I'm not in the church doesn't mean that God-fearing parishioners don't give me a full report.' Another Monday he had upbraided Stephen for misquoting a recent *motu proprio* of the Holy Father.

Stephen had had enough. 'I'm going to let you know right now that I'll not be treated like a seminarian. I'm nearly twenty years ordained, and if you attempt to correct me again, you'll count this money yourself and you'll get some other jackass to spend Friday night in the parish hall supervising bingo. So you know what you can do with your *motu proprio*.'

For a moment, the canon sat with a slack mouth and stared at his notebook. His face reddened. 'I could have you in the archbishop's office by tomorrow morning for this wicked challenge to my authority. I remind you that I'm a senior priest and now a canon of the metropolitan chapter. Have you thought of that, my good man?'

'Yes, my good man, I've thought of that. And all I've to say is – so what?''

When the sacristan, who had been hanging vestments in a wardrobe, became aware of the stand-up between the two priests, he scurried out the door.

'And here's something else I've thought about that you might wish to chew on,' Stephen continued. 'I'd be very glad to report to the archbishop, and while I'm there, I will have an opportunity to discuss with him your peculiar accountancy methods with parish funds.'

The canon crushed his cigarette in a Pan Am ashtray. Smoke billowed into the air. 'What an outrageous implication to make about your superior.' He glared at Stephen. 'Explain yourself! I've handled better men than you.'

'Certainly. I'll explain myself, and I'd be delighted to talk to His Grace about the curious fact that you make no distinction between your own personal account in the bank and the parish account. And secondly, while I'm at it, *my good man*, I'd like to get his opinion on the way you hold your hand over the total income for division among the priests when you ask your two curates to sign every month.'

'In all my years,' the canon said, a vein swelling in his neck, 'in all my years, I've never encountered such insolence. You have not heard the last of this.'

He gathered up his notebook and breviary and bolted out of the sacristy, hitting off the edge of the table and sending columns of coins crashing to the floor. After that, the notebook never again appeared, nor did he attempt to correct the curates' sermons, but he still continued to place his hand over the final figure for the monthly collection.   •

Things went from bad to worse between him and Stephen. One glorious morning in July when Galvin was getting into his car after saying the ten o'clock mass, the canon drove in.

'Where's Stephen?' he said brusquely. In his hand he was holding a sheaf of ticket books.

'I think he's gone for a cycle to Skerries.'

'No, he's not gone for a cycle to Skerries. He's in bed. Why are you covering up for him?' He made for Stephen's bedroom window and started tapping on the glass with his keys.

'It's his day off,' Galvin protested; 'he's entitled to be wherever he wants to be.'

The canon rounded on him. 'Day off, day off! He has cheque-books in his house and I need them right now to reconcile the parish accounts. And he didn't turn up for the bingo last week; it was his turn to bring back the bags of money from the hall. How d'you think I'm going to provide for the parish if I don't have funds?'

From the bunch of keys he always kept dangling from his wide girth, he selected one and began to fumble with the lock. Galvin intervened. 'I don't think you should do that – Stephen activates the internal circuit every night.'

Over his shoulder, the canon threw him an angry look and continued poking. The alarm box screamed.

Muttering about how Stephen should have provided him with a spare key like every curate is supposed to do, the canon paced the footpath until the alarm went silent. Stephen appeared, barefoot; he'd just thrown on a pair of slacks and a T-shirt.

'Where were you?' the canon snapped. Stephen ignored him and called Galvin. 'Come here a minute, Tommy.'

He held the door open while the canon and Galvin passed through his kitchen where the stale smell of cigarettes hung in the air. The table was littered with stained coffee mugs, an open bag of sugar, a container of Saxa salt and a blister sheet of Paracetamol.

By now the canon had calmed down. 'Where are the bank statements and the school chequebook, Stephen?'

Stephen turned to Galvin. 'Tommy,' he said. 'How am I expected to put up with this …?' He gestured towards the canon, who stood in the middle of the living room, a barrel of a man with a fringe of dyed hair sticking out over both ears – dye applied by Lizzie over the kitchen sink. 'I've had a splitting headache all morning. Mother was taken into hospital in London; she was on holidays with my dad, and I have to catch a flight today – and now I get this.'

'Today is Friday,' the canon reflected. 'Does this mean you're not going to be here for the weekend masses?' He kept waving the sheaf of ticket books in front of both curates. 'I was relying on you two to give the parish bazaar a good plug and be at the church doors to sell tickets after the masses.'

Stephen glared at him. Then, stretching out his arm, he pointed to the open back door. 'Out!' he shouted. 'Out before I lose my patience with you. My mother is in hospital and all you can think about is a parish bazaar. Have you any screed of humanity in you? Get out before I do something I'll be sorry for.' He made as if to strike the canon, but thought better of it. 'Ah, you're not worth it,' he said. 'Out.'

Like a cowering sheepdog, the canon sidled towards the door. When he spoke again, his tone had softened. 'If you find the statements, will you bring them to the parish office – and also the chequebook. I need them for the auditor.'

BY THEN, anyway, Stephen was making plans to leave the priesthood. He phoned Galvin one morning towards the end of the summer. 'Tommy,' he said airily. 'I'm on top of the world. Come and celebrate. Lunch on me. Won't take no for an answer.'

'You're on.'

They drove to a restaurant in Malahide and, before the waitress had brought the menu, Stephen made his announcement. 'Two things, Tommy. One, I'm in love. And two, I'll be falling in for a small fortune. An uncle, a Monsignor, who went to Florida in old God's time, bought up corner sites, then made a killing on the stock market ... left me the lion's share of his will.' He gave a hearty laugh. 'Had these corner sites all over the diocese; bought them when they were going for a song. So, Tommy Galvin, I'll be rid of that gobshite canon and free of his penny-pinching ways.' He raised his arms. 'For ever.'

'You're not, are you?'

'I'm off, can't take this crap any longer. Should never have joined the priesthood. It's a bloody epidemic in this country. Should carry a health warning.'

'I'll miss you; you were good to work with.'

'Like a lot of others in this country, I went into it too young. Seemed then it was the right thing to do. Not now.'

He rubbed his chin and looked away towards the other end of the restaurant where steam was rising from a coffee machine which was making a hissing sound. 'I was in quarantine,' he said, and related how he spent his summer holidays.

Every year, as soon as his parents got holidays from the school where they taught in Blanchardstown, they would hitch their caravan to the Austin Cambridge and head for France, or, if not, to the house they would rent in Tramore. And when Stephen was in St Paul's he used drive his three sisters to the Atlantic Ballroom Sunday nights where Sandra Dee lookalikes in buckram-flared shirts flirted in the streets, laughing with fellows who imitated Troy Donahue's sulky look and who wore their shirt collars turned up like they had seen him do in the pictures.

Stephen would drive as slow as a funeral car back to the house, where his father would be reading the paper, a glass of whiskey at his elbow, his face flushed with pleasure after a day's golf and, when the coast was clear at the club, throwing his arm around the nearest pretty woman.

Stephen's mother would have tea and apple tart ready for them both, which they would take in the kitchen, and she would delight in asking him, more or less, the same questions about ordination day at St Paul's. Once she told him how her brother, Monsignor

James in Florida, would be bringing him a chalice that summer for him to use at his first mass.

Stephen grew pale in the telling. 'When I went to my room I could hear the band playing in the distance, and I knew I was missing what any young person would want. But as the years went by in St Paul's, I didn't have the balls to pull out. I took refuge in the … you know … *no greater love*, and the nonsense we were fed: ontological change at the moment of ordination; marked off from all men, special grace from God, given only to … you know yourself. Our shared diet.'

To keep his thoughts from rambling on those summer nights, Stephen would pick out a book from the bundle he'd brought for the holidays: Dickens, Canon Sheehan or P.G. Wodehouse, and read until it was time to collect the girls spilling out of the dance-hall. Girls linking each other and singing, *'Que sera sera, whatever will be will be.'* Pink brush strokes in the western sky, the dying embers of a glorious Sunday.

But after swimming and walking for miles along the headland, he would fall asleep in the knowledge that he had a *calling* – given only to the chosen few.

'*Que sera*, bloody *sera*, I detest that song,' he told Galvin. 'Anyway enough of that. I've met the mother of my children – I hope.'

'So it seems.'

'Áine. She's small – *petite* the French would call her. Mightn't be considered a raving beauty, but I think she is. We love each other, and that's all that matters.'

Visiting a parishioner in hospital two years before, he had stopped at the nurses' station to ask for directions. One of the nurses had taken him to the ward. He'd joked with her on the way. 'I've this very bad knee, nurse, could you do anything for me?' He grimaced in mock pain and clutched his knee. 'Oh, unbearable, nurse.'

'Sure I can,' she said playfully. 'Come in here to the sluice room and let down your trousers and I'll give you a thorough examination.'

On his next visit they had a longer conversation, during which they discovered a mutual interest in hill-walking. When he asked her out to dinner, she cancelled drinks at Searson's with her nurse friends. The two of them did Lugnaquilla, the Sugar Loaf and other hills around Wicklow. And they joined a mountaineering club to climb in Snowdonia. His headaches left him and, under pressure from Áine, he gave up smoking.

They were laughing one day in a Clontarf restaurant – a safe distance, they thought, from prying eyes. Stephen was feeding Áine a wedge of pizza. They were having great fun. When she stretched with her open mouth for the wedge, he would draw back his hand at the last moment. Lost in each other, they were unaware that a stout little nun who ran a prayer group in the parish had dropped in for a coffee and a slice of lemon cake after visiting a friend in the Central Remedial Clinic. She watched from a far corner where the light was dim, and had a prayer said for him at the next charismatic meeting: she even got the canon to say a mass for a 'special intention' and told him what she had seen: 'For the father's own good, Canon. And to avoid scandal to the laity.'

'Whether I had a vocation or not, well, only God knows. One thing I'm certain of – fiddling with bingo bags and telling frightened women in confession that they could regulate their families only by the Billings Method ...' he laughed. 'The Billings Method. Jesus, do the Red Frocks in Rome think the people are children or fools?'

THE MORNING Stephen left, the canon was nowhere to be seen, even though his house was across the grounds from where the removal men were loading up furniture. Galvin arrived as the lorry was inching its way through the gates, the driver looking left and right at each side mirror so that he wouldn't strike one of the ivy-covered pillars. Stephen turned to Galvin. 'That's about it. You were a good support. We'll have a pint when Áine and myself are settled.'

He started to play with the keys of his new car. 'Tommy boy,' he said, giving Galvin a gentle poke on the shoulder, 'get thyself a wench, before thou loseth thy marbles.'

The two priests shook hands, and Galvin watched him drive through the gates. Out of the corner of his eye, he noticed a twitch in the net curtains of the canon's living room.

Stephen waved through the open car window. 'We'll meet up for a pint, Tommy. The three of us.'

'You're on.'

They never did.

THIRTEEN

SUNTANNED and with a close-cropped haircut, Irwin returned to Dublin after four years with his doctorate and a teaching post in Maynooth. When Galvin met him for dinner a few weeks later, he was wearing a charcoal grey suit and a navy tie.

'I like the style,' Galvin remarked while they were having a drink before the meal. 'Stylish but discreet. Washington?'

'Good God, no. They've no taste there. Roma – that's the place. You've got to go to Italy for a suit.' He looked Galvin up and down. 'Are you guys ever going to cop on that the world is changing? What are you all wearing mourning clothes for? Did the cat die?'

While Galvin was relating about the canon and Lizzie, he noticed that Irwin was beginning to fidget and shake his head. 'Jesus, Tommy,' he said at last, 'why are you wasting your time with someone like him? Ask to do further studies; you've a good record. At least you wouldn't be on a fucking one-way ticket to Palookaville.'

'It might seem like time-wasting to you, not to me, Damien. This is going to be my way of living out what I've taken up. And you know what?' He looked straight at Irwin. 'Even though I live with doubts, and see the whole thing as pretty shitty at times, I'll stay with it till I kick the bucket. I know that now. And maybe, if I can make a small change in people's lives – in my own life – that will be enough.'

Irwin tilted the wine bottle towards his own glass. 'I could still swing it for you. I'd be prepared to talk to the Nuncio.'

'No. I don't want you to do that.'

'Listen.' Irwin was irritated. 'Many of the guys here are just going to seed till they hand in their badge and gun. Are you going to be one of them? This life ain't a rehearsal, Tommy. It's a one-act play. You'd better believe it.'

'Things are moving on; there's hope with the Council. And, anyway … .'

'Nothing will change.' Irwin's forefinger shot up. 'Not in this rain-sodden country anyway. Bishops are afraid of their shite of Rome, and Rome is clawing back. John XXIII is dead, dead and buried, and the spirit he fostered is dying with him and, it seems, Paul VI, a decent enough man, but he's not able to stand up to them in the Vatican.' Irwin put down the wine glass. 'Make something of your life. Look at it like this: when you're having breakfast with the Pope and across the table is the head of the Congregation of Bishops, and Benelli, the second most powerful man in Rome, is beside you … .' He looked at Galvin to let the message sink in.

'How did you manage?'

'Networking, Galvin. When will you culchies cop on and learn to look after yourselves?' As ever, when he had wine taken, he was giggling. 'A stroll in the Vatican gardens can do wonders for one's future in Mother Church.'

'You've made it to Maynooth anyway. Congratulations. That's a start.'

'Creeping with conceited old bastards.' Irwin groaned. 'You'll find this hard to credit. One evening, a professor was served brandy not to his liking. "Take that back," he said to the old waiter who was trundling around the professors' dining room. "Not fit for putting in cakes, never mind drinking." They brag at the table; one trying to outdo the other, boasting about the prizes they won when they were students. First in Latin, Greek, canon law – you name it. Then when they've a couple of drinks on board, they give out yards about how they should have been bishops. I've no intention of ending up like those sons of bitches in the valley of fucking missed opportunities.

'Right now the cardinal is using his weight to get a white-headed boy – chap called O'Rourke – into a vacant diocese. One of the profs did the haka when he heard it. "He's pushing a fellow who only scraped through when he was here. I can read Plato in the original Greek, Proust in French. I've read all of Shakespeare. The anointed one was only a pass man when he was here. Now he's laughing his way into the hierarchy. Did some half-baked degree in America." Meant for yours truly, of course. I was in the corridor one day when I met these so-called geniuses.

'"Ah yes, the new kid on the block. And what are *you* lecturing on?" one of them says.

'"Pastoral theology."

'"Pastoral theology," he sneered. "You mean the theology of arsing around." They laughed like hyenas. They weren't interested in me, only asking about J. Desmond and how he is going to be one of the leading lights in theology before long. And a cert for the hierarchy. I'm not staying there.'

'What d'you mean?'

'Pastoral theology is a joke. No future there. I'm in touch with a curial bod. The archbishop should have his letter before long.' He grinned. 'We'll see, Tommy. There are always ways and means.'

That day he kept checking his watch. 'Got to keep an eye on the time,' he said. 'I've a date with the Communications Institute.

Television. Name of the game. And we're only beginning to see how important it will prove to be. The bishops and the Maynooth dons despise the media. Stupid bastards. It's the future. Biggest congregation sits down every night for the nine o'clock news. Make friends with the media, Tommy; they're the new kingmakers.'

THOUGH HE NEVER played golf, Irwin joined Galvin and his clerical friends for dinner in the clubhouse about once a month. He was usually in a flippant mood when they met, laughing and joking about the latest piece of gossip.

His interests lay in the political changes in the country and he was clearly well clued-up on the bishops' thinking. 'They don't trust FitzGerald, and, as for the intellectual wing of the Labour Party, like the Cruiser – can't stand them. But they think they can do business with Haughey.'

'How do you know all this?' one of the golfers asked.

He tapped the side of his nose. 'I've been asked by their lordships to offer some advice on a new religion programme for adults. Oh, nothing much. I wasn't the only one, so no big deal. In any case, I got to stroll around St Joseph's Square with the pointy hats and those looking for a leg up. Shower of yes-men. But Ireland won't hack this for much longer.'

'Not sure about that,' said one of the golfers.

'Read the signs,' Irwin said, chuckling, as they got up from the table to have one last drink at the bar.

NO SOONER had Rome announced that the Pope was coming to Ireland than Irwin secured a place on the organizing committee. And so, the morning after the Phoenix Park mass, when over a million people had arrived with their sandwiches and stools, holding little flags that would merge into a shimmering ocean of saffron and white, Irwin was among the guests at the papal breakfast in the Nunciature.

At the head of a long table, with the Cardinal Primate of All Ireland on his right and the Nuncio of his left, the Pope's cream soutane and skull cap stood out against the black cassocks and crimson piping of the archbishops and the scarlet zucchettos of the three cardinals. Jubilant, the Pope devoured the full Irish breakfast and talked casually about growing up in Poland, the weight of totalitarian Russia on his people and the enjoyment he used to get from skiing.

He listened to what each of the Irish clerics had to say about the state of the country and, when someone spoke, studied him with his deep-set eyes. A country bishop voiced his concern about certain political developments. 'The main party, Holy Father, called Fianna Fáil, is on the side of the Catholic Church. We can trust them.'

The Pope grinned. 'Ah yes, *Fee-ana-fawl*.' Now the penetrating look was turned on the bishop. 'But you have to remember, my Lord, a politician is *always* a politician.'

'Incontrovertibly so, Holy Father, but they are mostly on our side. If the Labour Party gets power in a coalition government, I could see them changing the laws that have served our country well.'

The smile faded from the Pope's handsome face. His powerful fist thumped the table. 'Then the Irish Church will have to work harder.' He seemed to grow bigger as he leaned over the table. 'Like those monks you told me about who lived out on the island. What was the name of it, Monsignor Magee?'

Halfway down the table, Magee, like a dutiful schoolboy, spoke up: 'Skellig Michael, Holy Father.'

'That's the place. They were rugged men and it is men like them who will defend the true faith. Like the Church of Rome established order to Europe. Remember my brother priests, *your endurance will win you your life.*'

The Pope was smiling again; he had unravelled a problem for dull pupils. Though the previous day had been a demanding one – he had celebrated mass in front of the biggest assembly in Dublin since Daniel O'Connell's mass meetings and had travelled to Drogheda to appeal on bended knee to the IRA to lay down its arms – he was brimming with energy.

Irwin finished his plate and gave it a slight push away. 'Yes, the Pope needed that fine Irish breakfast. He is now ready for another day's work.' His smile, familiar by now to television viewers around the world, was bestowed on the long table. He rolled up his napkin, inserted it in a silver ring and, rising from the table, said: 'My brother priests, let us pray and then go about doing the Lord's work.' All bowed their heads.

Afterwards, they stood for a moment, chatting. Bishops were going up to thank the pontiff for visiting their country. The Monsignor in charge of the papal mass joined them and beckoned to Irwin. 'And only for this man, Father Damien Irwin, Holy Father,' he said, 'I wouldn't have been able to get through the workload.'

The Pope studied Irwin. 'We've met, father. Remind me.'

'The Irish College, Holy Father.' Irwin was beaming. 'I played the piano at a St Patrick's Day concert.'

'Monsignor here tells me you are a very good worker and a fine scholar,' the Pope continued and, looking at Archbishop Devlin, added: 'If ever Your Grace could afford to release Father Irwin from his duties, we should be glad to have him working in St Peter's.'

'Holy Father, with God's grace, you will never find me lacking in obedience to the Holy See,' the archbishop replied.

The Pope turned to one of his Vatican aides. 'Now, Monsignor, I wish I had the same unquestioned loyalty from some of my Curial staff.'

'Thank you, Holy Father.' Irwin genuflected to kiss the Pope's ring. They chatted again until Monsignor Magee appeared, holding a black leather folio. 'I'm afraid, Holy Father,' he said, 'I have to interrupt this conversation and give you a further briefing on today's programme.'

FOURTEEN

ONE GLANCE was enough for Galvin to recognize the envelope hanging from his letterbox, for he received few letters addressed to *The Reverend Thomas Brendan Galvin, BA, CC* unless they were from the archbishop. He tore it open and skipped over the formalities – *the many blessings you have brought to the parish … your support to the parish priest … your work with young parishioners.* He read slowly the archbishop's directive. *I have great pleasure in appointing you to the parish of Allenmore. Please present yourself to the parish priest, Father Michael Kennedy, before 7 July to take up your duties. In Jesus Christ, James A. Devlin.*

STUNTED BUSHES leaned against one gable of the presbytery where Michael Kennedy lived. At the other end was a glasshouse with missing panes; the door hung at a slant and struck against the frame in the wind. Troublesome teenagers who drank cider under the bridge called the house Amityville.

Tall and with greying hair, Michael Kennedy still retained the lineaments of the youthful looks that had once caused girls from the town where he had been a curate to head for his confession box of a Saturday night. Father Gregory Peck was their secret name for him.

He brought Galvin to a small room just inside the front door. In it were a table and hard-backed chairs with worn leather seats that had sunk at the middle. A glass case containing old volumes of the *Summa Theologica*, photos and marriage papers stood against one wall. On another wall was a framed black-and-white print: cameos of young priests that filled every space with, at the centre, Pope Pius XII. Ghosting the cameos was the basilica of San Giovanni at Laterano and, at the bottom in calligraphy was written *Ordination Year 1954*.

While giving his new curate a rundown on the parish, Michael kept his eyes on the table in front of him, or else cocked his head and fixed on some point high up in the ceiling. Then he stood to open the door. 'On the whole, the parishioners here are on the side of the priest. You'll be fine.' His hand was already on the door knob. 'Right so, and if there's anything you need done to your house, just let me know and the parish will stump up.'

APART FROM counting the weekend collection on a Monday morning and meeting at the end of the month to add up the totals, the two priests kept at a distance from each other. But after a few months Michael lost some of his natural reserve and invited Galvin to lunch at the Riverside Inn; and from then on a pattern became established. They counted and bagged the Sunday collection, took it to the bank and then drove in Kennedy's car to the Riverside or the Grand or, sometimes, on a special occasion, to the Lord Allen.

Once a month or so, they went over the parish accounts in the sitting room, where, in summer, they had a view of the Dublin mountains through the picture windows. In winter, even with the heavy wine-coloured drapes closed, the old cast-iron radiators gave little heat, so Michael bought a Superser that filled the air with a gaseous smell.

They went over the cheque stubs and entered income and expenditure in a ledger. Each night before they started, Kennedy went straight to a cabinet and poured a whiskey for Galvin and a lemonade for himself. When they had finished their small talk, he always returned to his student days at the Irish College in Rome, and what he wouldn't give to spend a year there and stroll out on sunny mornings to the trattoria outside the gates for an espresso, then over to the St John Lateran Basilica where he had been ordained. 'Rome gets into your system, Tommy,' he said one night at he handed Galvin his Jameson. 'Whenever we had a free afternoon, I went off on my own, traipsing around the city. Heaven. And the hills, Tom, sure, there was nothing like it. I'd have loved to do postgrad studies there.'

'Why didn't you ask?'

'Ah no.' He gave a little laugh that showed a tooth missing on one side. 'You didn't do things like that in those days. That was up to the archbishop, who told me after ordination that my leadership qualities were needed in a parish.' He grinned. 'Must have taken me for a right eejit.'

With Galvin, he was able to shed the image he cultivated for the parishioners: the private figure in the long black coat walking tall up Castle Street after saying the ten o'clock mass. The one who read his homilies in a monotone and never departed from Church teaching.

Galvin was about two years in Allenmore when Michael phoned him early one morning in May. He had fallen and injured his ankle. 'Got out of bed during the night and turned over on my ankle. Must have been a dead leg,' he said. But when Galvin stepped inside the hall door, he was met by a strong smell of whiskey. 'Yeah, can easily happen in the darkness, Tommy.' He was sitting in the armchair with the swollen ankle resting on a footstool. 'You know the way at that hour of the night.'

When he saw Galvin staring at the bottle of Jameson he had forgotten to hide, his false smile dropped. With sad eyes, his collie looked up at him and licked the hand that was limp over the arm of the chair. 'Right, Tom, I suppose my secret is out. I wanted to level with you anyway, for a long time. For the past few years, I've been taking a drink or two, and only at night – that's all, I swear to you on my mother's grave. I hope you will keep it to yourself. You know the way priests ... .' He laughed shyly. 'On the golf course. And sure no one would blame me for taking a whiskey or two at night.'

'No one.'

Then, to Galvin's shock, he hung his head and dissolved into a fit of crying. 'It's the isolation, Tommy. Don't let anyone tell you otherwise. I never thought it would ... .'

'You're right. No denying that.'

'And it gets worse as you go in years. When I was in Rome I asked one of the professors at the Teutonic College: "Does one feel cut off, I mean, as a priest in one of them big presbyteries?" "Certainly not," he'd replied, "you'll have your priest friends and you'll be so busy you won't have time to think of loneliness." He was lying, Tom.' He shook his head. 'Them professors don't know what it's like in a parish. They have their lectures and each other's company in the college.'

The dog kept licking his hand. 'But, Tom,' Kennedy raised his head and blew into a handkerchief, 'it won't happen again. I promise you that.'

'Don't worry about that now, Michael. The main thing is to get you to A&E.'

His foot was in a cast for about six weeks, so Galvin was given the running of the parish, including the chequebooks and the ledger. Every day he went to the presbytery and prepared a meal when the parish priest's part-time housekeeper was on her day off. It was during that time, with his leg resting on a stool, that Kennedy started leafing through *Palgrave's Golden Treasury*. When

he was on his feet again and able to go to the Riverside, he sometimes brought the dog-eared copy with him.

'Ever read Marvell, Tommy?' he asked one day.

'No. Poetry was never my thing. A bit of Yeats or Wordsworth
maybe, but never ... who?'

'Marvell, English poet of the seventeenth century.' And he quoted:

> *The grave's a fine and private place*
> *But none I think do there embrace.*

Over time, Galvin became familiar with his parish priest's
moods: one day some parishioner was the very best, 'salt of the
earth, Tommy', but the tide could turn and the same person could
become 'a devious little man'. And Galvin too, though he didn't
know it, got a lash when Kennedy felt he was getting too much
praise. 'How is Father Galvin?' a woman asked him in Clerys. We
were very sorry to lose him when he left our parish.'

'I can't fault him; he's been a great support, but he has his eye
on higher things, you know. Oh yes. Ambitious.'

In the Grand or in the Riverside, Kennedy was likely to fall into
a silence: then, with a laboured sigh, he would come out with some
remark that would take Galvin by surprise. Like the day he said:
'When I wake of late, I have this ... I don't know how to describe it
... loss. A heavy weight on me.' His mouth twitched in a smile. 'Do
you ever have that?'

'How do you mean "loss"?'

'Ah you wouldn't ... you're young. Like I want to stay in bed,
not do anything. Like one's life has been a waste ... well, no, what
I mean is like dried up or ... .' He looked away towards the river.
'I suppose it has to do with age. Anyway, it clears as the morning
goes on.'

GALVIN WAS about four or five years in Allenmore when a big
change came about in his parish priest. One evening in late February

he noticed him, in dungarees and boots, uprooting the stunted bushes around his house, digging up the soil and replanting. Digging, lifting spadefuls, throwing it back and then stamping on the pedal and sinking the spade again in a way that suggested a floodgate of energy had been opened within him. He cleaned up and dug the fallow ground at the south side of his house for a kitchen garden, and got a tradesman to repair the glasshouse and paint the presbytery. Before long Galvin discovered the reason for his newfound vigour.

A young woman called Sighle who worked in a local branch of the Bank of Ireland where the parish accounts were kept began to chat with them when they took the bags of coins to the bank every Monday. At the counter, while she made out the lodgement slip, she talked to both, but the smiles were for the parish priest. 'Uncle Eugene is a missionary in Kenya. I used to spend summer holidays with him, so I kinda know the ways of priests.'

While putting an elastic band around the lodgement books, she said: 'By the way, Father Michael, as I've said to you already, if ever you want any help with the parish accounts, well … don't be shy about asking.'

'Yes, we might take you up on that, mightn't we, Father Galvin?' His look was that of the teenager who has been told that the village beauty will go with him to the carnival. 'Sure, you're an answer to a prayer,' he told her and turned to Galvin. 'Isn't this great, Father Galvin?' Sighle too looked pleased as she tapped her biro on the pad.

She did the accounts in the parochial house in her spare time, and when the Christmas and Holy Week services came round, she helped the part-time cook to prepare the meal for the neighbouring priests who had come to hear confessions. She also put up holly and ivy, and red-and-green swags in the dining room. And, for the first time since he had come to Allenmore, Michael had a Christmas tree with two sets of fairy lights winking in the front hall.

In a short length of time the house showed signs of Sighle's interest: empty shopping bags and stacks of yellowed newspapers disappeared; the television top no longer had a patina of dust, nor did the odd mouse scurry along the skirting board. New drapes and carpets transformed the look of the sitting room. And on the kitchen table a milk jug, which matched the butter tray, replaced the milk bottle.

Always conscious of the wagging tongues in his parish, Michael made sure they knew about Sighle's work. 'My new accountant,' he told them in Conroy's Foodstore while he was waiting for a few groceries. 'Neither Father Galvin nor myself, God help us, were trained to keep accounts. They never taught us about them things in the seminary.'

'Of course, father,' said Mrs Conroy, who was slicing his ham. And he was so taken up with his explanation, he didn't notice her winking discreetly at one of her customers.

He still invited Galvin to the house to go over the books with himself and Sighle, and to suggest ways they might fundraise or cut back on expenses. And when they were finished, the three of them went to the Grand.

ALL WENT WELL for a couple of years. Parishioners were telling Michael that he looked much better. 'Brighter, father,' one woman told him as she was arranging flowers for the altar one day. He even grew a beard while on a month's holiday with his sister and her family in Boston. They day before he returned, they took his photo before he shaved off the beard.

The confirmation ceremony came about in late May. The parish priest's garden was in flower. The tomato plants in the greenhouse were promising a rich harvest, and there wasn't a weed to be seen in the square of grass at the side of his house. Newly painted garden blocks marked the edges of the lawn. After the confirmation lunch, Kennedy accompanied Archbishop Devlin to his car, which was parked on the freshly tarred apron. The archbishop stood out of hearing distance of his driver, who was holding open the back door of the car. 'How long are you here now, Michael?' He sniffed and worked at his episcopal ring.

'Nearly twenty years, Your Grace.'

'Oh, twenty. Well now, I didn't know you were here *that* long. Right, time for a change then. As providence should have it, there's a vacancy coming up in Arklow. You'd like that.'

Conditioned by years of obedience to mother and Church, Michael, though shocked, could not get himself to question the archbishop's authority, but he did venture: 'There are things to finish, Your Grace. I mean ...' He fidgeted and looked away towards his garden.

The archbishop's fingers tightened on his ring. 'The diocese has needs, father; we can't be selfish about our little projects. Another parish will benefit from your leadership.'

'Yes. Yes of course, Your Grace.'

'You'll be getting official notice this week. I'm sending you to Arklow. Nice seaside town.' He sniffed again. 'Many would jump at the offer. One of the plums of the archdiocese. And they are good country people like yourself.'

'Right so. Thank you, Your Grace.'

The archbishop gathered his cloak around him and got into his car, and Michael was left staring at his own glum look on the gleaming surface of the tinted window.

Sighle would gladly have gone with him had she got a transfer to the Arklow branch, but her family stepped in: they thought it quite odd, anyway, that a young woman should be spending so much time with a man twice her age. The day he was leaving she got an hour off from the bank and drove up to the house to say goodbye and ensure that he hadn't forgotten anything, because lately he had had to phone her to know where he'd left marriage papers or when it was his turn to officiate at baptisms.

While Michael was giving directions to the furniture removal men, Sighle called Galvin into the waiting room. She broke down. 'He was one of the few men who ever looked at me without having only one thing on his mind. He'll not last long; I know it and I know him … . D'you know why he was moved? One of your good Catholics wrote to the archbishop. She's one of that shower of crawthumpers who huddle in the church after daily mass. Said it was a scandal that I should be in the parish priest's house so much. The dried-up old bitch.' She whipped a tissue out of her bag. Gradually, her frown disappeared; she brightened. 'He loved to dance, you know.'

'Goodness me.'

'Yes. After supper, he might say, "Right, Sighle, dancing time." And he would put on a record. But I could swear on the Bible, Tommy, he never laid a hand on me – you know, nothing sexual happened – but at the same time, and I make no bones about this, we loved each other. Of course, he'd kill me if he thought anyone knew about his dancing.'

Hearing the removal men's footsteps coming up the steps to the front door, she steeled herself for the final moment, rose from the chair and set about checking cardboard boxes that she had already labelled and sealed with tape. 'Not a word of this to anyone.'

'It will go with me to the grave.'

When she came back from her holidays, Galvin went to her hatch with the bags of coins. 'How's our friend?' he asked. 'I phoned last week. He's going to invite me down when he's settled in.'

She threw a cautious look around the bank hall. 'Let's have a coffee. Some evening or next Saturday. The Grand.'

'We'll do that.'

No sooner were they seated in the lounge of the Grand the following Saturday than she leaned across the table. 'What sort of crappy organization is this Church you priests belong to?'

'I've been asking myself that.'

'He's going to pieces in Arklow, and no sign of anyone visiting him. Wouldn't you think the archbishop would get someone in there to pick up the phone or hop in his car to motor down? Goodness knows there's no shortage of cars among you lot.'

'Well, he was always a private man.'

'Private man, my eye. Tommy, you wouldn't let a dog on his own like that if you had a screed of humanity in you. He can't remember where he left notebooks or the parish diary and he forgot to turn up for mass – twice. And I know he's pretending when I go down there. "Yes," he says, "and the air is so pure. And the sea. Ah, it's great. Sure I fell on my feet, child."'

He slipped up only once when she asked him about Holly, the terrier they had brought from the dogs' shelter one Christmas to be company for his collie.

'Who?' he'd asked, a flash of the Alzheimer's terror in his eyes, knowing that he had blundered. To deflect from his mistake, he invited her to join the parish pilgrimage to Lourdes.

'I'll go,' she said. 'Not that it means anything to me; stalls full of plastic Virgin Marys, and Holy Jesus opening and closing his eyes when you flick the cheap picture. Holy Jesus ...' Her voice trailed off. 'But I'll go for his sake.'

On his own in Arklow, Michael went into decline. To set his mind at rest and help him get a good night's sleep, he started to take an extra-large measure of whiskey while he sat watching the news and then waited for Sighle's nightly phone call. He tried to show her his best side, but he knew the darkness was closing in, and the isolation of the big old Georgian house, two fields away from the nearest farmhouse, was too much.

At first the parishioners regarded him as a holy man, preoccupied with his prayers, and therefore liable to forget. 'Ah, just a human failing,' they said and kept up the pretence until he forgot to hear confessions or neglected to turn up for a wedding. Then one June morning a farmer found him wandering, his trouser legs drenched from wading through a field of young corn. The farmer called out: 'Are you all right, Father Kennedy?'

'Yes, oh yes, I'm fine ... just going to the chapel to say my rosary.'

The parishioners covered up for him for as long as they could, telling the bishop when he came for confirmations that he was doing great work and was a 'very dignified and prayerful man'. He was a blessed relief from his predecessor, who quoted canon law every Sunday, and told his flock that if any of them were living in an 'irregular relationship' they should on no account present themselves for communion.

Every Sunday morning they knocked on the presbytery door to remind him about the masses. Even the single mother who had been upbraided by his predecessor for daring to come to the altar the morning her child was making his First Communion started bringing him soup and then began looking after his house along with her son. Sometimes Michael called her Sighle, and asked her who the lovely boy was.

Despite the parishioners' best efforts, however, he was slipping away. And when they found him one morning down at the strand digging a hole with a shovel, they phoned the priest in the next parish.

'Come on, Michael,' said the priest. 'You'll catch your death of cold.'

'But I have to finish here first. I'm building a new house for Sighle and myself.' He indicated towards the presbytery on the hill. 'The house is too big now for just the two of us. The family have all gone off, you see.'

'Come on up with me, Michael. My housekeeper will get you a cup of tea and then you can go back to the digging.' The priest laid a hand lightly on his arm while Michael was muttering in a way that made no sense to them. 'We don't dance much anymore.'

'I understand, Michael.'

'The two of us ... we were topping dancers. Every night we'd push the table aside and dance.'

'Yes, you did of course, Michael,' said the priest.

Like a child who has to down his plastic spade and bucket to go in for supper, Michael surrendered the shovel to one of the men who had called the priest, and plodded up the hill, speaking in a low voice: *'How beautiful on the mountain are the feet of him who brings good news.'*

'What's that, Michael?' the priest asked.

Michael stopped, held out his hands and examined the palms, first one then the other. 'I blessed them all on ordination day. My mother was delighted. I chose that for my ordination card, you know: *How beautiful on the mountain …* it was a lovely ordination card.'

'It was. A lovely ordination card.'

Michael raised his handsome head towards the Irish Sea. *'How beautiful on the mountain are the feet of the messenger who announces peace.'* Leading him by the hand, the priest joined in. They plodded up the hill, reciting Isaiah together as they had done many years before in the Pugin chapel. *'Who brings good news. Who announces salvation. And says to Zion, your God reigns.'*

Without knowing why, the men removed their caps and crossed themselves, instinctively aware that they were sharing in a sacramental moment. They felt it was the right thing to do, and even tried to join in. Someone looking on from a distance might be forgiven for thinking that the strange scene – the man in the long black coat, head and shoulders above the rest, and two dogs bringing up the rear – was enacting an ancient ritual. The sea, calm as an Easter morning, was mirroring the blue sky over Arklow.

The priest took Michael to his house, made tea and phoned one of the doctors in the town, who booked him into Roebuck Nursing Home. From then on, he went downhill. Sighle visited him three or four times a week, and the Little Sisters looked after him until he died of a heart attack a few days before Christmas.

At the funeral, when his coffin had been covered over, the grave-diggers, according to an old country custom, laid the shovels in the shape of a cross on the mound of fresh earth. Then they each got down on one knee and said a silent prayer. When they had gone, and the mourners also had disappeared across the road to one of the pubs for lunch, Sighle, who had been standing on her own in a dark gabardine that glistened with rain, stepped forward and bent low to place a red rose on the mound of earth. She remained still for some time until she heard the pub door open, releasing an explosion of Yuletide merrymaking.

FIFTEEN

GALVIN REMAINED on in Allenmore for two years after Michael had been sent to Arklow. Then one day, as he was about to take his golf clubs from under the stairs for the weekly four-ball at Royal Dublin, he received a phone call from the archbishop's house informing him that His Grace wanted to see him at three o'clock the following afternoon.

He put down the phone and tried to second-guess what it was about. He had been six years in Allenmore, so he could very well be a candidate for a change, yet he hadn't received the standard letter informing him of a new appointment, and it wasn't his turn yet to become a parish priest. Sleep that night was fitful.

Archbishop Devlin received him in the dim library, which had remained unchanged since the time he been given a crucifix from the High Command to ward off bad thoughts. He sat opposite the archbishop and, after the small change of polite conversation had been spent, heard him say: 'I'm appointing you to the post of diocesan secretary.'

The archbishop looked small behind the desk, as if he were a boy playing out a bishop fantasy. 'Discretion and loyalty, and a willingness to carry out my wishes are, of course, absolute requirements for any priest entrusted with this position.' His narrow lips jerked back and forth as he spoke and his skin stretched over his lean features. 'My sources tell me you don't lack those qualities. Needless to say, I make up my own mind on these matters.'

A woman with glasses hanging from a string around her neck padded in, bearing a tray with a pot of coffee and a plate of biscuits; after a brief introduction, while she poured the coffee, she left as quietly as she had entered. The archbishop hoped Galvin would be very happy as diocesan secretary. He listed his duties, and added: 'You will be expected to wear your soutane at all times in the house.' Galvin would live in the Victorian mansion that accommodated the chancellery and other diocesan agencies such as education and child adoption.

'Indeed, I'm not unmindful also of your kindness to Father Kennedy,' was the archbishop's parting comment at the front steps. 'Go on a fortnight's holidays before you take up your duties. Your work will be demanding, but, I trust, you will find contentment here. God bless.'

As soon as he had said the early morning mass in a local convent, Galvin's duties began: presenting documents for the archbishop to sign and sorting which letters he himself would open and which were for the archbishop's private mail. Usually Devlin joined him to read those in the personal tray. Occasionally the sluggish sounds of buses and lorries out on the Drumcondra Road invaded their concentration as the two men went over any issues that needed their immediate attention. Periods of silence were broken only by the slitting open of envelopes.

Except for Saturdays and the occasional Sunday, Galvin and one of the other priests on the staff had a working lunch with Devlin in the house. They were usually joined by the chancellor and the master of ceremonies who taught liturgy in St Paul's. After lunch they took a constitutional in the seminary grounds, where Devlin regaled them with stories of life in the college towards the end of the Second World War when the central heating was poor and they had to wear topcoats while studying in their rooms.

From January to May – the confirmation season – Galvin drove the archbishop to the various parishes and, during that time, learned to judge his moods: when to ask him for some favour for a priest, when to give him a wide berth. If he was in good humour, especially returning from the confirmation ceremony, the archbishop held forth on his favourite topics: his admiration for Winston Churchill and boxing, and Seneca, the Roman who lived during the golden age of Latin literature.

The haemorrhage of priests leaving the Church, a feature of post-Vatican Council days, was subsiding. Nevertheless, letters seeking laicization reached him a few times a year: leave-takings, which were followed by a deep sense of loss by their class colleagues and friends, and locker-room gossip among priests given to idle chatter. 'He couldn't escape, burning the candle at both ends,' or, with a derisive laugh, 'A mother's vocation – never should have been ordained.'

Each letter of resignation weighed heavily on the archbishop and dominated the lunchtime walk around St Paul's. In the middle of a conversation, he was likely to cut in: 'It's a betrayal of a man's sacred calling, fathers, and the promises he made at ordination. A serious sin.'

'Yes, Your Grace.'

With a new pope in Rome, the gloves came off. The word from St Peter's was that Paul VI was too soft in doling out laicizations. From now on priests would be refused laicization except when they had fallen from grace and were a scandal to the faithful.

It was all too late. Scornful of Vatican bureaucracy and fed up with the Church anyway, some priests packed their bags, threw the church keys on the vesting bench of the sacristy and got married in a register office. Those who wished to be granted a decree of laicization and then have a church wedding were advised to see Galvin. 'He'll tell you how to approach the boss.'

They picked up the phone. 'But, Tom, I don't want to see sight or light of that place,' they might say in reference to St Paul's, so they would meet in Wynn's for lunch or have coffee in Bewley's. And even though many of them had been in the seminary with Galvin, and their paths had crossed at clerical meetings or at the annual retreat, their hands trembled when they raised their coffee cups to their lips.

On a return journey from Lourdes with parish pilgrims, one priest had met a stewardess on board an Aer Lingus flight, causing Devlin to flare up when he received his letter of resignation. 'I had plans for that man, Father Galvin. Talent like his is getting scarce on the ground.' He pitched the letter onto the tray and began to work at his ring. 'Why, oh why? The first woman who pays them any attention causes them to lose any blessed bit of sense they have. Are they not saying their prayers, father? Don't they know that women, bless them, are … capable of leading any man astray? No matter how strong he is.'

In Bewley's one day, a priest gave Galvin an account of his meeting with the archbishop. 'I thought he would be supportive, give me some fatherly … Jesus, I was so naive. D'you know what he says to me?' He shook his head in frustration. '"I'd be concerned for your immortal soul."' He looked Galvin in the eye. 'Remember father, "anyone who puts his hand to the plough and looks back is not worthy of the kingdom of God".'

Having left the archbishop's house in a daze that day, the priest told Galvin how he had trudged out into the chilly autumn evening and waded across the senior playing pitch of St Paul's towards the river: with the dramatic drop in numbers, the pitch was no longer used for sports, so that the long grass soaked the ends of his trouser legs. He was trying to hide from the archbishop's fierce condemnation. Adam cast out of Eden. 'As your bishop, I advise you, father, to rethink such a rash decision and separate from this woman.'

He stopped wading. Catholic guilt and seven years of conditioning about the bishop being a father to his priests were driving him to distraction. He turned on his heel and shuffled up the hill towards the mansion. He would ask for a blessing at least; that would put his mind at rest.

The woman with the glasses answered the door, and, glancing at his anorak and wet trouser legs, was in no doubt that he was a toucher looking for a handout.

'I'd like to see His Grace for five minutes, please.' His eyes were red from crying.

'I'm afraid you cannot see him now. His Grace is at another meeting.' Her hand had edged towards the door handle.

'Please. Five minutes. I was with him only half an hour ago.'

'He's not to be disturbed.'

'Father Galvin?'

'Father Galvin is not here today.'

'Sorry you had to go through all that. I'll see what I can do,' Galvin said as they walked out onto Grafton Street. 'Try not to let it get you down. We'll find a way.' They shook hands.

'Thanks, Tom,' said the priest. 'Have to go. Kate is browsing in Weir's.'

The priest's story corresponded with others Galvin had heard, so he bided his time until the right moment: the day Devlin learnt that a nephew, a consultant in the Mater, had become a professor. The news put him in a sunny mood, so Galvin contrived to bring the conversation round to the upcoming summer appointments. When the archbishop remarked that they would be short five priests on the previous year – 'those who couldn't keep on their trousers' – Galvin grabbed the opportunity.

'All the same, Your Grace, it must be a difficult time for them. Many sleepless nights I'm sure.'

'Yes,' Devlin reflected, 'but then they ought to have prayed for perseverance and not run off with the first woman that gave them the glad eye.'

'With the greatest respect, Your Grace, I wonder would you reconsider the use of phrases such as: "I'd be concerned for the loss of your immortal soul." They're usually … well, very vulnerable.'

Devlin raised his head and sniffed. 'So you question my right to point out the error of their ways. You are now going to dictate to your archbishop. Is that it?'

'Of course not, Your Grace, it's just that …'

'*Anyone who puts his hand to the plough and looks back is not worthy of the kingdom of God.* Would you question our Divine Master's own words also?'

'Nor am I taking issue with your right to address the situations as you find them. It's just that … .'

'Good, father. You will answer to the Lord for your steward-ship, and I for mine.' Devlin showed one of his enigmatic smiles. 'No, one has – above all – to be faithful to the words of the Divine Master.'

'Yes, Your Grace.'

OTHER THAN Friday evenings, every hour of Galvin's day was filled with meetings and appointments. In September he went with the archbishop on the annual diocesan pilgrimage to Lourdes, and when Devlin submitted an account of the diocese – the *ad limina* – to Rome, he went also.

At night, when the stenographers had left the downstairs offices and the cook had gone home, the two of them were alone in the archbishop's house, a Victorian mansion set in from the road and hidden by mature trees. Apart from meeting at supper in the base-ment kitchen, each of them stayed in his own apartment: Galvin following up on some unfinished work of the day, Devlin preparing an address for a forthcoming assembly. Low-burning lights remained on in the wide corridors. Ambulance sirens speeding for the Mater Hospital burst in on the stillness of the house and then faded again.

The work conferred order on Galvin's day and was a welcome relief from the humdrum functions of a curate at the beck and call of a self-opinionated parish priest. As he eased into the job, he found great satisfaction in being a buffer between distressed priests and the archbishop. On the golf course, priests who had been calloused into cynicism claimed he was building a power base and had an eye to his future career. The best they would say was: 'Ah, he's not bad, but he's a fixer and a politician. That's plain to see. And a churchman through and through.'

'Sure, all of them who work in there have their eye on bigger things.'

'You never said a truer word.'

Galvin was meeting the requirements of the clerical life as had been prescribed by the rector in St Paul's – *keep the rule and the rule will keep you* – although patches of psoriasis on his arms, which he had had since his student days, flared up now and again and the faint drumbeat of anxiety that had worried him in St Paul's caused him fitful sleep, especially after a bad day. On a few occasions he had had mild panic attacks while saying mass and, some mornings, on waking, his head was in a mist: Michael Kennedy's fatigue crossed his mind during those moments. Traces of the doubts about the priestly life which had worried him in the seminary were seeping through the walls of his defence.

While they were opening the mail one day, Devlin handed him a slip of paper.

'I want you to go to that address. It's where a priest has been living until he betrayed his calling.' He released a heavy sigh. 'Look over the house and see what needs to be done before the next man moves in. I try to ensure that conditions for my priests are up to the required standard, especially for young men moving into a first appointment. Parish priests can be tight with the purse strings.'

Though unyielding in most respects, he was given credit in the diocese for the care he took with priests' houses.

The inspection became a constant in Galvin's work schedule, an inspection that the parish priests resented. 'Is it that he doesn't trust me, is that it?' one parish priest muttered as he stomped around the sacristy. 'How do I know where that man left the keys of the house before he reneged on his priesthood?' He fumbled in pigeonholes used for keeping sacred oils and rituals. 'Does the archbishop think I've nothing else to do than search for keys? I'll have to give that man a piece of my mind.' He slapped the keys on the vesting bench. 'There. And make sure you bring them back.'

'Certainly, father.'

He showed Galvin out of the church and headed for his car, his short bandy legs in a half trot. Galvin put the bunch of keys with the fob showing the logo of Liverpool Football Club on the car seat beside him and drove to the address.

Though in a street of fine red-brick houses with dahlias, gladioli or lupins in the front gardens, and bordered by low walls or picket fences, the priest's house looked unloved. The garden was overgrown, the curtain rod in one of the windows had fallen, buddleia was growing out of a chimney flue. When he turned the key, he had to push the front door against a mound of letters. Old trousers covered in paint stains lay in a heap on the landing. In the living room, papers and clutter were heaped on a low table that showed coffee-mug rings.

Galvin glanced with a sinking feeling at the dead spaces where the priest had lived for eight years. Their conversation over a beer they had had in the Leopardstown Inn came back to him. 'I'm out, Tommy. Can't take anymore.' He had wanted Galvin's advice about writing the formal letter of resignation to the archbishop. 'What qualifies me to go out there on a Sunday morning and preach to them about life, when they know much more about it than I do?' He looked for Galvin's reaction. 'I've no intention of being a messenger boy for Devlin's missives or for the old guys in the Roman Curia.' He smiled and raised the glass to his lips. 'Anyway, I don't believe any of it any longer.'

On an open bureau was a pile of ESB and telephone bills, papers and notebooks. Galvin picked up the *status animarum* book, a diary used by priests when on house-to-house visitations. He leafed through it. One entry showed: *5.05.1984. Visited six houses this evening. They were pleasant, and told me about a predecessor who used visit their house. 'Nice man, but he had no idea of time, father, and my husband having to get up in the morning.' I didn't stay long.* Another entry: *19.10.1986. Tackled by a bitch on Vatican wealth and priceless treasures. Who do they think I am? The Pope? Enough problems.* And right on the doorstep of Christmas: *22.12.1990. Children's confessions for the past few days; driving me demented: 'I spoilt love when I took me brother's marbles.' No life for a grown man.*

Signs of dampness showed on the ceiling of the bedroom and patches of fresh carpet were visible where the furniture had stood. On one of the beds was a heap of rumpled blankets and an eiderdown. A jotter with a marble design cover lay on a dusty bookshelf: nearly every page had set out the day's programme with notes added. One page was dated 28 March 1985:

> *Morning Prayer and reflection*
>
> | 10 | *Mass* |
> |------|--------|
> | 10.45 | *Visit schools until break time. Coffee with teachers* |
> | 2 | *Prepare homily* |
> | 4 | *Rehearsal with children for Holy Week and Easter* |
> | 5 | *Visitation of houses* |
> | 7. 30 | *Vincent de Paul meeting, and then youth club* |

He closed the copybook and trudged the bare floorboards until his eye caught a framed text in calligraphy that had been thrown into a wicker basket. The glass had cracked. *To live in the midst of the world with no desire for its pleasures; to be a member of each family, yet belonging to none, to share all the sufferings, to penetrate all secrets …* It was inscribed *To dearest Marty, from your loving auntie, Mother Mary Bernadette. Remembering you fondly on the anniversary of your ordination.*

He looked away through the window towards the pitiless granite church. He could recite the rest from memory; part of the diet at St Paul's: *… to have a heart of iron for chastity; and a heart of bronze for charity … O Priest of Jesus Christ.*

The following morning at his meeting with Devlin, he reported what he'd seen and how sad it was to read the Lacordaire piece. The archbishop interrupted him. 'You're being sentimental, father. Married people have to put up with struggles also. I'm sick to death of hearing sob stories from priests about how lonely they are. If half of them got off their backsides and did a proper day's work, they'd be too tired to think about loneliness. Now let's get on with our work.'

A few mornings later Galvin woke before five o'clock; his head was filled with another vague sense of his life growing more arid by the day. Fifty years old in a week. Where had it gone? The rain that had been lashing the roof all night was still pouring down. He sat for a while on the edge of the bed to come to terms with the niggling whisper: *You're not getting any younger. Is this the way you want to go to your grave – nursing crashed priests?*

Seven-thirty mass in the convent followed by a full diary, however, managed to keep at bay unsettling thoughts, and yet, like someone who denies the onset of arthritis at the first twitch of pain on a stairway, he knew the half-formed questions were ones he didn't want to face.

Just before Christmas of that year, Devlin felt a cold coming on and asked Galvin to represent him at a St Vincent de Paul benefit night in the National Concert Hall. 'I need to be in good health for the ceremonies. Please convey my apologies and best wishes to all for a happy Christmas,' he said as he gave him a cheque for the Society.

'I'll be glad to do that, Your Grace.'

SIXTEEN

WHEN HE arrived at the concert hall, two old ladies wrapped in tweeds were linking arms with each other on the icy steps. He held open the doors for them and then stood for a moment to inspect the gathering. Cast in amber, a party was in full swing: women in furs with hot whiskeys or cups of coffee raised daintily to their lips. Men in dress suits. A line at the box office. Young women in maroon uniforms stole a glance at themselves in pier glasses as they strode around selling programmes. The walls were festooned with red and green. The spicy smell of Christmas streamed through the opening between the glass doors. He'd seen it all before when accompanying Devlin, but on those occasions he had had just a walk-on part. Now he was the bishop's man, who would be shown around by the Knights of Columbanus and introduced to important people before the concert began.

Memories of the Main Hall as it was when the building was part of the university came winging back. He sees his comrades in black, young nuns with bird-like glances and briefcases hurrying to the lecture halls, Sarah Clifford in her cream mackintosh outside the door of the Kevin Barry Room, Mac's laughing face.

As soon as the knights saw him, they rushed to the door. 'Will His Grace be well soon?'

'Ah, yes. Just a cold, but he didn't want to run the risk of spreading it around.'

'Most thoughtful,' one of the knights nodded. 'And he needs to be in the full of his health for the Christmas ceremonies.'

A round of introductions followed. 'How do you plan to spend Christmas, father? Probably busier than ever,' a woman wearing a mink stole asked him. As she fidgeted, her jewellery glittered beneath the droplet chandeliers.

'Like other years. Go to my sister in Cork and spend a night with a brother in Rathfarnham and then I've to be back at my post.' Hearing his own voice, he caught sight of a Christmas Day stretching out ahead of him: nieces' and nephews' children playing and arguing over some game or other, and his brother, a garda superintendent, getting drunker by the minute.

From overhead came an announcement: 'The concert will begin in five minutes. Please take your seats.'

Shortly after the second half, the compère announced that he was delighted to introduce the next performer: 'A young lady just back from Milan, where she is carving a brilliant career for herself. Ladies and gentlemen, I give you Miss Muireann O'Dwyer.' The audience applauded. Galvin, who had been peering at his programme, removed his reading glasses and looked up to see her walking towards the centre of the stage. Her red lipstick matched the colour of her long dress. That lady will be in trouble with her weight before long was his initial reaction. He stole a glance at his watch: another blasted hour to go.

With much posturing, the conductor kissed her hand. She smiled to the audience as the conductor raised his baton. The orchestra played the opening bars of 'O Holy Night'. The stage lights caught the sheen on her black hair, gathered up from the neck. She began. *'O holy night the stars are brightly shining / It is the night of the dear saviour's birth.'*

Galvin sat up. The sheer beauty of her singing voice washed away any trace of the weariness that had enveloped him when he'd looked through the glass doors. His programme dropped to the floor. The main beam over the stage was dimmed so that the indigo backdrop with pinhead lights behind the orchestra became a starry night sky. He joined in the lavish applause. The soprano sang other songs and finally 'Jerusalem' for an encore.

By now he couldn't take his eyes off her. At one stage she scanned the front rows and he could swear she looked straight at him and smiled. A warm smile. The man on the street wouldn't give her a second glance, but something in her face hinted that she would have a great capacity for friendship: a woman he could spend Christmas Day with and not find it tedious. During the applause that followed her encore, one of the knights turned to him. 'Great, isn't she, father?'

It was an effort to appear casual. 'Yes. Fine voice.'

When the concert was over, Galvin strolled out with the knights to the foyer and joined in the chat, but quickly lost interest when he spotted her coming through one of the exits with members of the orchestra. She had let her hair down over her shoulders, and was wearing dark-rimmed glasses and a black coat that reached her ankles. One of the knights rushed over and asked her to join them.

Although he was used to meeting bishops and government ministers – even the Pope – Galvin talked too much when they were introduced. 'You've … that was beautiful. A great voice. The best rendering of 'O Holy Night' I ever heard. And Milan. Isn't it special? And did you take in Florence and Pisa while you were there? Where does your career go from here?'

He wanted to prolong the conversation but became aware of the others whose chat had lapsed and who were throwing discreet glances in his direction. 'We are taking Muireann across to the Hilton, father, for a sandwich.' One of them seemed amused at Galvin's flushed face. 'Would you care to join us?'

'Well, I suppose I should be getting back to Drumcondra.' Checking his watch was a put on. 'Yes. Why not? It's Christmas after all.'

In the lounge of the hotel, the pianist on the mezzanine was playing in the shade of a palm tree. Hanging from the walls between the green swags were Christmas wreaths, glitter and tinsel. The scent of mulled wine carried in the air. Galvin's earlier reluctance to be part of the celebratory mood had fallen away.

During his chat with Muireann O'Dwyer, while the knights were discussing meetings and programmes for the New Year, he lowered his voice. 'Perhaps you'd consider sharing your rare talent with the congregation at one of our churches some Sunday morning. Say the Pro-Cathedral or Westland Row?'

'Be glad to, father. I'm often out of the country, but if you give me enough notice, I'd be delighted.'

'Great. I'll have a word with the director of the Palestrina.' Their conversation confirmed his first impression, that he would be able to talk to her about anything – that dull ache when he wakes in the morning, doubts about the afterlife. About God. She had a turned eye and was inclined to squint but that for him was a beauty spot. He already loved the way she'd let out a sudden nervous laugh and gather her long hair to draw it together in a soft rope over one shoulder. Perfect.

HE GOT HER to sing in the Pro-Cathedral at the anniversary mass for the acclaimed soprano Margaret Burke Sheridan; then, against his better judgment, he wrote to her – news mostly, work he was involved in. In one letter, he told her *Your talent is something to thank God for.* Ignoring his outpourings of praise, she wrote back about concerts she was doing. When she returned from Milan that July, he suggested they meet for lunch, *just to catch up.*

That lunch was the first of many and, all the while, he clung to his own version of reality: this is a friendship, satisfying to us both, and that is the way any sane person should see it. And, anyway, spending hours listening to troubled priests, he needed someone to listen to him for a change. And she was great at listening.

Harry Sheerin rang him one Sunday night. 'So the dark horse is throwing off the traces. surprising us all.' He guffawed into the phone. 'Woah, boy.'

'What's wrong with you, Harry?'

'You and the diva, mate. You're a cosy item.'

'I don't know what—'

'Tommy, you know well when you're seen twice with the same woman in a restaurant, you're bedding her. I came across a diocesan gossiper in Eason's; he'd spied you in the St Lawrence. Apparently, he and his clique were having one of their long drawn-out lunches. The gobshite was laughing, said you were so taken up in her, you didn't spot them, even though they passed right by your table. Just marking your card, mate. Those shitheads would be only too glad to see you take a tumble, so *bith curamach*. In no time it would reach his nibs, if it hasn't already.'

'For God's sake – aren't there fourteen years between us? Muireann has a man in her life, an Italian conductor.' And to strengthen his hand, he added what he knew was a lie. 'She tells me her engagement isn't far off.'

'To whom? You?' Another guffaw.

A force within Galvin, which he had suppressed for many years, was now demanding to be heard, so that he frequently caught himself lost in a fantasy world with Muireann. He became distracted a couple of times in his work: once he forgot to make out the confirmation list for the archbishop; another time he left a priest who was applying for laicization waiting in Wynn's Hotel for half an hour.

That taught him a lesson. He needed help. One evening when he had finished work, he rang the religious house where the spiritual director he had consulted in the early years of his priest-hood lived.

'He is no longer a priest,' the receptionist told him. 'He's a psychotherapist now.' Galvin left his telephone number for the therapist to ring him back.

'If you wish to avail of psychotherapy, my office door is open,' the former Franciscan priest told him when they spoke over the phone.

'This could be a major turning point in my life, so I need to consult a professional like yourself.'

'Then I advise you to think about it for a couple of weeks. This is not spiritual direction. We will have some preliminary meetings. Thing is … you may not want to continue as a priest when you have finished. You may discover a desire that has lain hidden all your life, one that is fundamental to your being.'

'I'll give it a try,' Galvin said when the three preliminary meetings had been completed. 'Anyway, if you're out at sea and you're sinking, like I seem to be, you'll grab at anything. Yes, I'll take a chance.'

Twice a week, Galvin lay on the couch and told the therapist about Muireann. She is unique. The smell of her perfume. The exciting world in which she lives, the company of talented artists and conductors, the way, in an abstracted moment, she smooths her hair into a rope and draws it down over one shoulder. 'My aim is make up for the disappointments she has suffered in her life.'

'What disappointments?'

'The chap from the London Philharmonic who left her high and dry after they had been going out together for three years. Told her she was a spoiled child and that no one could live up to her dad.'

'Really! Something you might bear in mind.'

'No. We love each other. And that's all that matters. Love conquers all.'

The silence of the therapist was unnerving and yet, it gave him a free run to say whatever came into his mind, such as the few days, every six weeks or so, they were able to get away to M.J.'s summer house, west of Dingle town. 'After dinner we watch the sun going down behind the Blasket Islands. Arcady.'

He recalled the evening he had returned from Dingle town with groceries, wine and cheese, and he found her crying while *Madama Butterfly* played in the background – the parting of Butterfly and Pinkerton. He dropped the groceries on the draining board and fell to his knees beside her. 'What's wrong, Muireann?'

'We listened to that together only a month before he ... .'

'Who, love? Who are you talking about?' Fearing she had in mind her former lover, he drew her close.

'My dad.'

While she snuffled, her face took on the aspect of a lost child, but, after a while, she dried her eyes and a weak smile showed as she described how the two of them used listen to all the great composers. 'Saturday mornings I was in heaven because he didn't have to go to the College of Music where he was a professor. You know what he used to do? It drove me crazy.' Her face brightened. 'He would buy three different records of a Mozart or Beethoven symphony, play them in succession and note down the slightest shade of difference in arrangement. I would be fit to strangle him.'

Holding her hand, Galvin rested his back against the sofa while she talked on about the times when she would devise a plan to be alone with her father in the car when he was going to buy tobacco or a paper. 'Then I would say, "Dad, it's a beautiful day. Let's drive to Dun Laoghaire and we'll be back before the others know it."'

A wave of defeat coursed through Galvin and a whisper of warning from within told him that he would never match 'Dad'; nonetheless, he drew her to him again. 'We've created something good. And I will make up to you what you lost when you were a child.'

She looked strangely at him, but he continued to reassure her. 'As soon as the time is right, I will apply for laicization. I will.' He kept stroking her hair while staring over her shoulder at the

Blaskets, turning dark and gloomy and abandoned, in the middle of the ocean.

'Life would be too bleak to even contemplate if she weren't … .' he told the therapist.

'Weren't what?'

'In my life.' Instead of receiving answers or words of consolation and 'everything will be well, and keep your crucifix beneath your pillow', all the therapist said at the end of the half hour was: 'It's not easy, but it's part of the human condition. Could be a fruitful time in your life.'

The weeks turned into months, the months rolled on and, all the while he was trying to justify his being in love. 'I am working harder and, after all, the spiritual books nowadays are saying that a priest needs to have "a significant other".'

'You said. Now how did you put it? "I threw myself into seminary life to forget Sarah Clifford." And the girl you met in London, how you "mourned her loss".'

'So I haven't grown much. Is that it?'

'Love is blind. Isn't that what we say? Right. We'll stop there. See you on Thursday.'

Angered because the therapist wasn't seeing how special Muireann was, or how unique was their experience, Galvin made up his mind that he wouldn't be back. But in spite of himself he continued to return and began making snide remarks about priests who desert their calling. His frustration at failing to get a response turned into rage. 'This pagan thing that you are practising. Very obvious to me you've lost all screed of faith. I was advised to steer clear of therapists and to go to a good spiritual director. That's what I should have done.'

'Very likely he or she would give you plenty of advice. I don't dole out platitudes, certainly not to someone with your awareness of life. But I will support your struggle, even if you will do most of the work.'

While all this was going on, a change was coming about between him and Muireann. They started to argue about small things. She was often late for their appointments and a couple of times she forgot completely. Then one night after a gin and tonic each, and a bottle of wine with their meal, she lured him into an argument about music. When he was trying to bluff, she let him have it. 'Oh, come on,' she said with sarcasm. 'You wouldn't know an oboe from an elbow.' That was the night she confronted him again about their future. 'You've nothing to lose.' Gone now were the endearments, the soft looks emanating from her brown eyes. Nights in Arcady. And the sun going down behind the Blaskets. Instead, sitting upright with her arms folded, she glared at him across the restaurant table.

'Last year you said you would apply for laicization. Well? Where's the letter? We've been over this before.' She had raised her voice and those at other table were throwing guarded looks in their direction. When he began to stammer and hedge, she threw her linen napkin on the table, picked up her bag and, before she stormed out, whispered in his ear: 'You want it both ways. Go and fuck yourself.' He looked away through the window at the rainy night and spotted her getting into a taxi on the Terenure Road.

That was the first of many arguments: she demanding an answer, he pleading that she be patient until he found the right moment and when that didn't happen, she making excuses about meeting. Eventually she made her declaration: 'Live in the real world and, when you've done that, you may be able to relate in an adult way. I'm not one who hangs around.'

Some months later, he got a card from her. *Despite it all, Tom, thanks for everything. I'm off to Milan for a couple of months.* That was the last they heard from each other.

For weeks he woke at four and stared into the darkness until it was time to rise, yet he had to continue as if everything was fine. *I got on OK before I ever met her*, he told himself. *It was only a passing fancy*. And, anyway, people did split up, even those who had invested years of their lives in a marriage and had reared families together. That attempt to raise his spirits, however, was short-lived, like an unusually mild day in late winter when everyone is saying that spring has arrived and the next day hailstones are dancing on windscreens. So when a woman wearing Muireann's perfume passed him by on the street, she brought it all back: exciting moments when he had searched the glass display units of Brown Thomas for Nina Ricci's *L'Air du Temps*, or for earrings at Christmas, all the while keeping a weather eye out for anyone who might know him.

In the void that followed, he let fly all the more at his nearest target – the therapist. 'What are you doing anyway?' He was staring at a picture of the Goose Girl above the couch. 'Sitting there like the Buddha. Have you any idea of the pain I'm going through?'

It was as if he were drunk or that a frenzied creature had been living inside him and had now taken possession of his mind. Jekyll and Hyde. The man who was 'good to talk to', the one who tolerated Devlin's moods, was cursing and swearing at Catholic Ireland, at himself. 'How could I be so deluded as to take on such an insane way of life? Answer me that, you who have read all these books.'

Then, when he calmed down, like someone coming out of a drunken state, he was full of shame and apologies, and guilt for 'Going on in a way that isn't me. I made a promise to myself coming up to ordination that I would give women a wide berth. I thought I had my life under control – archbishop's secretary, priests looking for my advice, golfing friends – and then this happens to me! I thought falling in love was only for young blokes. Now I'm a slave to these bloody feelings.'

'No. You're doing good work … much-needed work. See you Monday.'

SEVENTEEN

DESPITE HIS FRUSTRATIONS, Galvin continued to be a cushion between the archbishop and those priests who were looking for leave of absence. Some were on the edge of a breakdown, telling him how they were crying themselves to sleep. 'Burn-out, Tommy. I need time to recharge the batteries, if you know what I mean.'

'I understand what you're saying.'

From behind his desk in the archbishop's house, or in some café, he listened to them and, despite his resolve, his mind strayed towards Muireann, wondering where she was at that moment. He had the urge to say 'Yes' to priests who were carrying the burden of defeat on their shoulders. 'Yes, I know well what you're talking about. And I think compulsory celibacy is nothing more than the Church's way of controlling our lives and, furthermore, a kick in the teeth to women.' But he couldn't say those things. He was Devlin's bag-carrier.

At times he emerged from the twisted skein of his life to hear some priest say: 'You know, I feel better now, Tommy. And you never judge anyone. You're in the right job. I wish I had control of my life like you. Don't know how you do it. And you're so grounded.'

But he was still slipping. Once he missed Benediction in the convent where he was chaplain. Instead of bringing it up with him in the convent parlour where she was dropping in to say a polite 'hello' while he ate his breakfast, the reverend mother phoned the archbishop. 'I wouldn't mind but it was the feast day of one of our elderly sisters and she was very upset, Your Grace. And I'm only making this telephone call out of concern for father.'

'Very thoughtful of you, mother,' said Devlin. 'I will speak to Father Galvin. He is very busy at present. He has a lot on his mind.' When he put down the phone, he sniffed and said to the books that lined the far wall of his library: 'Your concern is edifying, Reverend Mother, and, yes, father has a lot on his mind right now. God help him.'

The following day while they were going over the mail, the archbishop glanced out of the window. 'The laburnums are in all their glory.' He indicated the hanging yellow blossoms in the back garden.

'What's that, Your Grace?' Galvin raised his head and looked to where Devlin was pointing. 'The laburnums. Oh yes, the laburnums are beautiful.'

'Can be toxic – did you know that, father?'

'No, I didn't.'

'Oh yes,' Devlin returned to his letters with a sigh. 'As so often happens, God's great beauty reflected in nature, or indeed, embodied in special people can, if we go too near, flatter to deceive – cause us pain.' He sniffed. 'Look at what happened to our friend Icarus.'

'Icarus? Oh yes, Icarus. Got his wings … .'

'Scorched. Flew too close to the sun, father. We have to be careful that our heads aren't turned. The bard was usually good on these human situations, now what's … ah yes: *When the blood burns, how prodigal the soul lends the tongue vows.*'

During all this time, Galvin's estimate of his own life was plummeting. He was a dogsbody, Devlin's trusty retainer who opened his letters but was kept at arm's length from discussions the archbishop held with the vicars general. He understood now Michael Kennedy's waking in the morning and being sick in his heart, and he cursed the day he was ordained. He should have become an engineer and worked with M.J.

How could he have known in the seminary what he was now denying himself, like the deep satisfaction when he woke in the small hours to hear the rise and fall of Muireann's breathing when they slept together in the Dingle cottage? In St Paul's when he had talked with others about the sacrifices they were making, they had glossed over them with a trite comment: 'Well, all the priests that have gone before us have managed. And since the eleventh century. And anyway, we get the grace of ordination. You worry too much, Tommy.'

The argument seemed convincing and got lost in preparations for the next soccer game against Holy Cross, or the next debating contest against All Hallows.

'Becoming a priest was one unmitigated disaster,' he told the therapist. 'What am I? Can you answer me that after all your studies?' Lying on the couch, his hand swept over the books that lined the walls and, knowing by then that he would never get an answer, his hand fell to his side. And he cried for the first time since he had hunkered on the riverbank when Mac had been expelled. 'No. I'll tell you what I am. I'm a toady. A fucking toady who is at the beck and call of the archbishop. Hah, archbishop. D'you know what? He'll be like all the others … .'

'What have you in mind there?' The therapist's tone was steady but paternal.

'One day he'll be wheeled down to the crypt of the Pro-Cathedral and he'll be piled on top of the other coffins to make way for his successor. That's what will become of him. Forgotten while he gathers dust.' Breathing heavily, he rested for a while in silence. 'I'm kicking myself I didn't take up my brother's invitation to join him.'

'You'd be happy building houses?'

'I'd have something to show for it at the end of my days. Yeah, I think I would be happy. Something manly and natural, not the company of those who fill their days pirouetting and prancing around in lace albs. The best of us of gone, you know.' He raised himself on one elbow and turned around to look at the therapist. 'I was drawn in by the power of the message – the heroic thing, you know, *give and not count the cost*. Well, I'm afraid the cost is too high.'

With a slight gesture of his hand, the therapist indicated that Galvin should lie back. 'I did tell you at the beginning that you may not wish to continue in the priesthood. You are making a major decision about your life, maybe for the first time.'

Galvin rested his head on the bolster. 'I think I'm going crazy.'

'You most certainly are not.'

'Jesus, what a mess. I don't know what I'm going to do. If I leave, I still have a chance to meet a woman, start a family and one Sunday when my children are grown up and have their own children, they'll come and visit me and we'll go to the beach, erect a wind-breaker maybe, buy ice-cream … ordinary everyday things that normal people do.'

'Normal, hah, I wonder what that is?' The therapist's creaking chair indicated that the session was over.

With a hangdog look Galvin got up from the couch. 'More normal than this crucifixion.'

GALVIN ASKED Devlin for a three-month sabbatical to reflect on his life. 'Your Grace, I'll be celebrating my silver jubilee this year and I'd like time to pray and reflect.'

'I see.' The thin lips were twitchy. 'But it won't be easy to replace you at relatively short notice. Of course I won't stand in your way, much as I need your support and, indeed, friendship. I'm fully in agreement with priests taking time off to reflect on their spiritual lives. So often, yes, temptation can test our vocation. Events and people can upset our plans, and the lure of the world's attractions and, of course, our own fallen nature.'

'Thank you for your understanding, Your Grace.'

'I hope you find the sabbatical a time when you will be able to pray to Our Divine Saviour for guidance. I will remember you in my masses. The Church needs men like you. Keep that in mind. I hope you will come back to us; you show great depths of humanity, but that could be your tragic flaw. In another, Thomas, your vices would be virtues.'

EIGHTEEN

GALVIN SPENT a month at the Benedictine monastery in Santa Fe. Then he stayed with Mac in California, close to the city of San Diego and, since Mac was away all day working as a chaplain in the state penitentiary, or else trying to help ex-prisoners settle into an apartment and find a job, Galvin had time to drive to Carlsbad and lie on a deck chair, gazing out at the young men and women surfing the cascading waves of the Pacific.

He was like someone getting back his strength after a draining sickness. When he dozed off, a constantly changing pattern of colours and figures filled the screen of his thoughts: Muireann, Sarah Clifford, days behind the cement mixer in High Wycombe, the spiritual director and his transistor and the pale face of his young brother lying dead in the mortuary chapel.

On dull days he mooched about Mac's apartment, gazing at the pictures on the walls or the stand-up photos on low tables beside the armchairs: one was a black and white of the two of them, in

Roman hats and sopranas, walking down the driveway of St Paul's on their way to the Pro-Cathedral; another of Mac on the Cork minor football team; a beautiful collage in watercolour of his family farmhouse in West Cork of St Paul's, and of his first parish, Star of the Sea. It had been painted by a prisoner on death row. Many times while browsing in Barnes & Noble, he was tempted to choose a postcard from the rack for Muireann and write it while sipping a coffee.

At night, he and Mac had dinner at home or in a restaurant and then they would stroll along the promenade. During the meal Mac would finish most of the bottle of wine and invariably call for another. He had put on weight and his hair was flecked with grey. They talked about Dublin and laughed at the Phantom stories and the rector's posh accent. All traces of resentment were gone. One evening a self-conscious look showed on Mac's face. 'By the way, whatever happened to the love of my life, the one and only Lovely Legs?'

'Life seems to have been good to Lovely Legs. By all accounts she trained to be a nurse in Leeds and married a surgeon she used to assist in the operating theatre.'

'I'm glad,' said Mac. 'I'm really glad; that kid deserved the best. We'll drink to Lovely Legs and her surgeon.' They raised their glasses.

On the last night before Galvin left, Mac was strangely subdued. Getting into his car after their meal, he asked: 'Will you hear my confession, Tommy?'

'Of course.'

'D'you mind if I ramble?'

'Ramble to your heart's content.'

Mac described how he and three others, newly ordained in the Thurles seminary, had taken the same flight to New York, seven hours to Kennedy and then on to Los Angeles. The palm trees that lined the route out of the airport, the open cars, the golden tinge to the houses – just like in the pictures – were new and bright and filled with promise. Even the sky looked bigger. They wouldn't have been surprised if Angie Dickinson in sunglasses were to pop out of a shop at any moment.

While he spoke, Galvin looked away towards the shops that lined the far side of the mall: Pizza Hut, Kentucky Fried Chicken, Tony Roma's. Over the low roofs, crimson brushstrokes lined the salmon sky.

'Off playing golf with the lads once a week; big steak dinners and wine, and then back to the house for nightcaps. The Mustang parked in the driveway. Del Mar for the horses. Motor over to Torrey Pines for golf. A dream come true.

'Pastor at Star of the Sea before my thirtieth birthday, Tommy. A big office and desk and my word was final. I knew it was all a sham, so I opted for the state pen.' He stopped and looked away. 'There's something I haven't told you.'

'Take your time.'

He kept running his fingers along the steering wheel while he spoke of the morning in St Mark's parish when a young nun had come to the sacristy after he had said the 6.30 pm mass. She wanted his advice. Swept along by the high tide of freedom emanating from the Vatican Council, the six nuns who made up her community were joining the flow from convents all over America. She was trying to make up her mind whether or not she should leave with them.

The following week he came across her in Mission Valley, where they had coffee. Very soon it was dinner and, after she left the convent at the end of that summer, they started going away for a few days. They did Route 66 as far as Denver, had their photo taken on the Golden Gate Bridge, flew to the Grand Canyon and, in a hotel just south of Tijuana, their child was conceived.

'I know I've sinned, Tommy, but Valerie was my salvation.' His arms opened wide in a bid for understanding. 'Saved me from the madhouse or ending up like priests who worked with me – inviting themselves to parishioners' houses for dinner; leaving thousands in the bank for nephews to buy real estate back in Ireland. One poor bastard died, left fifteen thousand bucks in a tin box beneath the stairs. Half-starved himself. It helped to make a doctor out of his nephew back in Mohill.

'I was willing to leave and marry Valerie: drive a truck … anything … but she wouldn't hear of it. Said it wouldn't be fair to me. She met someone else. A decent guy who has given our son a good education.'

As Galvin raised his hand in absolution, tears trickled down Mac's face as he recited the Act of Contrition. 'I knew then that I'd have to mend my ways. I asked the bishop for prison chaplaincy. Atonement, I suppose. I don't spend too much time over these things. If I remember, *you* were more into agonizing.'

The sabbatical did Galvin much good, and when he returned he continued in therapy. 'I was living in a fool's paradise,' he told the therapist.

'And what are you going to do now? These longings will not disappear. This woman Muireann awakened desires in you. Desires you thought were met by working. By the way, why didn't you leave and marry her? Many do, as you know full well from your work with the archbishop. Your own friends have done so too.'

'This might sound over the top, but I still believe in the Christian thing, you know: forgiveness, compassion, trying to offer some help to those worse off than myself. I've been thinking about it a lot out in California. Seems to me as good a way as any of spending my few short years in this world. I want to have a share in that mission. And now that I've fallen, I might be more understanding of others. Will I fall again? Can't say. No one knows what the future holds.'

'Indeed.'

OTHER THAN visits to Rome, or if they were down the country for a funeral, Galvin rarely had a meal out with Archbishop Devlin. On his return from America, however, the archbishop asked the woman whose glasses hung about her neck to book a table for them at the Marine in Sutton. 'Less conspicuous than the flash hotels for someone in my position,' he said as they finished looking through the mail. 'I've invited the chancellor along, and a couple of other priests also.'

That day in the Marine they were given a table beside a window that looked out on the palm trees and a stretch of Dublin Bay. A cruiser was making its way out to sea. Before they began the main course, Devlin raised his glass. 'Now,' he said, 'good to have you back, Father Thomas. God grant you will be all the better for your desert experience. Bon appétit.'

'Bon appétit, Your Grace.' The priests raised their glasses.

At the table all Devlin said about Galvin's sabbatical was to describe the climate of southern California and the beauty of the oleanders with the same assurance he maintained on any subject, from the culture of ancient Egypt to the political career of Chancellor Adenauer or why Jack Dempsey was the greatest boxer of them all.

When one of the priests mentioned the recent publication of J. Desmond's book on theology, he beamed. 'My most brilliant student when I taught in the Gregorian. His publishers sent me a copy last week.' Grinning wryly, he added: 'I'm relieved to see Desmond has become, well, shall we say, prudent. A splendid achievement and much less likely to raise Vatican blood pressure.'

He went on to praise his *most brilliant student*. 'Along with teaching at Maynooth, Desmond is now one of the leading theologians in the country, as well as being an advisor at the bishops' spring and autumn conferences. Each summer he is a guest lecturer in Berkeley or Cambridge. Prodigious worker. Another book every couple of years; books that are put on the curriculum for students of theology.' He sniffed. 'Regrettably, as we all know, seminaries are now closing down, but, thank God, forward-thinking rectors are responding to the times by opening up the colleges to lay students and drawing up courses of study in humanities and education for the training of teachers of religion. That can only benefit the Church in these times of growing secularism.'

Before his latest book had been published, J. Desmond had come across a bishop in Maynooth from one of the smaller dioceses down the country. They had strolled around St Joseph's Square during a break at the spring episcopal conference.

'It's as simple as this, Desmond,' the bishop said. 'If you continue with your line of thinking regarding, well … shall we say, sensitive subjects, Rome won't touch you, no matter how often your name appears on the *ternus*. The word is – and this is the death knell of your chances – "you're soft on the contraceptive issue" and that is still the litmus test for high office.'

While putting a word in Byrne's ear, he greeted his colleagues with a broad smile. 'You know you've been on the *ternus* for Kildare and Leighlin and other dioceses, and now, well, as soon as Devlin retires, only a matter of a few years … .'

'Thank you.'

'To my mind you are eminently suitable. Indeed, my colleagues at the episcopal conference share that view.'

After more smiles and 'beautiful day, thank God', he had leant towards Byrne. 'You were too closely linked to Garret FitzGerald. An honourable statesman, but the pointy hats didn't trust him – his crusade to free Ireland and all that.' And with a twinkle in his eye, he added: 'Guilt by association, Desmond. All I'll say is, beware. Many loose tongues and itching ears in the Church.'

They stopped for a moment to greet other bishops on the wide avenue where the purple of the flowerbeds and the episcopal crimson stood out against the grey of the Gothic square. When they had passed, the bishop looked around. 'Finally, a priest of your own archdiocese is not helping your cause in the Eternal City. A certain Dr Irwin. Be careful of that Trojan Horse. He's ambitious and he's hinting that you have a liking for a drop of the craythur.'

It was time to return to the meeting room. They joined bishops and theologians waiting their turn to enter the small door set into the big wooden gate.

'I appreciate the heads up,' Byrne said in a low voice.

Since any sign of weakness against *Humanae Vitae*, the papal encyclical which forbade contraception, could end his prospects of one day wearing the mitre, Byrne grew more guarded from then on. And coming from a family of high achievers, he had ambitions that he revealed to only a few. 'Whatever a Byrne takes up, he does it well' had been his father's canon for his children around the dinner table.

He shed over a stone in a year, and mineral water replaced wine when he joined his companions from the teaching staff for a confab on Saturday nights. Just before the summer holidays that year, when exam papers had been corrected, he was entertaining a couple of his trusted friends in his room, which looked out on the square. The laughter of the students, free now from soutanes, answering bells and baking for examinations, rose and fell. One of the priests said in a throwaway manner: 'Odds are shortening that you will succeed Devlin when the time comes, Des.'

Byrne looked him in the eye. 'If the call comes, I'm ready. Nothing whatever wrong with ambition,' he went on to say as they sipped their after-dinner drinks and the slanting sun lit up the diamond windowpanes. 'Oliver Plunkett begged the cardinal prefect in Rome to get the Pope to give him Armagh, and now he is numbered among the saints.'

They raised their glasses. 'Here's to wannabe saints.'

From then on, J. Desmond's articles in theological journals in Britain and America and papers he delivered to seminaries showed a marked increase in quotations from papal encyclicals. He was appearing less on television. But he still urged Catholic Ireland to wake up to what was happening, and to implement the recommendations of Vatican II. At a talk in All Hallows College he declared: 'It's not the Jesus of Nazareth who is my primary concern, it's the Jesus of the hi-tech age who concerns me most, and how to communicate His message to modernity.' He had added: 'It is absurd to send out healthy young men and not to recognize the urges of the flesh, especially since they will be meeting men and women in situations charged with emotion. And time will tell how foolhardy it is to gloss over the complexities of human sexuality.'

AFTER HIS RETURN from America, Galvin sensed a changed atmosphere in the archbishop's house, one he couldn't put into words. Cryptic comments were being passed between Devlin and the chancellor in his presence. And Devlin was selecting the times when Galvin would join himself, senior clerics and J. Desmond at the long table in the Chapter Room.

Galvin would take the minutes and give them to one of the stenographers in the basement, unless something of a delicate nature came up at the meeting, when he himself would type them. Whenever an item appeared on the agenda marked *sub secreto*, Devlin would wave his hand. 'Right then, Father Galvin, you have other duties needing your attention, so you may leave now, or wait in the room across the hall until it is time to return. The chancellor will let you know.'

This happened also on the odd occasion when a priest was being taken out of a ministry. Once when he and the archbishop were working on clerical appointments in the library, he asked in inno-cence why a priest was being given leave of absence so suddenly. Devlin turned his dreaded stare on him.

'The trouble with you, father, is that you want to know too much. Remember your position as my secretary. Certain matters of a highly confidential nature are reserved to me and to the vicars-general of the archdiocese.' An awkward silence followed until he spoke again, once he had recovered his composure. 'You understand, father, that I cannot break the confessional seal; some matters relating to my priests fall into that category. And now,' he surveyed the appointments sheet, 'we will move to the next item.'

Later that evening Galvin was so taken up with typing minutes of another meeting that he didn't hear Devlin slink through the open door of his study until he was standing beside him. Working at his ring, he paced the room, stopping now and again to glance out of the window as if he were expecting someone who, at any minute, might climb the steps to the front door.

'Tiring meeting today,' he said.

'Sorry to hear that, Your Grace.'

'A minute of your time, father.' He was sniffing. 'Come to the library.'

Galvin followed him into the dull fug of old books. Devlin sat himself stiffly behind the big desk and started to rearrange things: his diary, the holder for his pens and pencils, a stand-up image of the Virgin Mary.

'This is a matter of strict confidence.'

'Of course, Your Grace.'

'My God, how perverse is human nature.' He was running his fingers along the rope moulding of the desk. 'The priest who is being moved has committed an unspeakable act of depravity, so I'm sending him to a psychiatrist: a professor at the university and a good Catholic man. He will give me guidance in regard to his state of mind and his future in ministry. I am not at liberty to discuss this man's sin in detail. Confessional matter.'

About six months later this priest returned to parish work, and one evening shortly afterwards Devlin explained to Galvin that the psychiatrist had given the priest a clean bill of health.

'I am giving him another appointment, fully confident that he will not offend again. This priest is receiving good spiritual direction; he's been to confession and received a suitable penance. So we can leave it in the Lord's hands from now on. It's best this way. Something of this nature is open to misunderstanding, and could harm the work done by the majority of priests who are good men.'

'As you say, Your Grace.'

NINETEEN

ON THE THURSDAY MORNING of the retreat, as the confrères are sitting down to breakfast, Sheerin says, his grey curly head bent over his sausage and poached eggs: 'D'you know why so few of us are leaving the priesthood nowadays, lads?' He had to raise his voice to be heard above the din of conversations and the clash of metal as lids are lifted off and banged down on the steaming *bains-marie*.

The priests are paying him little attention. One is filling cups from the huge stainless-steel teapot, others are drawing back chairs to sit down. Another has brought a newspaper to the table and is deploring the way the media never misses an opportunity to put down the Church. He flings the paper onto an empty chair.

Feeling ignored, Sheerin turns to Galvin. 'Tommy, do you know why so few of us are leaving?'

'Many reasons, Harry.'

'The urge has died, that's why, mate. We're shagged, can't move our arses.' His broad shoulders shake as he releases his squeaky laugh; a laugh that echoes back through the years to morning walks around the ambulatory. It could be heard especially on Mix Days when juniors tagged along to hear his latest quip: they thought he was 'a gas man' and when he cast a jaundiced eye over the grounds and declared that 'this place is a shithouse', he had them in stitches.

Straight-backed Sylvester O'Flynn blesses his porridge with two fingers and raises a spoon daintily to his lips. Beside him Cyril is quiet, but his eyes are darting from one priest to another. He raises his head. 'Do you remember after the Council, fellows were leaving like the new time?'

'Yeah,' says Sheerin, 'but the sap was rising then.' He adopts his presiding pose, sitting sideways and resting one hand on the table. 'Did you know, lads, that when he was ruling the roost in Westminster, Cardinal Heenan closed down a renewal house for clerics and religious in London? He claimed it had become a dating centre for priests and nuns who'd thrown off the habit. That's what happens when you start paying attention to feelings and finding yourself.' He looks around for a reaction. 'They used to hug trees, but it wasn't long before they were hugging each other – much more satisfying, if you ask me.'

They go through a list of those who have left and scorn the loss of men with great energy and potential. 'And many would be back in the morning if compulsory celibacy were relaxed,' says a priest who is on the edge of the conversation.

Sylvester O'Flynn cocks his head and sneers. 'I don't care what anyone says – celibacy has served the Church well over the centuries.'

Cyril loses interest and leans over to Galvin. 'Tommy, did I tell you? I've found a way of making it easier for myself when I'm in the house, especially during the long winter nights.'

'Even longer still in the Wicklow hills, I'd say.'

'I leave a radio on upstairs, or in another room.' The look in his pale blue eyes suggests he has made one of life's great discoveries.

'Gives the impression there's someone else in the house with you. You should try it sometime.'

'Yes, I might.'

'The evenings are the worst, no one to talk to … you know. When something goes wrong in the parish and you're blamed for it, and some old hairpin lacerates you in the sacristy, and you have to take it, I'd love to have someone … really love to have someone to talk to. Thrash it all out over a whiskey. That would be great.'

Encouraged by Galvin's listening ear, Cyril suggests they take a walk outside before the retreat director gives his morning reflection.

'I was getting a headache in there, I hate all this argy-bargy. Put years on you, wouldn't it? Harry, God love him, goes a bit far at times.' Cyril says as they step around the black cat who is unwilling to surrender her place on the sunny steps of the front door. They take the Abbey Walk where a priest is examining the leaves of a eucalyptus tree. 'The small things. That's what I miss, Tommy. Hearing the kids talking in the classroom about pancakes on Shrove Tuesday evening. Or the fun on Halloween. Or someone to be there at the airport when I return to Dublin. I mean, after all, we're only flesh and blood. What are they expecting from us? Or d'you think that I'm a needy person?'

'No. And I know well what—'

'Oh, thank God. You're sound. They all say you're very grounded. I can see why. Are you still going to the monks down in Roscrea? Gosh, you're great.'

'Nothing great about it, Cyril. I need it. A time to celebrate the Liturgy of the Hours with them. I'm someway drawn to it. Don't know why. *The heart has reasons* – remember Pascal?'

Galvin studies Cyril's pinched face as he stops and gently strokes a young beech leaf. 'Yes, and the monks have each other. Don't you think there's something sad about presbyteries, Tommy? I mean they lack the ordinary things. Children arguing over the remote control, teenagers in a huff, banging doors – at least it's for real. You know, the cut and thrust.'

'Put like that, yes.'

Cyril is picking at a scab in Galvin's soul that hasn't quite healed. 'When one of my nephews was a child, he hated visiting the parochial house in Ashford. And, Tommy, d'you know what he said on the day of his First Communion – I'll never forget it as long as I live – "I like my Uncle Cyril, but his house is spooky."'

The soft tone of the bell rings out over the grounds and brings an end to spooky presbyteries. They hurry to Coghill for the morning reflection.

WHEN THE BLINDS are pulled down that day and the grounds deserted, Galvin takes a diary from the batch and heads for a favourite garden seat at one side of the quadrangle, near where the prie-dieux were put out on the grass for the First Blessings.

He opens one of his diaries at the page he had marked the night before. *Letter from Rome; Irwin gets his wish at last* jumps out at him.

They were reading the mail that day when Galvin sensed Devlin grow tense. He stole a glance across the table to see the archbishop's eyes move back and forth over the page of a letter with the Vatican crest. He put the letter aside and didn't speak until they had finished looking through his personal mail.

'Your friend, Dr Irwin, has finally got his wish. Have a look.'

The letter was from the Vatican Secretary of State suggesting that Dr Damien Irwin might be considered among the candidates for Rector of the Irish College now that a vacancy has arisen with the death of the incumbent. *Of course*, the Secretary of State wrote, *the Holy See unreservedly acknowledges that appointments to the Pontifical Irish College are made by the Irish Episcopal Conference. This, Your Grace, is merely a tentative suggestion to help you and your fellow bishops, guided by the Holy Spirit, in your selection process. Dr Irwin is a man of proven ability and it must be a great blessing for you to have priests like him in your archdiocese.*

'You can rest assured Armagh will also have received a similar billet-doux.' Devlin knew well that, even though he was an important figure in shaping Church policy in the country, he was down the pecking order in Rome.

Galvin proffered a sop. 'Without wishing to interfere, Your Grace, might I suggest that you still have control over all clerical appointments?'

'Thomas,' Devlin said, 'I learned a thing or two from my years in Rome, both as student and teacher. One thing you don't do: you don't say no to the Holy See. If you do, you will come off second best.' His forefinger shot up. 'Always. They haven't survived for nearly two millennia and not learnt a thing or two about getting their way; and indeed, I'm sorry to say, tightening the screw on someone who *does* say no. Dr Irwin has been chasing Rome for a long time. The barque of Peter, Thomas, is very susceptible to human frailty. As the fallen sons of Adam, our motives are rarely pure. But, let the almighty be the judge of all that: the parable of the wheat and the cockle should be sufficient for us. Remember, father: in the fullness of time, all will be revealed.'

'Yes, Your Grace.'

The clerical version of Devlin's own appointment, recounted in golf clubs and at retreats, was part of diocesan lore. How a couple of Monsignors had made tracks to Rome and how they had taken out members of the Curia to Sunday lunch to lament the growth of secularism in their country. 'And what a shame to see such a faithful people led away from the correct path by erring politicians,' one of them stressed. 'Which is why, Monsignori, the vacancy in Dublin needs to be filled by a strong and able leader.' The Pope's men were studying him. 'Someone, in my humble opinion, with the moral force and intellectual capacity of James Devlin.'

'Yes, very fine man,' says one of the dinner guests, a member of the Congregation for Bishops.

Before the Monsignors returned to Dublin, they left them a copy of Devlin's latest book, *Humanae Vitae: At the Heart of Respect for Life*. The book sealed his appointment.

'I have no option except to give the nod to a man who has had Rome on his agenda ever since the day he set foot inside St Paul's.' Devlin replaced the letter in the envelope and tossed it in his personal tray. 'Anyway,' he raised his hands in a resigned gesture, 'nothing new under the sun.'

With an impish grin, he handed Galvin another letter. 'Now, cast your eye over *that* missive and my reply. And tell me if I'm being uncharitable with one of my priests, father.'

The letter was from a curate in north County. Dublin. *During the week, Your Grace, while I was on my day off, my parish priest was visiting the chapel-of-ease adjacent to my house, and afforded himself the freedom of my lavatory facilities. My housekeeper informed me of same when I returned. I find this an invasion of my privacy and appeal to Your Grace to reprove him.*

Devlin grimaced: 'This is what we have to endure – and all too often. Now read my reply.'

Galvin read the terse note – Devlin was famous for his brevity. *Dear Father, in the event of an emergency, anyone would be entitled to avail of your lavatory facilities. May the Lord continue to bless your work. James A. Devlin*

'Brief and to the point, Your Grace.'

Both men were smiling as they rose to take their coffee.

That evening Devlin wrote to the Secretary of State saying he was glad to be of any assistance to the Holy See, and agreed that Dr Irwin was a man of proven ability and, indeed, if his talents were needed elsewhere in the vineyard of the Divine Saviour, he would not stand in his way and would recommend him at the next episcopal conference. He enclosed a substantial cheque from the archdiocese to be disbursed at the Holy Father's discretion, sealed the letter and sat for a while at his desk. Acceding to Irwin's craven desire for a career in the Church and to the Secretary of State's machinations would be a small price to pay for Rome's goodwill, especially now, when his retirement would be up for review in two years' time.

IRWIN'S TRANSITION to Rome was seamless. The dream, hatched as a child, when he had draped a rosary beads around his neck for a pectoral cross and chain, and later, when he kept a *cappa magna* in his cupboard, was now taking shape. In no time he was broadening his circle of Vatican contacts and going with them to prominent families for Sunday lunch. In fluent Italian, he charmed the Romans with jokes, gifts of cognac and Galliano and piano recitals. They in turn were his guests at the Irish College on St Patrick's Day and during the Christmas period. Within a few years he was a Monsignor of the papal household and, as often as he could, was hosting dinners at the Irish College for distinguished visitors from Ireland, and accompanying them to St Peter's to be presented to the Pope.

'Come out in October or November,' he said to Galvin on their way to Dublin Airport one summer. 'Rome is sweltering till then. The rash of tourists with their stupid cameras will have gone. And anyway, rednecks like you would blister in the heat.' Galvin went out that October and stayed for a week at the Irish College. From then on, it became part of his annual holiday.

One evening they were going across to a restaurant on the Piazza di San Giovanni when Irwin noticed a fat priest in a soutane sitting with a group of students at the trattoria outside the college gates.

'Don't look now,' he whispered. '*Mo dhuine* – O'Rourke thought he would take my place at the captain's table. He has a couple of bishops, including Armagh, in his corner. I told you about him before. Teaches in the Biblicum and plays the jokey card.' Irwin glanced across to where O'Rourke was laughing and giving an explanation with much movement of his hands. 'Make no mistake about it. Falstaff, for all his jolly ways, carries the major's baton in his knapsack.' Irwin cast a cold eye on his adversary.

From their first meeting, Armagh took a dislike to Irwin. And, after a few years, when word reached him that he was spending too much time loitering around the Vatican and hobnobbing with Curial figures instead of attending to his duties at the Irish College, he started putting pressure on Devlin to call him ashore.

Irwin got wind of the cardinal's intentions and immediately set about a plan. Now was the time to enlist the help of one of his influential friends – the British ambassador to the Vatican. Of old Catholic stock, the ambassador, educated at Ampleforth, was a friend of Armagh's going back to the days when he was a senior civil servant at Stormont and the cardinal a parish priest in West Belfast. Irwin had shown himself to be the perfect host when the ambassador and his wife visited the Irish College for Christmas drinks. The ambassador, in turn, invited Irwin to different functions at the British Embassy, such as the millennium celebrations. 'A capital fellow' was how the ambassador described the rector of the Irish College.

Irwin did a perfect impression of the ambassador's clipped tones to Galvin: '"If I may venture to say, Dr Irwin, and at the risk of scandalizing you, Rome is about introductions, about networking. About being cordial with people of influence. If you like, it's about fixing things. Been that way since Caesar's time." Chortle, chortle, chortle. Anyway, I had a plan.'

He laughed and became the ambassador again. '"Monsignor Irwin, before you return to Ireland for your summer holidays, do come to Sunday lunch at the Embassy." The word is that the wife wears the trousers and has a passion for yellow roses so, for the Sunday lunch, I turned up with a dozen. The roses became my 'welcome' from then on. Armagh wants to sing off the same hymn sheet as the Brits, especially to consolidate the Peace Agreement. Show a united front – Church and State. So the ambassador was able to put in a word for me. And herself too.'

At a social event in the embassy one evening, the ambassador's wife whispered to Irwin: 'You leave this to me.' Then, beneath the decorated ceilings and portraits of Her Majesty, she introduced him to the other *chargés d'affaires* and delegates.

Rather than ruffle any feathers, Armagh shelved his plan. Irwin was cock-a-hoop. 'The trouble with you, Galvin, is that you don't give your Bible a close reading. If you did, you'd learn that *the children of this generation are more shrewd in dealing with their own age ...*'

'*... than are the children of light.* Yes. I know.'

'I came across Armagh a few weeks later when he was staying with us. "You got me this time, Monsignor," he admitted. Don't want to get on his wrong side, though.'

Galvin's visits followed a routine. Irwin was busy during the day, so he pottered around the city, visiting churches and, while having a coffee at a trattoria near the Spanish Steps, ploughed his way through the pages of *L'Osservatore Romano*. In the evening Irwin would call a taxi to take them to Trastevere for dinner, or else they would eat in the college dining room.

By now, Irwin had lost the paunch he had acquired in previous years. He wore fashionable suits and good Italian shoes – his speech, too, had a hint of Rome.

One morning while they were having their espressos in the loggia where bougainvillea formed a red and pink canopy over the walls of the courtyard, he slipped a business card from his wallet and held it out to Galvin. 'Treat yourself to the full works while in Rome. Go on – there's my hairdresser.'

Galvin hesitated.

'Come on,' said Irwin, 'put your redneck roots behind you. I have a manicure and the whole shebang done once a month.' He grinned. 'The pride of our country is at stake. Tommy, look, we make enough sacrifices, we deserve to indulge ourselves now and again.'

When they had finished and were bringing their cups in from the table outside, he added: 'By the way, I've a dinner organized before you go back. You'll have a chance to meet one of the cardinals, Luigi Alphonso Giordano – dripping with Roman aristocracy – so fasten your seat belt. A few others will also join us. I do a bit of work for Giordano. Nothing much. Keeps the brain from atrophying. By the way, he likes to be addressed as *Eminenza*. So, when in Rome ... .'

At the dinner were the vice-rector and three priests. One, a German, worked in the Curia as a member of the Pontifical Commission for the Appointment of Bishops. While the waiter was pouring the drinks, Irwin announced that they should greet Giordano at the front door, so they all trooped down the stairs, out into the evening sun and congregated around the fountain. And though he joked and worked his way around the guests, recharging their glasses, all the while Irwin was keeping a peeled eye on the main gate. As soon as Giordano's taxi pulled up, he cut short his conversation and hurried out to the huge wrought-iron gates.

Cardinal Giordano was silver-haired with a Roman nose and a slight stoop. He spoke in a hushed voice, as if he were in a basilica or was nervous that someone might be listening in. At the table the priests deferred to him, so that he dominated the conversation, speaking about his family's long military service to Italy and its contribution to building up the country after the devastation of the Second World War and Mussolini. Then he held forth on the unpopular but necessary work that the Curia is charged to carry out.

Irwin broke into Italian. *'La Curia e per difendere la Chiesa dagli errori.'*

'Certamente, padre. Certamente. Ah yes, how right you are, Dr Irwin. Cardinals and even – dare I say it – popes come and go, but the Curia is there to remain steadfast and guide the bark of Peter.' Cardinal Giordano was in lecturing mode.

'Our function before God is to have a wide perspective on all developments: *nihil sub sole novum*. We don't get any thanks for that, only contumely, but see what has become of the Anglican Communion. Disarray, fathers.' His gold fillings showed when he smiled. 'You need order in the world, that is what is wrong today. The Anglicans are bickering about the election of women to the episcopacy. They ruled in favour of contraception back in the nineteen thirties and it's not helping their cause.'

He turned to Galvin. 'Undoubtedly, in Ireland, Padre Tomasso, like everywhere else, the Curia is regarded as the stumbling block to progress.'

Galvin did a courtesy protest. 'Well, I wouldn't say it's that strong, *Eminenza* ... .'

'No.' He raised his hand. 'No, I can understand. We're the ones who are destroying the great work of John XXIII. And of course, they all love the saintly man from Bergamo. We're used to that.' His brown eyes shone. 'We have a duty, Padre Tomasso. A duty to defend the true faith, and not whimsical versions that come and go according to fashion. We got much grief over *Humanae Vitae*, but what many don't understand is that the Holy Father is being faithful to the age-old teaching of the Church on the nature of human sexuality. The Creator's imprint is stamped on nature. The function of the sexual act is to reach its natural fulfilment, that is, to be an act that is procreative, or has the potential for such. There is no other way to see it.' He waved his hands. 'Now, in the western world, it's feminism. That too will pass.'

Just as he had done many years before when the rector was laying down the law, Irwin made sounds of agreement, and now muttered: '*Sì, sì, cardinale, hai assolutamente ragione.*'

'What we are preserving is the beauty of sexuality as created by Our Divine Master. The world forgets that the so-called spoilers of progress are often the ones who have a deep sense of what is beautiful. Look at Julian II. Now there's someone who would put the Borgias to shame and yet he is the one who was first to denounce slavery; he engaged Michelangelo to paint *The Last Judgement*. That's not a man who lacks an appreciation of beauty.'

When one of the priests tripped on a landmine by mentioning the possibility of a married clergy, the cardinal beat out an angry tattoo on the table. 'My brother priests, the day the Church allows priests to marry is the day the Church loses all control.' He graced them with a benign smile. 'Ah, women. What a mystery! No. Divine wisdom will never allow that to happen.'

They had their coffee out in the loggia and, before Giordano left, he turned to Galvin. 'Padre Tommaso, please convey my best wishes to His Excellency the Papal Nuncio, in Dublin. I trust the climate in Ireland is in every way suitable to his gentle disposition.'

'I shall convey your best wishes, *Eminenza*.'

'*Buonasera, fratelli*. Until we meet again.' He raised his hand in a blessing.

Irwin stood and thanked his guests and, in Italian, had a special word for his guest of honour. 'And one last request,' he said, looking towards one of the high doors where a little man with a camera stood waiting. 'I'd be obliged if you would all arrange the chairs so that we can sit for a photograph to honour the visit of His Eminence.'

He accompanied the cardinal to his taxi and when he returned, suggested they go to his rooms and leave the kitchen staff to tidy up; but now that they had stirred themselves, his guests were of a mind to leave. One man was checking his watch, another was doing a stretching act and praising the company and the food.

'Did you hear Giordano about the Nuncio?' said Irwin to Galvin after they had seen them off and were making their way up to Irwin's rooms. '*Gentle disposition*. Balderdash! His job, as everyone knows, is to bring every tittle-tattle here to Rome. You know what he said to me once at a function in Dublin Castle? "My recommendations are always accepted in Rome, father. Now remember that."'

'So much for the Holy Spirit.'

'And as for his Creator's imprint – the day after one of the American bishops held a press conference to lay down the law about *Humanae Vitae*, he flew off in a private jet to the Bahamas with a few millionaire businessmen.'

'Pharisees. Laying heavy burdens ... .'

'Yeah, but look, Tommy, if you were to get uptight about Church teaching, you'd never do anything.'

He stood and Galvin watched him go to the drinks cabinet, where on the top shelf was a row of cocktail glasses. Lower down, bottles of whiskey, cognac, port and Galliano were ranged.

'The main thing,' he said over his shoulder, 'is that, even if it gets some things wrong, it is a force for good in the world and it has the power to influence. And Tommy' – he turned round – 'as I told you all those years ago, this is where I want to be.' He opened a bottle and poured cognac into two global glasses. 'I mean look at the celibacy issue. It will never change, I hear them here – the liberals – they go on about how unjust it is. Waste of breath. Rome will never change on that. Your health.'

'*Sláinte.*' They raised their glasses.

'They won't allow girls to serve mass, so why take on a losing battle? The mother used always say, "choose the battles you think you can win".'

TWENTY

THE MORNING AFTER he had drafted his letter of resignation
to the Pope, which he was required to do on reaching seventy-five,
Archbishop Devlin woke early, opened the curtains and looked out
over the city where he had wielded influence for nearly a quarter
of a century. The thought of retirement horrified him. In a matter
of months he would be no more than a memory among priests at
a confirmation dinner and, with the passing of time, his rigid ways
would dissolve into amusing anecdotes. They would laugh and cite
him as one of the last of the feudal lords. No sooner had the thought
crossed his mind than he felt ashamed, but he still prayed that Rome
would see fit to reject his submission when he visited the Pope.

It was his opinion that he was still the most suited to lead the
archdiocese through what could be stormy times ahead. He could
find little common ground with the younger crop of bishops, who
were either afraid of, or trying to court popularity with, the media.
Few of them now had his background in classics, or a doctorate in

philosophy from Freiburg. Instead, they had second-class degrees in business management, or diplomas in catechetics or one of the social sciences; paltry derivatives of fundamental modes of scholarship.

During the episcopal conferences in Maynooth he had, as a rule, kept to himself and, each day, enjoyed a quiet lunch in the presbytery of a local parish priest. In that, he was following the example of the High Command, who always dined alone with his priest-secretary on these occasions.

In the big bedroom with its decorated ceiling, he knelt at his prie-dieu, rested his forehead in his hands and tried to track the source of his depression. It came to him: the early morning dream just before he woke. He was standing outside the Gresham Hotel watching his own funeral passing by. No one was paying the slightest bit of attention. Even the hearse driver and his colleague in the front were laughing and smoking cigarettes. Buses were stopping for passengers. Young people were going into the Savoy Cinema. Taxi drivers were loafing around Cathedral Street and talking about a football game.

He looked down at his ring, his mother's ruby housed in a gold band. The plucky comments of that fiery curate – Mayo, the priests called him – came back to him from one of the open forums he had set up to promote consultation with his priests. 'Archbishop,' the young priest had said, 'why do you and others bishops have to live in mansions, be driven around in big cars and wear gold rings?'

The senior priests – Devlin's henchmen – rounded on the upstart. 'Have some respect for our revered archbishop,' Winters snapped.

Mayo did not back down. 'This is supposed to be an open forum. The Catholic Church in Ireland is dying on its feet, and when that happens finally, it will be too late.'

Mayo's last visit while home on holidays from Kenya came winging back to James Devlin as he rested his elbows on the crimson-upholstered prie-dieu. His whole body had been consumed with his description of the red earth of Kenya.

'And the sun when it lights up the snow-capped Kilimanjaro, archbishop, well, that's something you would never forget.' Not a sign of resentment, even though they had parted on bad terms. 'I'm helping the people to run the parish, rather than them helping me.' Along with a team of young men and women, Mayo was building a clinic and a school. No priest for 200 miles and he lived in the same compound as the nuns and lay volunteers. 'You should come out and visit us some time. You'd be very welcome.'

Devlin shifted on the prie-dieu.

'Yes, maybe I will,' he had told him. 'I'm delighted to hear of the work you and your community are doing, father.'

But a twinge of regret had crept into his heart at the way the young priest seemed fired by a spirit that had once been his. His own dream to be a missionary, the one he had shared with the spiritual director when he was a seminarian, had met with a sudden death. *Surely there's nothing greater than to be a harbinger of the Word in Africa or perhaps the Far East, father. Carry no purse or wallet, no haversack ... the Lord will take care.*

The archbishop swept his eyes over the pictures and photos on the walls and stopped at the crucifix. Africa had no chance against the academic successes that had come his way. 'You've a great future in the Church, Mr Devlin,' his professors had told him. 'Many will benefit from your brilliant mind.'

Sent to Germany for philosophy and to Rome for theology, he had come up against some of the brightest young clerics in Europe. From then on, the wheels of his life gathered speed. Ordination day on a Pentecostal morning at St Peter's basilica. Lying prostrate on the marble with 200 others: symmetrical rows of white albs filling the vast sanctuary. And after that, postgraduate studies at Tübingen, the youngest in Ireland to hold a chair of theology. 'What does it profit a man if he gains the whole world and suffers the loss of his own soul?' came to him as he gently rubbed his ring.

What he had revealed to Father Galvin only a week before

flashed across his mind. 'If my resignation is accepted by Rome, I'll be the first bishop in the history of the archdiocese to be taken to the crypt of the Pro-Cathedral while not in office. That would be more than I could bear to think about.' Hearing the echo of his own words, he scorns the shallows to which his spiritual aspirations have contracted.

He stood. When they opened the mail, he would remind Father Galvin to book two tickets for Rome, one of the few places where he found consolation in a world where the tide of faith was being sucked out into raging waters. Terracotta peeling from the houses in Trastevere, the golden aspect of the Seven Hills in the early morning, the classical ruins that bespoke history, grandeur and power had never failed to excite him.

He gave Galvin his instructions. 'And reserve accommodation at the Casa Internazionale del Clero for four days, father.'

Galvin hesitated. 'You usually … not the Irish College, Your Grace?'

Devlin eyed him. 'I find the Irish College uncongenial at present. Christian charity forbids me to say any more.'

On the morning of their departure, Devlin, wearing his black gabardine, paced the main hallway that ran from the main door to the high window on the back, which looked out on what used to be the croquet pitch. Galvin busied himself checking their bags, passports and flight tickets.

While waiting for the driver to bring the Audi around to the front, the archbishop stared out at the garden. He noticed a shower of cherry blossoms drifting to the ground. *'Gather ye rosebuds … .'*

'Yes, Your Grace, a reminder to us all.' Galvin gestured towards the umbrella. 'You may not need it. The forecast for Rome is good.'

'Father, I keep reminding you. Conditions in Rome can be changeable: one needs to go prepared. And the weather around the Holy See can be decidedly volatile.' A wry smile showed around his mouth.

'Yes, entirely.'

As in the days when Devlin had been one of the theological advisors to the Irish bishops at the Vatican Council, he kept to himself at the Internazionale del Clero. And his only departure from that habit of a lifetime was to sit out with seminarians and sip a coffee on the Piazza Navona. There he teased them while testing their knowledge of Italian and irregular French verbs and affected shock when they professed never to have heard of the ablative absolute in Latin.

'Look,' said a priest to Galvin as the two of them were returning from a walk through the city and noticed Devlin at the centre of the student group. Galvin nodded discreetly. '*Monarch of all I survey.* Never gave up being the university professor.'

'A safe haven from the Irish newshounds.'

Devlin beckoned them over and called the waiter to serve them, then returned to his lecture – how the Catholic Church, now reviled in Europe, had saved the same continent from marauding forces such as the Huns and the Barbarians.

The following morning when Galvin pulled open the curtains, his eye was drawn to the figure of the archbishop in the atrium below with his hands resting on his umbrella. He did not move for at least ten minutes; then, like someone with a heavy heart, he began to poke at a pebble near the fountain. 'The loneliest man in Rome,' Galvin said to the oval mirror on the wardrobe as he walked past it on his way to the bathroom.

After breakfast they drove in a taxi to St Peter's and were met by a curial Monsignor who smelt of cigars and had the body of a wrestler. He spoke Italian to Devlin in an American accent and, after a half-hearted greeting to Galvin, proceeded to ignore him. He led them to one side of St Peter's, past the Swiss Guards and down a cobbled yard to a long colonnaded loggia leading to the papal offices.

The Monsignor rapped on a high double door and another Vatican official let them all in. Sitting behind a big desk at the other end of the room, the Pope looked old and frail but, nevertheless, gave the sense of one who is thoroughly in command. He stood and came around the desk to greet them and, with practised charm, welcomed them both to Rome. He asked after the archbishop's welfare and, patting him on the forearm, remarked: 'Your Grace, you and I are not getting any younger.'

The heads-up wasn't lost on Devlin. The Pope was cordial with Galvin, asking him about Ireland and recounting how Pope John Paul II retained fond memories of his papal visit. 'The Church in Ireland is still an example for Europe, father,' he said, reaching up to lay his hand on Galvin's shoulder: all the while his eagle eye was taking the measure of them both. For all the influence he had wielded over the years, Devlin was now a little boy at the mercy of the surgeon about to remove his tonsils. The Pope thanked Galvin for his commitment to the Lord's work and for his support and kindness to Archbishop Devlin. '*Molto grazie*, Padre Tommaso' – Galvin's cue to leave the room.

For most of an hour, Galvin walked up and down the corridor, stopping to look at the oil paintings that covered the wide panels of the walls: Moses on Mount Nebo looking across at the Promised Land he would never reach; Jesus handing keys to St Peter; St Paul's Damascene conversion. His tour came to an end when Devlin appeared at the door of the papal office, accompanied by the Monsignor with the cigar breath.

'Now, father,' Devlin said before they got into their limousine on the Via Conzolatione, 'we've done our duty. I'd like to rest for a while when we get back to the college. I've arranged to meet the students at the trattoria at four o'clock. I must keep my promise and I should like you to join us.' He looked old and chastened.

'Most certainly.'

'I received an invitation from the rector of the Irish College but I have no desire to share that man's table. I shall have a quiet supper at the Internazionale and an early night. This has been a trying day, and a disappointing one, but that need not deter you from taking up the rector's invitation, which was for us both.'

'No. I'm tired also. I will join you for supper, if I may.'

'Most certainly, father. And you are very kind to keep an old man company.'

On the way back the archbishop brooded: now and again he released a heavy sigh and, all the while, kept tapping the floor of the limousine with his umbrella. When they were driving up to the Internazionale, he said: 'Father, ours is not to question the Holy See. It's not what one expected but *fiat voluntas tua.*' The limousine came to a halt at the front door and he raised the umbrella as he stepped out. 'I did tell you, father, that conditions in Rome can be unpredictable.'

He was mostly silent again that evening at dinner and, just before wiping his lips with his serviette, said: 'The rector of the Irish College has done me a grave disservice, father. He has intimated that I no longer have the capacity to meet the demands of a changing culture. I have my informants in Rome too, you know.'

'I'm sorry to hear that, Your Grace.'

One eyebrow peaked, he looked at Galvin. 'Don't be, father dear. There has been treachery among the clergy since the time of our Divine Saviour.'

Soon after Devlin returned from Rome, he called Galvin on the intercom. 'I should like to speak to the boys in St Paul's, father, before they go on their summer holiday. Will you please make arrangements with the rector? Tell him I should also like to take Benediction afterwards.'

'I'll attend to that immediately.'

The following Friday evening when Devlin was walking down the wooden corridor towards the Academy Hall where he would address *the boys*, he cast a sad eye towards the playing pitches and remarked to Galvin: 'Now that Rome has seen fit to dispense with my services, do you realize, father, this is the last time I will ever speak to my seminarians?'

'Yes, Your Grace.'

The quiver in his voice caused Galvin to glance sideways. To his astonishment, tears were streaming down the archbishop's cheeks, but before he went in to the Academy Hall, he paused, took a handkerchief from the folds of his purple soutane and composed himself. 'Now then, father,' he said, straightening his shoulders and with the hint of a smile, *Once more unto the breach, dear friends, once more ... .'*

IN THE MONTHS that followed, Devlin receded into himself. When Galvin was typing late into the night he was aware of the archbishop's light reflecting on the asphalt apron and catching the sheen on the magnolia trees at the back of the house. At lunch he picked at his food, sometimes emitting a heavy sigh. It seemed to Galvin that he was on the brink of revealing a worry, but, after a while, he just took up his knife and fork again.

He hardly ever played his favourite Bach or Beethoven pieces, like he used to do of a Friday evening. Instead, he retreated to his library to read Virgil 'the greatest poet of them all, father' and his beloved Seneca. The only time he brightened was when the Dominican nun, his close friend, visited him every Saturday afternoon, as she had been doing for years. They had tea and cake in the downstairs kitchen and his driver brought her back to her convent, and always before nightfall.

'Sister ensured that I didn't become a stuffed shirt by being *ex aequo* with me every year at university' was the way he had introduced her to Galvin who had come across them in the garden. 'I have told her many times, I will reproach her before the Lord on the Day of Judgment: she didn't use her unique talent and go on to do her doctorate. I have no doubt but she would have succeeded to the chair of classics.'

TWENTY-ONE

THE ARCHBISHOP'S VISIT to the Pope was the death of him. He was listless, especially in the morning, yet he put off going to his doctor. Nearly every night, Galvin was woken in the early hours by coughing and the creaking floorboards in the corridor outside his room. 'Would you consider going ... I mean, would a check-up put your mind at rest?' he suggested when Devlin complained of having no appetite.

Devlin rounded on him. 'Father, if I need to consult my GP, I will do it when the time is right.'

'Of course, Your Grace.'

When he did go, his doctor referred him for a scope to the Mater Hospital. 'The truth. I'd prefer it that way,' he said, sitting upright before the surgeon.

'Your Grace, there are two tumours. One is quite advanced: size of a golf ball, and I'll need to wait for the lab report, so there's no use in speculating until that is available.'

'Could we be talking about metastasis here?' Devlin sniffed.

'I'd prefer not to speculate until we carry out further investigations.'

The lab reports showed that the disease had spread to the archbishop's spinal cord and to his liver.

'How long?' he asked the surgeon at the next consultation.

'It wouldn't be prudent to, well, set a time, but ... .'

'From your experience, how long?'

'Eighteen months or so. Hard to say with certitude.'

'Thank you for your honesty.'

From then on, Devlin swung between depression and fear, and sat in his library while the auxiliary bishop, the vicar-general and the chancellor took over the running of the diocese. Word got out among the clergy that the three wise men were now calling the shots.

Devlin had grown into the habit of inviting Galvin into the library mid morning to indulge his Roman taste for a double espresso. Now he sipped cranberry juice and stared out of the window at the front garden.

'Dying is a lonely business,' he said one day without taking his watery eyes off the trees. 'I'd like you to sit with me for a while, if you would. I pray to God my courage won't desert me when the time comes.'

'Be assured, Your Grace,' said Galvin. 'We here in the house will do anything we can to help.'

As he weakened, the medication, or else the realization that nothing short of ventilating hidden truths would satisfy him in the face of death gave birth to a figure very different from the one who hardly ever questioned Church teaching. He seemed to recover some of the liberal views he had held as a young theologian until he had been advised to change his tune if he wanted to be considered for a diocese. *The mess of pottage*, Thomas, I and others like me – the clever boys – yes, we took the mess of pottage. Renounced integrity for power.'

Much of the time he spent mooching around the house, staring at the books that lined the walls of his library. 'What did we ever learn?'

'How do you mean, Your Grace?'

'One of the greatest scholars the Church has known, Aquinas, said when he had finished the *Summa Theologica*, "So much straw."' He gave a scornful laugh. 'Time was when we had all the answers. We were on the crest of a wave. Two thousand clerical students in the country, full churches. Not a year went by without a new church being opened and blessed. Ministers coming to us cap in hand before they dared pass a Bill in the Dáil that might upset us and cause them to lose their seat.'

Another day it was his regret at unmet needs. 'Never knowing what it's like to experience the intimacy of love with a woman. Whatever qualified me to, well, pontificate … . Oh I don't know.'

'Maybe it's not all it's cracked up to be,' Galvin ventured.

He turned from the window and trained his arched eyebrow on Galvin. 'Are you speaking from experience, father?'

'I stand corrected, Your Grace. But maybe we overestimate … . I mean, look at all those who are separating, getting divorced.'

He wasn't listening. 'Power and control,' he said, looking away again towards the garden, where bluebells lined the sides of a meandering pathway through the trees. 'We had the truths, you know. And another thing: I was too hard on priests. No sympathy for the men who came for laicization. You pointed that out to me. "Hand to the plough", what an appalling … "whoever flings his Calling in the face of the Almighty is not worthy" … . God forgive me.'

Like a shuttlecock, he swayed from one mood to another. One day he bemoaned missed chances of love, another day he trumpeted the glories of Maynooth and Rome. In the library lined with bound volumes of theological works, the Popes' encyclicals, Greek and Roman classics, he rummaged through the past. 'I was regarded as sound in theology, taught the prescribed texts, *peritus* to Archbishop Browne at the Council – a ready-up – as the racing punters are fond of saying. Only a matter of time before my name appears on the *ternus*. The nuncio gave his approval. I was on my way. At forty-two I was handed the shepherd's staff. Did you know that I was called "the boy-bishop" in the newspapers?'

'Didn't know that, Your Grace.'

'Oh, yes. The boy-bishop.'

LATE SUMMER becomes autumn with a bite in the air, especially in the evenings. The beeches and oaks turn brown and it was becoming a struggle for Devlin to take his customary walk around the garden. When he did, a foul odour of rotting leaves rose from the moist earth. He called weekly meetings of the Wise Men, but much of the time took only a passing interest in what they reported. The vicar-general and the Monsignori came for monthly meetings, which were held in the Chapter Room where the walls were lined with Devlin moments of glory: Devlin the young theologian, delivering a lecture at Louvain; Devlin a *peritus* at the Council, walking up the steps of St Peter's with the High Command; Devlin being consecrated in the Pro-Cathedral, alongside it the occasion when he received the pallium from Paul VI. Two stained-glass windows to the east picked up the rising sun and flooded the Chapter Room with colour.

For the meetings with the Wise Men he made a special effort, rose earlier than usual and put on an appearance of good cheer. 'Best foot forward, father dear,' he said as they were going down the hallway one morning. 'The contenders and their seconds are making tracks to Rome. Can't wait to dance on my grave.'

Galvin made the most of the rare flash of dry wit. 'Difficult thing to do, Your Grace, since all archbishops are taken to the crypt in the Pro-Cathedral and the roof of that hallowed space is too low for dancing.'

As they stood, out of respect for the archbishop, the Wise Men and senior clerics were relieved to see both men laughing as they entered the room.

While Devlin was dying, Catholic Ireland was unravelling. Attendances at Sunday mass were plummeting; the only seminary in the country now open, Maynooth, was down to sixty students. In the 1960s they had close to 600 and were turning many candidates away and advising them to consider the missions. Convents were closing; some were being sold and converted into restaurants or health centres for yoga and aromatherapy.

Visionaries were warning that the Second Judgment was imminent. Elderly women were bringing back messages from Medjugorje. 'If Catholics don't renounce their sins of lust, they will be doomed.' On cold days they huddled together around the statue of Father Mathew in O'Connell Street to recite the rosary: 'To thee do we cry, poor banished children of Eve, to thee do we send up our sighs, mourning and weeping in this valley of tears.'

Divorce made it onto the Constitution, homosexuality had been decriminalized without a dissenting voice in Dáil Eireann. Contraception for all over eighteen had also been passed. The government parties were continuing their crusade to wrest the last vestige of control from the Catholic Church. 'Never again,' TDs were saying in the bar of Leinster House, 'will that shower do what they did to Noel Browne.'

In the final months before he died, Devlin's moods continued to fluctuate. 'We come into this world, father,' he said one evening, 'kicking and screaming, and we leave it in pain and distress. You'd wonder at times. How right you were, Beckett: "They give birth astride of a grave."' He shrugged his thin shoulders. The smell of death hung in the archbishop's house and infected everyone, including the secretarial staff. In the wide hallway Devlin was often seen staring up at a print of Michelangelo's 'Last Judgement' and, when a young woman from the chancellery was passing by one day with a sheaf of folders, he gestured towards the picture. '*Nine times the space that measures night and day to mortal men, he with his horrid crew lay vanquished … .*'

'What's that, Your Grace?' The woman was startled.

'Lucifer, child.'

'I'm afraid I don't understand, Your Grace.'

'Conceit, my dear.'

Holding the batch of folders to her well-formed breasts, she glanced at the archbishop. 'Can I get you something, Your Grace? A cup of coffee?'

He smiled and patted her shoulder lightly. 'No thanks, Gemma. I'm afraid it would take more than coffee to … yes. You are very kind.' He pointed towards the picture again. 'Lucifer – bearer of light – what a beautiful name. So much potential and lost it all because of pride … many a good man's failing, Gemma. *Non serviam.* You could say, Lucifer got his comeuppance.'

Gemma turned to the picture again and affected interest. 'Yes, I see what you mean, Your Grace. Well, Archbishop Devlin, I'd better take these files to the chancellor.'

'Yes, you do that, Gemma. You're a great girl.'

In this twilight world, he spoke to Galvin one evening. 'Father, I have set the process in train for you to be made a Monsignor of the papal household.'

'I feel very honoured. Thank you, Your Grace.'

'You will have clout in dealing with the spiky members of the presbyterate who might be inclined to defy you by virtue of their seniority.' Devlin raised himself from the desk, shuffled to the high window and stood, looking out at the garden. 'Yes, you deserve it, if only for putting up with me and my moods.'

He turned to Galvin. 'What if all that has been rejected by the new thinking is true, Thomas? What if, as Jesus said – and mark you they are his words – "sheep on my right; goats on my left". What if that's the real situation – none of this candyfloss theology, penitential services and general absolution – and we all love each other?'

'There's the Prodigal Son. God's infinite mercy.'

'Yes, that's the presumption of those who espouse the woolly thinking of modernity. I can quote you at least two or three opposite statements from the Bible that would challenge that assumption.' He turned to the window once again. *Goats on my left*. I think about that lately, father. Yes, especially of late.'

When he suffered the first of a series of minor strokes, he grew even more frightened of death and, in addition, worried that he might not be able to reach retirement age, which was only a few months away.

One evening before dinner when he was sipping cranberry juice and Galvin, along with the vicar-general and the chancellor, was having a gin and tonic, he recalled his time as a professor in Maynooth. 'Strutting around, haughty as peacocks, we were – the flowering of the crop, and we knew it.'

While he spoke, commendations from priests who had passed through Maynooth many years before were coming back to Galvin. 'Devlin was what kept us in that place. The only priest on the staff who would pay you much attention. You could go to his room and he might open a bottle of beer or a lemonade. It was great. Discuss your doubts. He loved a challenge. He was Newman to us.'

DEVLIN WAS right about the contenders and their seconds. Aspiring clerics were making trips to Rome, securing a mentor and taking influential figures out to dinner in Trastevere. And for the first time three names were appearing in the newspapers as candidates: J. Desmond Byrne, Damien Irwin and an outsider, Oisín O'Rourke.

Though they weren't always pleased with what they read when they opened one of the clerical journals, such as *The Furrow* or *The Tablet*, the bishops were relieved to see that Byrne couldn't be accused of departing from Church teaching. They were glad when they noted how often he was quoting the Pope's encyclicals. That would go down well now that his name was again on the *ternus*.

'They have me in the crypt already,' Devlin said to Galvin one morning when he was glancing over the papers, The silence that followed was broken only by the rustle as he turned the pages. And when Galvin didn't hear his customary sniffing or angry throat-clearing, he knew there wasn't another Church-bashing headline. Devlin folded the newspaper and heaved a sigh. 'He's saying the right things.'

'Who's that, Your Grace?' The vicar-general raised his head. He was sitting stiffly in his well-tailored suit, a high shine on his black shoes. On his knees rested a folder.

'Our man in Rome. Your friend.' Devlin gestured towards Galvin. 'The inestimable Dr Irwin.'

He cast aside the paper. 'I'd hoped that Desmond Byrne would succeed me. Not sure now. Pity. He was one of my brightest students in the Gregorian. Too independent. Too impatient with lesser mortals. He never learnt that it's not always the brightest and the best that … ah well.' He lapsed into silence and when he spoke again he was peevish. 'It's getting too dark in here. I must get the gardeners to cut down some of those trees. They're obstructing God's sunlight.' In a suit that was too big for him, he trudged around the room, stopping to glance over the shelves before sinking into an armchair and saying, almost to himself: 'Will I ever reach heaven?'

The priests exchanged cautious looks. The chancellor was the first to reassure him. 'Your Grace, sure if you don't, what chance have we?'

'Absolutely true,' said the vicar-general, dainty fingers tapping on the folder.

But Devlin paid no heed to the assurances and kept looking away where the trees were showing the first signs of flowering after a long winter. 'You know, my greatest fear, fathers.' He glanced from one to the other. 'That the good Lord would show the same severity to me as I have shown to others.'

The vicar-general smiled bravely. 'With respect, Your Grace, I think you're being unfair to yourself. You did great work. Your commitment to the Church is what Irish Catholics need in this age. A strong hand.'

Instead of being comforted, Devlin turned on him. 'You are forgetting, father, it's the motivation that counts. Motivation. In my twenty-five years as a bishop, I failed to address the recommendations of Vatican II.' He stopped. 'And, father, would you mind ceasing from that infernal tapping?'

The vicar-general gave a little start and blushed. 'Oh, I do apologize, Your Grace.'

Devlin waved it away. 'We who made it to the hierarchy, well, some of us were the bright young priests, *trailing clouds of glory*, gentlemen. We learned how to keep in step; never challenged the powers-that-be because that would scupper our prospects.' He threw a jaundiced look at a bird pecking for worms in the garden. 'The good Lord graced us with ability, but we used it for our own advancement. Oh sure, we convinced ourselves that we were doing it to serve the Word. We've a lot to answer for.'

The vicar-general, who had stopped tapping, shifted in his chair. 'But the Lord is a compassionate … I mean.'

An impish grin showed on Devlin's face. 'And you are able to divine the mind of the Almighty, father!'

The following day, Devlin asked Galvin to drive him to the Jesuit house at Milltown Park. 'I am in need of the sacrament of penance. I wish to talk to my confessor and receive absolution for my sins.'

'Of course.'

While Devlin was with his confessor, Galvin wandered the grounds. Small pink blossoms were appearing on the cherry trees. Soon there would be a frothy canopy on the hawthorn, then the pink clematis. The slow movement of nature towards summer.

Scanning the grey buildings, he was reminded of weekends, ages before, when he had brought his pupils from the technical school to discover themselves. In one of the buildings, Tabor House, young Jesuits back from Berkeley had got them to sit around on bean bags while they read extracts from *The Little Prince* and *Jonathan Livingston Seagull* and played *I Am a Rock* on a hi-fi. 'To help you to connect with your inner self,' the Jesuits told them. God was in His heaven. The mercury was soaring.

Galvin's thoughts turned to speculation on Devlin's successor. The Wise Men were already meeting in secret and making tracks to the Papal Nuncio's residence. 'Politicians wearing Roman collars and crimson belly bands' was the way an American nun had described 'the male-dominated Church' a few evenings before at a lecture in Trinity College.

In the distance, the sound of a door opening in the main house disturbed Galvin's reflections. Devlin emerged from the building with a tall, silver-haired man in civvies. They were in conversation until the tall man raised his hand in a blessing over Devlin's bowed head.

As Galvin cruised down the driveway, the archbishop was quiet; yet, from the way he sat, with his hands resting on his umbrella, he was more relaxed than Galvin had seen him for a long time. 'The Jesuits were my schoolmasters, father.'

'I didn't know that, Your Grace.'

'Yes. I've the highest respect for them.'

As they drove through Ranelagh, Devlin began to show an interest in the houses lit up by the slanting sun. 'The red brick comes into its own in springtime.'

'It does.'

'I wonder will the Lord in his wisdom spare me to see such spring beauty again?'

'None of us knows when.'

'Yes indeed.' Looking away, he said, as if to himself, '*It is the blight that man was born for.*'

'Excuse me?'

'Hopkins.'

Still admiring the red brick, he half turned to Galvin. 'My mother died when I was only twelve. For reasons best known to the Divine Will, God chose to take her at an early age. Poor woman stirred out on bad winter nights to bring comfort to those who were destitute. On one such night she got soaked to the skin and died a week later. The loss of a mother is a big blow to a young boy, father. The one consolation is the thought of meeting her and my dear departed father in heaven.'

When Galvin pulled up on the gravel apron in front of the arch-bishop's house, Devlin made no move to step out. Instead, he was more interested in continuing to talk about his childhood, some-thing he had never done before.

'Only a sister and a brother. But we were at a distance from each other, and my father, God rest him, was busy at the dispensary. You know, I'd read most of Dickens and Thomas Hardy by the time I was in second year at Clongowes. Hardy is a much finer writer, but his view of life is dark. I wouldn't share it.'

He fell into silence again and, after a while, added: 'If the Lord spares me, I hope I get to France, just for one more holiday.'

'Of course you will. And many of them. Probably see us all down.'

Once, on a journey back from confirmations in Wicklow, he had told Galvin that France was his great joy. For many years he went every July with two priests who had studied with him in the Gregorian. When one of them died and the other's arthritis wors-ened, he'd travelled on his own. Having corrected examination papers, he would pack his bags and take a flight to Nice. Then over the course of two weeks or so, he would work his way up to Paris by train, staying in different monasteries. In Paris nothing gave him greater pleasure than browsing through the bookstalls in the Latin Quarter and sharing in the explorer's joy when he came across an early edition of Malebranche, Mauriac or Péguy.

He died the following year when the clematis was at its most beautiful. At least he avoided his worst fear of being taken to the crypt of the Pro-Cathedral while out of office.

TWENTY-TWO

ON THE DAY the Month's Mind Mass for Devlin was celebrated in the Pro-Cathedral, the Hegarty Report on clerical child abuse appeared in all the newspapers. For weeks it was the top story on all chat shows and current affairs programmes on radio and TV. Irwin devoured every bulletin in his rooms at the Irish College. He was frequently on the phone to Dublin to hear the reaction from every angle. In Rome, too, the television was full of it for a couple of days; it even filled a couple of pages of *L'Osservatore Romano*.

If Irwin was having a double espresso in a trattoria and the BBC was reporting on the 'cover-up' by Irish bishops, he would forget his espresso, becoming fastened to the screen high up behind the counter. And although he decided to give it all a wide berth, he was, once again, confirmed in his belief that the priests he had considered a privileged set when they arrived in St Paul's in tonsure suits and smoking cigars on prize-giving day regarded themselves as above reproach. The triumphant Church was now getting it in the neck and he wasn't losing any sleep over it. Full of themselves they were; thought they were God's gift. And he became more convinced that his style of leadership was all the more needed.

The tidal wave that was hitting the Church was too much for the auxiliary bishop who was in charge during the interregnum. A scholarly man, he had taught philosophy at university and, during the summer holidays, had been happiest amongst papers and fragile manuscripts in Louvain or traipsing from one archaeological site to another in Greece or Rome. He was a popular choice among the priests when the Vatican appointed him as auxiliary, but he was now looking forward to retirement and to finishing off a commentary on the *Summa Theologica*. His scholarly pauses – a knee-jerk from years of research and the effort to be accurate in his choice of words – came across as evasive in the fast world of television. For this he was lacerated in the media. Men in pubs, who had nipped in from the bookies, watched him hesitate and swore at the television. 'You shifty fucker' … 'Get out of it, you perv ' … 'Look, the fat bastard is lying through his teeth.' Eventually he came down with an attack of shingles.

Before the Hegarty Report was published, the hierarchy had been concerned by rumours about standards of discipline dropping in the national seminary. Diehard priests were sidling up to bishops at confirmation ceremonies with stories about seminarians drinking in the village pubs and returning to the college late at night. 'And from what I hear,' one priest told his bishop out of the side of his mouth. 'Not always getting into their own beds! Furthermore, My Lord, the authorities have lost control.'

And so, two weeks after the bishops' spring conference, O'Rourke was made a Monsignor of the papal household and called back from Rome to join the staff and be 'a steadying influence'. The man with the wide girth and the jolly face – Irwin's nemesis in Rome – quickly became the voice of the hierarchy. He seemed to flourish in the job: facing the cameras, giving interviews to journalists and appearing on the nine o'clock news. Rome was impressed: *He is the one bright spark in a dark episode.*

The tide was going out for Irwin and he knew it, yet he kept in touch with Dublin. And before he returned to Rome after a visit to Ireland, he invited Galvin and a couple of other priests to a late supper and drinks at his brother's Edwardian house on Mount Merrion Avenue. The divorcee brother, once a car mechanic, was now the owner of several garages across the city. He was at his Cap Ferrat hideaway with his partner, previously his secretary, so Irwin's guests had the house and dining room, with its high, decorated ceiling and droplet chandeliers, to themselves.

Seated at the head of the table, Irwin was becoming increasingly flushed as he drank one glass of wine after another. Gone now were the jokes and the mimicry. Instead, he was sullen and downcast and scowled at his own troubled world. And though the others kept up a conversation that flitted from one topic to another, they were uneasy and exchanged furtive looks across the table.

Galvin had seen it all before – after prize-giving when J. Desmond had swept the boards, the day before the summer holidays when he had been passed over for Rome and after ordination when he was sent to America. But never this bad. And, in his drunken stupor, Irwin kept returning to how a vicar-general, who had clout in Rome, had let him down. 'That slimy turncoat bastard jumped ship when Giordano died and O'Rourke's star began to rise.'

He came to his senses when the fitful conversation swung towards the Hegarty Report.

'The ruination of the Church, that's what it will be. We're buggered if we don't face the scourge of child abuse and accept that we have been covering up.'

Galvin cleared his throat. 'Even if those in authority, the bishops and others, were doing what they could, not much was known about the effect of this at the time. Not even by the medical profession. I came across a psychiatrist one night at a social gathering; he assured me the archbishop was sending every accused priest for medical assessment.'

'Did *you* know what was going on?' A priest with whiskey breath looked balefully at Galvin.

'No, I didn't, and I could swear to that on the Bible. I was told to mind my own business. And for your information, I was excluded from the discussions. I don't believe they knew at the time the full extent of the damage.'

'I find that hard to believe.' The priest with the whiskey breath was on the attack. 'To think that anyone who was abusing a child should be allowed back into the ministry! Hogwash. I suppose you would also defend that cardinal in Boston … what's his name? Law.'

'You're saying they were in bad faith then. Hiding and moving around criminals.'

Irwin intervened. 'Look, the wind will be whistling through every church building in the country unless people get a full explanation.' He was on the brink of tears, so Galvin drew back.

'I love the Church,' Irwin continued, his voice filled with emotion. 'And I've a lot to be thankful to it for. A lot. The Church is there when we come into this world and there when we kick the bucket. When children with hungry bellies were scampering barefoot around Mountjoy Square, the High Command – for all his faults – put shoes and clothes on them.' The conversation stopped when the Polish cook came in to remove the plates.

'And now Armagh and the rest of the bishops,' Irwin took up again as soon as she had gone, 'think that the arrival of Falstaff will clear up the mess. Make no mistake about it, Falstaff isn't the laughing giant that people think he is. One Christmas while I was in Washington I went to mass in the cathedral. He preached in front of the cardinal. Not an empty seat in the place – families, children, visitors. Your man had them eating out of his hand with his laid-back delivery and the odd joke against himself about his weight.' He rapped on the table with his knuckles. 'Believe you me, the bottom line was the evils of contraception and abortion. On Christmas Day!' He stopped and looked around the table. 'Most of the congregation wouldn't be there for another year. Children there! So he's going to be your leader. Well, you're welcome to him. Thank God I don't have to stick around.'

The following morning when Galvin drove him to the airport for his flight to Rome, he showed no signs of the previous evening's gloom. Instead, he was upbeat about plans for the Irish College. While they were having a coffee at the departure lounge, he looked at Galvin and grinned. 'D'you remember how I stymied Armagh when he wanted Falstaff to be rector of the Irish College?'

'Yes. With the intercession of Ampleforth and the yellow roses.'

'Well, looks like he's trumped me in the end. Giordano couldn't influence it, but then his star was waning. Swings and roundabouts, Tommy. If the train left without me this time, there'll be another coming down the line. Two other dioceses will become vacant in the next few years: backwaters, but they'd be a stepping stone. Never give up, as the mother used say.'

It was time for him to go to the gate. 'I'll not leave Rome until I'm a bishop. You mark my words.'

O'Rourke held press conferences in Wansborough, in the very room where students had vested on the morning of their ordination. Seated behind a battery of microphones and confronted by a hive of journalists and photographers, he seemed in control, unlike the diocesan administrator, who had a hunted look in his eye and beads of sweat on his forehead; he had to stop from time to time to take a sip of water. When cornered, he handed over the microphone to O'Rourke and wiped his slack mouth with a handkerchief.

IN THE WEEKS that followed, the festering resentment against the Church for its years of imposing Catholic teaching on legislation and public life, for compelling members of the government to appease the hierarchy, erupted in a torrent of rage and resentment and was played out daily on television and radio.

Journalists popped up when Galvin was shopping in town or visiting the Pro-Cathedral to drop on his knees on the spot where he had knelt many years before as a student and the High Command had presided from a red-upholstered sedile in the sanctuary. They ambushed him in the vestibule one day and a journalist with a notebook rounded on him as he dipped his fingers in the holy water font.

'You were one of those who knew all along. Have you anything to say, Monsignor Galvin, about the cover-up?'

'I was not privy to some decisions made by the archbishop.'

The following day he was described in the papers as *an evasive man who has learned nothing from the scandalous way the Church has behaved*.

'This is the sort of deception,' said a deputy in Dáil Eireann, 'with which the Irish people are fed up to the back teeth. I am a practising Catholic but I can no longer abide the chicanery of Church leaders who care nothing for vulnerable children, and whose only concerns are their own careers.' The TD finished by saying: 'As a Catholic, I don't mind saying we need honest priests like that Father O'Rourke.'

Articles appeared in the papers about the disgraceful way the Church had behaved; the letters page was full of calls for wresting the control of schools and hospitals from the bishops and the religious congregations. And proposals were made in Dáil Eireann to compel priests to break the seal of confession if an abuser had confessed. Galvin's photograph, taken at confirmation ceremonies and other occasions when he was accompanying the archbishop, appeared beside these pieces. He started getting hate mail and abusive phone calls at all hours of the night. One midnight caller shouted in a drunken slur: 'Get out of that palace, you pervert. You're all fucking queers in there.'

Guilt for not confronting Devlin about child abuse caused him to wake each morning at three and stare at the ceiling until it was time to rise. And even if Devlin had kept him out of the loop, he should have spoken out. Psoriasis had his arm the colour of raw liver. When he started getting pains across his chest, his GP sent him for an ECG: the result was negative. 'Nothing to be concerned about in the heart region, father,' the doctor told him at the next visit. 'Stress is the most likely cause.'

'I need something to calm me down.'

The doctor, who had been winding up the blood pressure instrument, studied him. 'I'm slow to prescribe sleeping tablets. There's a danger of being hooked.' His trained eye noticed Galvin's slumped shoulders. 'Yes ... well, a light course, baby strength, but only on the short term. Sleepers are not a solution.' He rested the sphyg on his desk. 'Would you – and I'm speaking here as your doctor who knows you for many years – consider moving out of that stressful job you're in?'

Galvin was putting on his jacket. 'I'd be reluctant, John, to leave a sinking ship.'

'But there's the issue of your own health. You could – and here I'm not trying to scare you – end up with a cardiac arrest. Your blood pressure is up.'

'I'll think about what you've advised,' Galvin said. 'I might ask for a sabbatical. I've a priest friend out in California.'

The doctor began to write on his prescription pad. 'Even if you find a temporary respite, you'll still be carrying the problem with you. And eventually you'd have to come back, unless you plan to stay out there.'

Two weeks later Galvin resigned his post as bishop's secretary and asked the vicar-general for 'a quiet country parish'.

'Then St Jude's is your place,' the vicar-general said. 'One chapel and a small school, golf course up the road and the strand is only a half-mile away.'

'St Jude, hmm,' Galvin smiled. 'Patron saint of hopeless cases.'

'Ah no, Tom, many more years left in you.'

The change to St Jude's along with the upheaval of moving his property unsettled Galvin for a while. On a daily basis he was now learning the full extent of the clerical abuse of children. Palpitations and one or two episodes of sleepwalking, a feature of his adolescence and seminary life, were recurring. One night he woke himself in the front hall of his house, asking: 'Why? Why didn't Devlin let me know?'

J. DESMOND was doorstepped frequently. He was crossing St Joseph's Square to his rooms in Maynooth after a lecture when a female journalist and a photographer pounced on him. 'At this stage, Dr Byrne, you and those who had hand, act or part in this cover-up must be ashamed of yourselves.'

When he turned to them, the photographer began snapping in rapid succession from different angles. Despite his outrage and anger that mere journalists were upbraiding him, he spoke in a deliberate and restrained way about the efforts that were made to send perpetrators for assessment and to therapeutic centres in Britain and America. How the archbishop and his advisors never returned a priest to the ministry without getting clearance from professionals. 'This is by no means an attempt to try and justify our response to these abominable crimes. We readily admit our limitations, and if we'd had foresight, we would have done things differently. But as the minister for justice said in relation to the response of the gardaí: "It was a different time then." Like the statutory bodies, we were on a learning curve.'

The journalist opened fire. 'Oh, so you are telling the Irish people that you're excused because it was "a different time"? Surely that's a weak defence. Priests were moved from one parish to another. Predators were let loose on unsuspecting people so that they could violate innocent children. And you tell me you were on a *learning curve*?'

'We readily admit serious errors, but ... .'

'How you continue lecturing in theology beggars belief.' She noticed the flash of impatience in his eye and continued to provoke. 'You did precious little while monsters continued to do their evil work.'

'I admit the limitations of our procedures.' J. Desmond's tone became even more measured in order to contain his mounting anger. 'We were given counsel by professionals – psychiatrists, psychologists, lawyers even. We followed the best possible advice, but that advice was sorely lacking and we didn't know then the extent of the damage that had been done.'

'A lame excuse, Dr Byrne.' She closed her notebook and walked away with the photographer, who continued to snap the quadrangle.

TWENTY-THREE

OMINOUS CLOUDS hang over the grounds on the second-last evening of the retreat. Later that night, a downpour brings the spell of fine weather to an end. Throughout the following day, a wholesome smell of summer rises from the freshly cut grass and the flowerbeds. As they have done every afternoon, priests take a siesta: some disappear to the common room to watch Wimbledon, but no sooner are they seated in front of the television than the wine at lunch begins to take effect. Heads start to nod. One of the priests reaches for the remote control and lowers the volume so that the commentator's modulated voice and the occasional cut-glass applause seems to come from the other end of a long room.

Galvin had been heading towards the Long Walk when drops of rain on the tarmac cause him to seek shelter in Senior House and, as he is about to turn the cast-iron door handle, his mobile phone vibrates. His curate is hysterical.

'There's a leak, Monsignor, right on the altar of the Adoration Chapel!'

'Phone our handyman. I'll be back tomorrow,' he tells him.

'Oh I'm greatly relieved, Monsignor. Oh thank God.'

Along the stone corridor, he passes pictures of students throwing their mortar boards in the air, but in his mind's eye, he is seeing the curate fussing about the leak with the elderly women who run the Adoration Chapel and give him socks and handkerchiefs every Christmas.

Galvin had taken the curate to lunch one day. 'I have to say this, but I don't want you to take offence. Some parishioners have complained to me about the way you preach repeatedly on divorce and the pill. I mean … .'

'I'm obliged to obey the teachings of the Church, Monsignor; to defend the sanctity of marriage and uphold the natural law which governs conjugal love.' His head jerked to one side like a bird's.

'For goodness' sake, most of them are in their seventies, I don't think they'll be filing for divorce, and they are long past child-bearing age, unless there's a Sarah among them.'

'Sarah? I don't follow, Monsignor.'

'I'm sure you've heard of the Book of Genesis.'

'No need to be so patronizing, Monsignor Galvin,' he said, hurt showing in his baby-blue eyes. As if getting ready to defend the purity of Catholic teaching, he sat rigidly at the table, his monogrammed cufflinks matching his ring. 'Monsignor, I have to point out to you that my loyalty to the Holy Father takes precedence before that to my parish priest.'

Twenty years before Galvin might have challenged him but now, battle-weary, he considers such a confrontation to be futile. Anyway, he resigns himself to the thought that the few who shuffle into the church on a Sunday and wedge themselves between armrest and seat couldn't care less what the curate says about the pill so long as they fulfil their obligation to attend Sunday mass and get in a rosary as well.

'I'm sure you understand I'm not undermining your authority, Monsignor.'

'No, of course not, but bear in mind what I'm saying.'

Galvin had repeatedly asked that the curate stop calling him 'Monsignor' but it made no difference. Nor did it make any when he approached him about wearing his soutane around the parish. 'This is not the nineteen fifties, and we're not in Rome or Poland.'

The curate cried when he told Galvin about the day he wore his soutane going into town in the bus. A young man selling illegal cigarettes spotted him on Henry Street. He'd called his mate. 'Hey, Anto, will you look at your man with his fuckin' black dress.'

They'd laughed and headed for him and started to thrust their hands up his soutane and, when the curate ran, they gave chase as far as O'Connell Street. Shoppers took it at first to be a jape or a publicity stunt for some play in the Abbey when they saw the ridiculous figure dashing by, holding up the ends of his soutane with one hand, a briefcase in the other. 'Run, Forrest, run,' they'd shouted, doubled up with laughter. 'Go on you fuckin' weirdo,' the young blokes kept on shouting until they spotted two policemen standing in front of the GPO. They'd slunk into the crowd and made their way back up through the stalls on Moore Street.

On the final night of the retreat Galvin sits with a few priests watching the nine o'clock news. Some have gone to the Skylon Hotel or to the Cat and Cage; a few are strolling the grounds. Outside the high windows, the shadows are lengthening. The priests have one eye on the news while they carry on a low-burning conversation, like men in a hospital ward comparing their operations.

They talk about their dogs and their medication. 'In the past,' says one, sheepishly, 'you had to make sure you had your passport and your driver's licence when checking for the holidays. Now you have to be doubly sure you have your pills.'

'The pill organizer is your man,' says another.

'Now you're talking. I'd be lost without it.'

Their tone becomes querulous as they flit from one topic to another. They don't think much of the Wise Men who are helping the administrator to run the diocese.

'The sooner an archbishop is appointed, the better for everyone,' one of them says.

'The way they're asking us to synchronize masses and expecting old people to take a bus to a neighbouring church for weekday mass.'

'After a lifetime of contributions.'

'A scandal.'

'Wouldn't happen in the High Command's time.'

'Certainly wouldn't.'

'I'm on my own now.'

'Are you?'

'And after a belt last year.' The priest rubs his chest. 'The ould ticker, you know.'

A cough breaks the silence that follows. 'What did you think of the retreat director?'

They laugh. 'Naive. "Let go of the steering wheel in your parishes, fathers. The Holy Spirit speaks through your parishioners." That's monks for you.'

'And leave it to a few crackpots. Ah, I'm afraid Father Clement and his Oxford accent – lovely man – is living in cloud cuckoo land. He and his like don't have to take responsibility for parishes.'

'You're dead right. Freewheelers.'

'Sure if we didn't keep control, the whole thing would be a mess.'

'Now you're talking.'

When the news is over, Galvin leaves them. Out in the vestibule and in the stone corridor, the lights along the skirting board glow in the falling darkness. He stands for a moment at the front door of Coghill. Someone has a radio on low. Canned laughter is followed by applause. Across the lawn by the chestnut trees the red tip of a cigarette glows and then fades. Long-legged herons have flown in from Dollymount to high-step on the wet grass and sink their beaks into the fresh earth. They stop to eye him suspiciously, then lose interest and go back to their foraging.

He goes down the steps and, following the perimeter path towards the river, catches the rich perfume from the fusion of verbena and cow parsley. The bells of a nearby church ring out and, like a flock of birds flying overhead, the air is suddenly filled with the sounds of boy-priests in their soutanes surfing on the high tide of promise. The rector is promising a glorious future: 'The new extension will be open for the next group of freshmen in October; over a million Catholics in the diocese by the turn of the century. The harvest is great, gentlemen.'

EARLY the following morning, before they return to their parishes, a few of the priests take their bags out to where they had parked under the trees in readiness to leave after the first talk. Most, however, stay on for lunch and linger at the tables, sipping the last of the wine and draining every drop of pleasure they can from these shared days. With the schools closed for the summer, many of them, after saying ten o'clock mass, might not see another soul over the course of the day. Rossiter and his cronies would fare better: they would meet for leisurely lunches and fill each other in on the latest gossip. And the few priests who were still able to move around a golf course would continue to play Royal Dublin every Tuesday.

Beside Galvin at the table is the priest he had met on the Sunday evening, hauling his bag up the stairs of Coghill House. He leans over. 'I don't care what anyone says, Tommy, meeting the lads is the best part of these retreats. The old bit of banter. Breakfast, dinner and supper on your own. Ah no, not human. Don't care what anyone says. We have nice houses, oh, the best to be sure, but what's the use?'

'You're right, and the puppet-masters don't seem to be too concerned so long as the trains are on time.'

'Trains?'

'Masses are said, confessions heard. You know.'

'Ah, I'm with you. Yes, the trains are on time.' He chuckles. 'Sure they're only doing what was done to them.' The priest pushes back his plate and crosses himself. 'Well, Tommy, that's it for now. Only God knows how many of us will be back next year.'

'Ah sure, we'll hope for the best. May God go with you.'

'And with you.'

He stands and says: 'I'm going on my holidays next Sunday evening. A good hotel in Killarney. I hope I'll enjoy myself.' The joyless look in his eye was sucking life out of the day.

'I hope you will.'

'That's it for now till next year. God bless, Tommy.'

'God bless.'

When nearly all have driven off, Galvin takes the Abbey Walk around by the back of Senior House. He wants to have a last look at that rich vein he had been exploring during the week. He glances at the Pugin chapel and remembers the words of the retreat director when he went to him for confession there the day before.

'Make no mistake about it, father, your calling in life was and is to be a minister of the word. You wouldn't have persevered for over forty years if it were otherwise. Despite the almost empty churches nowadays, the jockeying for position you've witnessed among your confrères, your own sins of weakness, you have remained faithful.' He stood and proffered his hand. 'Pray for me, Father Galvin.'

TWENTY-FOUR

BACK IN THE PARISH, Galvin collects Sam, his Labrador, from the kennel and listens to the midday radio while having his lunch. Apart from the dog bounding around the apple trees in the back garden in anticipation of his afternoon walk, the house feels strangely empty after the cook has gone. Fragments from the retreat cross his mind: the fencing between Sheerin and Sylvester O'Flynn, and Cyril's radio on upstairs to ward off isolation.

In the afternoon, as filmy clouds float towards Blessington, he takes the lawnmower out of the garden shed and cuts the grass around the apple trees. 'Exercise is good. Walking – in fact, you need to walk,' his doctor had told him after he had put him on medication for blood pressure. 'But don't overdo it.'

'No, I won't.'

When he has finished, he rests on a chair down at the back near the shed and casts his eye over the solid bulk of the presbytery. Surrounded by a high wall, the limestone house with steps up to the front door is one of the biggest in the parish. It was built in the nineteenth century when Catholics wanted their man to have a house as good or even better than the parson's. He had thought about selling it or converting it into a parish centre, but the director of finance in the archdiocese had said no.

'It's counter to the message we're trying to preach, and especially at a time when people are now going through austerity. And the house is impossible to heat in winter,' Galvin had argued.

'That house is a parish asset' had been the director's final words. 'You won't always be there and your successor might like to live in it. Or a retired priest and his housekeeper.'

As in the case with his curate, Galvin didn't have the will to put up a fight or to appeal to the diocesan administrator, who had enough on his plate. Anyway, what difference would it make apart from raising his blood pressure, he reasons as he shades his eyes from the sun. Things would remain the same: those like Rossiter and his henchmen would haunt the archbishop's house and ingratiate themselves with bishops over a nightcap in Lourdes. Irwin would network in Rome until he got a diocese. The Book of Job comes winging back: *Where is the place of understanding? It is hidden from the eyes of all living.*

A week later, while he is pulling in at the local station for petrol, a news bulletin announces that a successor to the late Archbishop Devlin has been chosen. Galvin slows to a halt by the bales of briquettes and bags of charcoal. 'He is a priest from the archdiocese of Armagh, the Right Reverend Monsignor Oisín O'Rourke.' In the back of the car, Sam emits a growl from deep in his throat and cocks his ears.

'Yes, I agree with you, Sam. That won't go down well with our friend Damien, sure it won't?' Galvin turns around but Sam ignores him: he is taken up with a bitch who is sniffing around the bundles of kindling.

'How do you feel about being called to this high office, Monsignor O'Rourke?' the religious affairs correspondent asks.

'I must put up my hands here and tell you that it came as a shock. I resisted at first, but after prayer and reflection, I decided to accept the honour conferred on me by the Holy See. But, yes, it comes as a surprise. I was teaching in Rome, and then Maynooth. I'll miss my students. However, I look forward to the challenge.'

The report ends with the announcement that he would be installed as archbishop in the Pro-Cathedral on the feast of the Assumption of the Blessed Virgin Mary.

Irwin phones Galvin a few nights later. 'Come out for a couple of days. I need to talk. We'll shoot the breeze.'

'In a week or so, if my curate will hold the fort. He spends a lot of time in the archbishop's house. "My life revolves around meetings, Monsignor," he tells me. Did you ever hear the beat of it?'

'He is modelling himself on his parish priest,' Irwin says, chuckling.

GALVIN CATCHES a flight to Rome and as his taxi pulls up at the Irish College he sees Irwin walking slowly around the fountain and laughing into his mobile. When he spots Galvin, Irwin puts away his phone and hurries to meet him.

'Leave your bags here for a minute,' he says when they are in the hallway. 'Let me show you something I came across today. We'll have a drink then before dinner.' He goes ahead of Galvin down a stone stairs at the back of the college and along a dim corridor, then down more stone steps where stale air rises from the uneven flagstones. A cupboard stands against one of the stone walls.

'This place is creepy, a goddamn crypt.' Irwin opens one of the cupboards, filled with robes and lacy vestments in the old Roman style.

'I want you to see these.' He takes out a musty-smelling scarlet cape and zucchetto and holds them in front of Galvin. 'You think I'm bad? Well, take a look here. Cardinal's colours. Story goes, one of our illustrious archbishops who has long gone to his reward had been rector here and a cert for the Red Hat. Everyone told him it was only a matter of time. In any case, he went out and bought the full rig-out but Armagh pipped him at the post. Apparently, he went on the sulks. Wouldn't talk to his staff for a month, only sending notes. And didn't talk to Armagh for a couple of years.' He closes the cupboard door. 'So it's not the first time Armagh beat us to the post.'

After dinner they have drinks in Irwin's apartment on the first floor. And, as if the previous week's disappointment had never happened, he was his old self, taking off priests of the diocese, including Winters, now a canon of the chapter. But as the night wears on, he becomes maudlin.

'You know you helped me, and you never judged me, because I can be a difficult bastard, and downright unfair at times. But you never failed me.' His face flushed, he tilts his drinking glass, looking intently into it as if it held some secrets. 'You remember the day outside the Pro. The day the father was calling me.'

'I remember.'

'On Holy Thursday. All that was needed was for a cock to crow. Jesus! Despite my efforts to bury him, he keeps turning up in stray thoughts and in dreams. I know, *I know*, no one takes any notice of dreams. And yet, the other night I had this strange, and so bloody vivid ... .'

In the dream his father had staggered into the Irish College while Irwin was receiving a delegation from the Vatican. They had come to talk about Giordano's recommendation that Irwin should be appointed an under-secretary in the Curia – a post that would lead in time to the Red Hat. Having forgotten that Irwin was fluent in Italian, the Roman delegation began to talk among themselves. 'Look what a drunken fool Irwin's father is.' 'No class.' 'Must be low-born, and we thought Irwin was from better stock. That's the end of our mission. He would never have the subtle skills that are required in the Curia.'

'I woke, Tommy, pleading with them not to write me off.'

'Well, as you say, it was only a dream.'

'I'll get there, Tommy. Falstaff and Armagh beat me to it this time, but I'll get there.' He raises his arms to the high ceiling and to the portraits of bishops on the walls. 'I made it this far; not bad going for a lad from St Brigid's Terrace. And, as I told you many years ago, I'd do a better job than many of them.'

Galvin puts down his empty glass on a side table and does a stretching act. 'I'm knackered, Damien. Have to rest my weary bones.'

As he shows him to the door of his apartment, Irwin grins. 'Another thing – nearly all rectors of this college ended up with a diocese. See you in the morning.'

Down the corridor in a guest room, Galvin, as always when he has taken more drink than he intended, is awake as dawn is breaking over the green domes of the city. He opens the shutters, throwing light on a shadowy portrait facing his bed of an austere-looking bishop on the wall, probably one of the rectors who *ended up with a diocese*. He goes to the window and looks down at the fountain where Devlin once poked at pebbles. Rome is coming to life: scooters are streaking down the Via dei Santi Quattro. At a junction beyond the high wrought-iron gates, traffic is building up. A pointsman with white gloves is blowing on a whistle.

His thoughts stray to the previous night. He hears Irwin's vow. 'I'll get there, Tommy.' A wave of sympathy washes over him for the lone figure, who, since his days as an altar boy, has been fascinated by the drama and rituals of the Church. The parish priest of East Wall declaiming from the pulpit, the murmur of Latin from the young priests saying mass at the side altars, a packed church on Christmas morning for High Mass: the canon, deacon and sub-deacon, one behind the other on descending steps. Lace albs and braided chasubles.

244

O'ROURKE'S installation ceremony takes place at the Pro-Cathedral while the summer sales are still on in Clerys and herds of youths in Kilkenny and Cork hurling colours are waving flags, shouting and rushing up a sun-drenched O'Connell Street, past the Gresham, to Croke Park. In less sunny Marlborough Street, priests are making their way to the Pro-Cathedral, their white heads bobbing like bog cotton in the breeze.

Ahead of Galvin is a cluster of youngish priests. One of them has exciting news. 'The Nuncio and the Vatican secretary of state – the new guy – have just driven up with O'Rourke.' Alongside Galvin, Sheerin is in his element. 'Not surprised at all. Didn't O'Rourke work on him while he was in Rome?'

'Work on him? How do you mean?'

'Held a potty for him.' He guffaws. 'Oh, Mother Ireland, you're still rearing them. The word is, if Giordano hadn't popped his clogs, Irwin would have acceded to the throne. Swings and roundabouts, mate.'

'And no one's as dead as a dead king.'

Inside the main door, the chatter ceases as the administrator of the Pro-Cathedral gives instructions to the priests about reverencing the altar and where to sit in the cathedral. Double cuffs and gold cuff links show beneath his soutane; his accent has a hint of Rome. Galvin takes in his surroundings. The mingling of beeswax and incense and the hollow sound of footsteps flood his mind with something like a batch of old, dog-eared photographs.

Tall and solemn as a church spire, de Valera is at a prie-dieu in front of the high altar for St Patrick's Day, his chaplain robed in surplice and soutane at his side. Winters was giving a guided tour one Sunday after mass when Galvin was a first year. 'Paul Cullen, the first Irish cardinal, the man who built up the archdiocese; indeed, transformed the face of the Irish Church,' he announced. Now, as then, the stolid giant in cold marble casts a shadow over a whole corner beside an abandoned confessional. 'And over there, a deeply spiritual and cultured man, Archbishop Murray.'

Winters had pointed towards another giant, one raised hand frozen in a blessing. Forgotten in a dark nook at the other side of the main door is the baroque pulpit that once faced the congregation. Galvin hears the High Command, just back from the Vatican Council. 'No change will worry the tranquillity of your Christian lives.' His reverie is broken by the administrator indicating with stylized gestures that the procession will begin. Hands joined and with measured steps, the priests process up the centre aisle in twos, just as they did many years before as seminarians.

The cathedral is full. In royal blue bibs emblazoned with a cross, the Knights of Saint Columbanus are checking invitation cards and handing out booklets of the ceremony. High above, the organ is warming up while the conductor fusses with sheet music and instructions for the Palestrina Choir.

THE ACADEMY HALL, now a lecture room, is crowded for the reception that follows the ceremony. Priests who had often said they could see through O'Rourke's lust for power and had called him a lickspittle and a pipsqueak are full-hearted in their praise of him as they lay into the buffet of smoked salmon, cold meats and salads.

'After all, isn't he the only credible voice in the Irish Church?' one of them says, catching sight of the wine waiter passing by with two bottles. The others nod. 'We need him at this time. Right man for the job.' He stretches out his glass. 'Red, please. I mean, look at him: no one can work a room like him. Sheer class.'

'Wouldn't he put new life into you.'

'And God knows we need that.'

They gaze at O'Rourke, a jolly potentate surrounded by his entourage, as he moves about. He is introducing the Vatican secretary of state to a former Taoiseach who once crossed the floor of Dáil Eireann to vote in accordance with his Catholic principles. The British ambassador and his wife who has a weakness for yellow roses are in the happy circle, as well as a couple of bishops. Sunny smiles and handshakes all round. The catering staff are rushing to help elderly guests with their plates of smoked salmon and salad. Chuckles of apology when a serviette falls to the ground. Like a proud father at his son's wedding, an Italian Monsignor who had been O'Rourke's mentor in Rome is beaming his way around the room. Waiting for their opportunity to congratulate the new archbishop and get a selfie with him are a few young priests, carrying cameras and iPhones.

'You'd have to hand it to him; he lifted us out of it. Things are looking up, lads.' The priest who likes red wine is getting loud.

'No one could do it like him.'

'Great communication skills.'

'His forte.'

'When all is said and done, better choice than Damien or J. Desmond. Fine men too.'

'Yes, indeed,' another priest says, and laughs. 'Sure, aren't we all fine men.'

'Precisely. Here's to us.' He raises his glass. 'Anyway, J. Desmond's goose was cooked when the Hegarty Report came out.'

'How's he taking it?'

'Crushed, and who would blame him?'

'Oh, that's a pity.'

'Ah, he'll be alright. He has more books to write.'

When O'Rourke waves and gives them a broad smile, they raise their glasses. '*Ad multos annos*, archbishop,' they chorus.

After the new archbishop has thanked his guests and hoped that he could rely on their prayers and support in the years ahead, Galvin slips away. He hurries along the wooden corridor and down the main stairway, and stands for a moment at the front door of Wansborough. Every space for parking has been filled with rows of cars stretching right across to Coghill and up to where the back pitch once stood. Car tops gleam in the afternoon sun. A mighty surge of cheering reaches him from Croke Park.

One of the Eastern European attendants with a high-vis jacket guides him out. Through the open car window Galvin drops a five euro note into his hand and drives slowly down the main avenue, past the beeches and the chestnuts, past Beresford's Folly and the gingerbread house where Lovely Legs once lived with her family. He waits until the road is clear to drive away.